THE GREEK VIRGIN

by

S. T. DARKE

CHIMERA

The Greek Virgin first published in 2002 by
Chimera Publishing Ltd
22b Picton House
Hussar Court
Waterlooville
Hants
PO7 7SQ

Printed and bound in Great Britain by
Cox & Wyman Ltd, Reading.

THE GREEK VIRGIN

S. T. Darke

Athena's skin simmered with the humiliation of standing there, naked from the waist down. Her hands hung by her sides, with him staring at her lower belly. Her heart hammered mercilessly against her ribs, showing her no mercy at all. Each breath was a tremulous pant as it flowed hesitatingly between nervously parted lips. But she felt something else, too. She wanted to be looked at in that way, and in that place. To herself she admitted that fact, and found it to be liberating despite the humiliation and embarrassment she felt so strongly.

'Turn around,' I instructed her firmly.

'What?'

'Turn,' I said forcefully, 'now.'

Athena obeyed slowly, her heart racing.

'Bend forward and hold the armrests. Your woman needs punishing to show her that you are really the boss. Doesn't she?'

Athena did not believe what she was hearing. Her heart hammered in her ears.

'Who's the boss?' I prompted. 'You or her?'

'I—' she began, but he cut her off.

Chapter One

This is a story about a Greek girl... a virgin... a Greek virgin, or at least she was... until she met Him, her Master... only she didn't know that at the time because she was only a woman. He didn't know that either. Yes, she was a woman... a Greek woman... but not for long. Then she became a Female... and a Slave... and a very happy natural human being. And so was He who birthed her that way... only He didn't know what he was doing... until He did it... but when He did do it... He did it perfectly!

On Friday I had visited the hypnotherapist to help me give away smoking. Now it was Monday and I hadn't smoked since before visiting him. Not only that, but I couldn't for the life of me remember what happened with him after he had me focus on a spot on the ceiling and then began to count down from one hundred. I think ninety-one was the last thing I could remember.

I was amazed that it actually worked. I'd always thought hypnosis was all rubbish for deluded minds to play games with when interacting with other deluded people of like nature. Now I did not think like that. Now I believed that hypnosis, in the hands of someone who knew how to use it, was a very interesting thing indeed.

Leaving work early I went to the library and took out all the books I could find on hypnosis and hypnotherapy – thirteen in all.

For the rest of the week it was after midnight before I

fell into bed exhausted with visions of people falling under my hypnotic power, one after the other. By the time Saturday morning came around I had read them all, some twice, especially the ones with pictures. I was anxious to try it out on someone and began to think of potential marks while I made myself breakfast and ate it. Thoughts of the covertness and moral ethics involved crossed my mind, not to mention the legality of it all, or rather, the illegality of it all, but I brushed them aside in my excitement to see if I could actually do it. The way I looked at it, if I followed the directions in the books I'd read then it should be a piece of cake. It had worked with me.

It was all a matter of preparing someone for hypnosis, with or without them being aware of it being done. That was the way I saw it. Now all I had to do was to find someone, and then, with or without his or her permission I would prepare them and then do it.

I decided to begin with playing it safe and obtaining permission first, just to make sure I was doing everything properly. I had someone in mind by the time I'd done the breakfast dishes. She was the daughter of a friend of my wife's who came to clean the house each Saturday afternoon while my wife was at her tennis club till five, and I was usually fishing till later than that. Her name was Nicola. She was Greek, she was eighteen years of age, and she was utterly beautiful.

Chapter Two

Nicki arrived promptly at midday. By that time my excitement had built to almost fever pitch. I'd had several erections come and go throughout the morning as visions of my success filled my imagination and body with adrenaline – sensations I hadn't felt since I was a teenager.

'Hi, Mr Davis,' Nicki bubbled as he let her in the front door. She liked Mr Davis, although she never saw him much. His wife told her that he was always out fishing whenever she called. His wife was nice, too. 'Beautiful day, isn't it?'

'You bet, Nicki,' I replied, anxious to begin my preparation of her. 'Too nice to be indoors working. We should all be down at the beach somewhere, just relaxing and letting the cool sea water drain away all of our tension and take it back down into the peaceful deep blue sea.'

'Sounds wonderful,' Nicki answered as she headed for the closet to get out the vacuum cleaner to begin her chores. He was right about that. All she wanted to do was get it all done before it got too hot.

I went into the lounge then and waited until she had finished vacuuming the house. By that time she should be a little tired, I figured. After all, it was a hot afternoon, and the middle of our summer. I waited until I heard her packing away the vacuum cleaner back into the closet. When I heard her bang the mop and bucket against the door getting it out I went to her with a tall cool drink.

'Thought you might like this,' I said with a smile. I handed her the cool glass. She grinned a grateful grin and took the glass from me. Then she held it against her forehead and moved it back and forth a few times. Her forehead was covered with a light sheen of perspiration from her vacuuming efforts and the heat inside the house, even with the windows open. Nicki upended the glass and drank the lot. Then handed it back to me.

'That was great!' Nicki said with a wide, grateful smile. 'I really needed that.' She could feel her body cooling down slightly from the inside out.

'Why don't you take a little break for a while?' I suggested. 'You've got all afternoon, unless you have to go somewhere? You've only got the mopping and dusting still to do.'

Nicki looked at me evenly for a few moments – not suspiciously. She would never figure me for doing anything like that. I was just the man she cleaned house for with the friendly wife. Then she smiled.

'I'd love to,' Nicki said. 'But I'd better keep moving or I just might stop permanently and get nothing finished. It's so hot!' It was too soon for a break, she thought, not that she wouldn't have loved one.

'Okay,' I said smiling. 'Just a suggestion I thought you might like to kick around while you mop the floors of each room in this heat. Might make you feel a bit cooler while you push that heavy water-filled mop up and down the floors if your mind thought about putting your feet up and just resting through the hottest part of the afternoon. Would you like another drink to cool you down from the inside?' I was excited, and I really wanted to see if I could do it.

'No, thanks.' Nicki smiled gratefully, knowing she could easily down another two of those beautiful cool drinks. 'I'd better keep moving. If I slow down for too long in this heat I might stop altogether.' She laughed and headed for the laundry to fill the bucket with hot water.

I walked back into the lounge and sat down to plan my next move. So far so good. I'd planted the seed, at least. It was so hot she must be thinking about it a little bit, at least.

Chapter Three

After about an hour Nicki came into the lounge room where Mr Davis sat reading a book. She sat down opposite him on a single chair and collapsed with a sigh, glad to finally be able to sit for a bit.

'Thought I'd take that break you talked about,' Nicki said, sprawling down deeply into the comfortable chair. 'I've only got the dusting to do now. That won't take me long. I wanted to get the heavy stuff done first.'

'Smart girl.' I smiled at her. 'Would you like another long cool drink?'

'Great!' Nicki said. 'I'll just vegetate here for a few minutes before I do the dusting, if that's all right with you?'

She then relaxed even more with a long sigh, feeling her body just seeming to deflate.

'Sure,' I answered, getting up to fetch her drink. 'Put your feet up and chill out for a while. It's so hot. Just imagine you're somewhere nice and cool – cold even, like a cold room.'

'I used to work in one of those at the supermarket,' Nicki said to his back as he headed for the kitchen. Then she pictured the cold room at the deli. God, what she wouldn't give to be able to nap out inside there for a while and catch a few Z's.

'You look so tired and relaxed,' I said to her as I came back into the lounge and handed her the glass. 'This should cool you down and relax you even more.'

I watched Nicki struggle a bit to open her eyes. She

must have been somewhere else in her imagination. Then she smiled and took the glass, downing half the contents in one go. She sighed again and licked her lips, and what lovely lips they were. She wore a light cotton halter-top and cut-off denim shorts that were loose around the upper thighs. When she had first collapsed into the chair her legs had been tightly together. Now they were relaxed and slightly parted. By the time I had settled back down myself and smiled at her she'd finished the drink and was placing the glass back down on the occasional table that separated us.

'How was it?' I grinned.

'Mmmmm,' Nicki murmured, then added, 'I feel cooler already.' She did, too. All she felt like doing now was resting for a bit, then back into it to finish her day's work completely.

'You look more relaxed than you did when you first sat down,' I said to her. 'In fact, twice as relaxed, I'd say.'

'I feel it,' Nicki answered as she closed her eyes and sighed deeply. She felt as if her whole body was shutting down. He was right. She felt much more relaxed than she had only a moment ago. Must be the heat, she thought, as she took another long deep breath and exhaled slowly.

I waited a few minutes more, and then I spoke again.

'You know, it's amazing what the power of your own mind can do,' I said with a smile. Her eyes opened slowly and gradually focussed on my face. 'I'll bet you could really feel it before when you were imagining you were in that cool room at the supermarket, when I was getting your drink. Would that be true?'

'Yes,' Nicki answered. 'I could feel it, and you're right. The mind is very powerful – mine is, at any rate, I think.' In fact, she knew exactly how strong her own mind was, especially when it came to giving up chocolate.

11

'And I'm sure you have a very strong and powerful mind, too, Nicki,' I went on. 'I think I read somewhere that the Greeks have one of the most powerful subconscious minds of all races. Don't know where I read that, but I remember it because it made me think of you. You're the only Greek I know.'

I laughed then and Nicki laughed with me. I could see a little puffiness beginning to form under her eyes.

'Really?' Nicki said, a note of amazement in her voice. 'I didn't know that, but it's probably true. Dad is very strong-minded, and mum's no slouch, either.' She finished with a knowing grin, suddenly aware of how heavy her eyes were feeling. She actually felt as if she could go off to sleep right then. And it was so hot. She could feel her forehead and the heat on it.

'I read somewhere, too, that a strong subconscious mind can easily override a weaker conscious mind, if it really wants to,' I told her interestingly.

'How do you know if you've got a strong subconscious mind?' Nicki asked him, curiosity mounting on her forehead, which had now stopped sweating. She was still wondering about that when he answered her again.

'Well,' I began. 'I guess it would be sort of like when I suggested to you that you would really like to take a break and chill out for a while, instead of working so hard in this heat. Your conscious mind wanted to get all the work finished. Isn't that true?'

'Yes, I did,' Nicki answered. 'But only in the beginning. Then I changed my mind.'

'Actually,' I said, 'you didn't. Your subconscious mind changed your conscious mind for you, without you even knowing it, because chilling out here with a cool glass of drink seemed a better suggestion than slaving away in the heat of the house. It's the natural nature of your

12

subconscious mind to always go for the deeper levels of relaxation, learning and pleasure. I read about it in a psyche book.'

Nicki looked at him for a few moments before answering. She felt heavy-lidded, and had to refocus several times while he'd been speaking to her, but now she finally got it together enough to answer him lucidly.

'That's amazing,' she said.

'Yes, it is,' I replied. 'And the only reason you're feeling so tired right now is because I suggested it to you, and your subconscious mind must have decided that letting go completely and being tired was better than being wide awake right now. So, now you're feeling more and more tired by the second – more and more heavy in your eyes, as if they just want to close right down all by themselves and take time out for a little while so your body and conscious mind can have a well-earned rest.'

'Gee,' Nicki said through a yawn. 'I never realised my subconscious mind could take over and make me feel something I hadn't felt or wanted to feel before. I do feel really tired, now that you come to mention it.' She couldn't understand her fatigue. Every part of her body felt loose, limp and relaxed.

'Yes, amazing, isn't it?' I said, driving the concept home. 'Your subconscious mind will always go very strongly for the deeper levels of relaxation, learning and pleasure. That seems to be just the way subconscious minds work, in order to take care of us when we try to do too much consciously, without enough rest planned to happen. And you have been working hard in all this heat. Isn't that true?'

'Mmmm,' Nicki said slowly with heavy blinking eyes. 'It was hot in the house, especially mopping.'

'Yes,' I continued. 'So you can understand now that if

13

your subconscious mind wants to accept a suggestion it feels more like doing than your conscious mind does, your subconscious mind will win every time, because in the long run, it's good for you.'

'Mmm, I suppose so,' Nicki said slowly. In reality she couldn't care less about it right then. All she wanted to do was go to sleep.

'And your subconscious mind does seem very strong, today, especially,' I said. 'Isn't that true?'

'Mmmm, seems so.' Nicki answered slowly and tiredly. 'I wasn't this tired when I sat down.' It was getting more and more difficult for her to grab onto and then focus on a single thought.

'That's because,' I confirmed to her, 'your subconscious mind has been following my suggestions of how nice it would be to just let go and relax and chill out for a while, even though you hadn't really planned on it. Isn't that true, too?'

'Yes,' Nicki admitted. 'I hadn't planned on stopping, either. But I have now.' She chuckled tiredly; it was almost too much effort to laugh.

'Which means,' I said, closing down and becoming more excited by the second. 'That your subconscious mind will accept, follow and act upon each and every suggestion I give you that's of a highly beneficial nature to you by way of deeper relaxation, deeper learning, or deeper pleasure. That must be also true then, don't you think?'

Nicki was having real trouble keeping her eyes open now, let alone being able to focus on his face.

'I don't know.' Nicki answered very wearily. 'I suppose so.'

'Nicki, listen to me carefully,' I said, getting really excited now. I felt like a hunter closing on its prey for the

14

final kill. 'I'll bet if I suggested to your subconscious mind right now, that within a few minutes you would feel as if you were wide awake, fresh and alert, because you'd have something new and fascinating to learn about yourself, then your subconscious mind would simply see to it and make you feel wide awake, fresh and alert when I counted to three and snapped my fingers. And even though your conscious mind would still be chilling out and relaxing, your subconscious mind would allow you to feel wide awake, fresh and alert. But only until I said the words, "Nicki, chill," again. Then you could join your conscious mind and rest a bit longer, until I wanted to suggest more things for you to learn. Then it would follow my suggestions to the letter and allow you to feel happy and willing to do each and every thing I suggest to you. And without question and without doubt would you believe that everything I suggest to you will happen, exactly as I suggest it will, so that you can benefit from the outcome in the manner you desire most. And that's what you want, anyway, to benefit from all of my suggestions so you can feel good about yourself, without feeling guilty. Isn't that true?'

Nicki felt her head nod slowly from where it had fallen to her chest. Her breathing was deep and peaceful. Her arms hung limp and loose on the chair beside her and her thighs had fallen wider apart. It was too much. Everything he was saying was just too much to take in.

'Good,' I said. 'One… two… three…'

Chapter Four

I watched. Nothing happened for a few seconds. Then her eyes slowly opened and she took a deep breath and stretched long and loudly with a groan. When she stopped doing that she looked at me. Her eyes were a little red with lacrimation, but becoming whiter by the second. Slowly she smiled.

'How do you feel?' I asked with a smile.

'As if I've just woken up from a long sleep.' Nicki smiled. 'If I listened to you long enough your voice would put anyone to sleep.' She just couldn't believe it; a moment ago she was dead to the world, believing nothing on planet earth would have caused her to rouse.

'Are you saying I've got a boring voice?' I grinned at her.

'No.' Nicki grinned back at him, feeling more awake by the second.

'See how strong your subconscious mind is?' I said. 'A few moments ago you were dead to the world, and ready for sleep. Now you feel relaxed and fresh and alert, simply because I suggested you would and your subconscious mind just made it happen, even though you probably didn't want to feel awake. Isn't that true?'

Nicki laughed, and her breasts shook a little. She was actually amazed to think her subconscious mind was actually as strong as that.

'You're right,' she said. 'While I was listening to you I was betting my conscious mind was stronger because I wanted to stay like that and go to sleep. I was feeling sooooo tired. But now I don't.'

'See what I mean?' I pointed out. 'Your subconscious mind will do whatever I tell it to, if it means you will benefit from my suggestions by always going to the deeper levels of relaxation, learning or pleasure, and learning more and more about yourself as you do so. Can you see that?'

For the first time then I saw a hint of suspicion in her eyes as she smiled back at me.

'Well,' Nicki said, dropping her gaze from his for a second, 'I do feel wide awake now. I didn't want to, but I do.' She wasn't really sure. She trusted Mr Davis and his wife, although his wife wasn't there. He was quite good looking, too, in a mature sort of way.

'We can test the strength of your subconscious mind, if you like,' I put to her, leading her into acceptance.

'How do you mean?' Nicki asked, a little more suspicious now. She wasn't quite sure what he was talking about. Surely he wasn't going to come on to her – the daughter of his wife's friend?

'Well,' I began, 'I could suggest something to your subconscious mind that it might like to experience a deeper level of, even though your conscious mind might not want to right now. Then you'd be able to see that the more your conscious mind tried to resist the suggestion, the more your subconscious mind would make you feel like following it to the letter until it was done. Want to try and learn a bit about the strength of your own subconscious mind, Nicki?'

She held his seemingly sincere gaze for almost thirty seconds before answering.

'Okay.' Nicki smiled, the suspicion still there. What harm could it do? It was broad daylight and they were in the middle of an open lounge. Also he was her boss, in a way, anyway.

'Good,' I said, and tried mentally to still my thumping heart. 'Now, I think your subconscious mind would find it much, much cooler and more relaxing if you were to stand up now and take off all your clothes. That way the refreshing air can drift around your body and cool you down quickly and revitalise you, knowing the more you try not to take them off, the more you will. The more you try to resist your subconscious mind the more you'll do exactly what it's making you feel like doing. Try to resist your own mind now, and find that you can't. Try and find you simply can't.'

Nicki's eyebrows remained fixed and frozen high on her forehead where they leapt to when he told her to remove her clothes. Her mouth also had dropped open when he'd confirmed her growing suspicions, but she wasn't moving, wasn't saying anything, just staring at him, eyes as wide as a skittish chestnut mare.

'Try and "not" take off all your clothes to really cool off, Nicki,' I pushed home, 'and see that you can't, and that you will, and quickly now, too, before you lose all the cool air.'

Nicki remained frozen in the chair. She just couldn't believe what he had said. Her face seemed frozen as well – but suddenly she got the shock of her life. Slowly her hands came up and took a light hold on the T-shirt she was wearing, but they didn't attempt to lift it. They just remained there. She just couldn't believe it. She didn't do that, did she?

'No,' she said quietly but definitely, holding his gaze in hers – yet her hands didn't move either way.

'Yes.' He smiled. 'Why fight your own subconscious mind? You know that's exactly what you feel like doing. Why delay the pleasure any longer when you can stand

18

up now, take them all off, and let that breezy air drift around your body and really cool you down? You know you have a very powerful subconscious mind and you know you're already feeling like standing up and taking off your clothes without feeling embarrassed or guilty so you can feel really cool.'

I watched and I waited. My heart thumped in my chest and my pulse beat a tune in my temples, but I forced myself to remain calm. I also had the hardest erection I'd felt inside my pants for a long time.

Nicki felt her fingers unbelievably grip the material of her T-shirt, and then they relaxed. They tensed again, and then they relaxed. They gripped it again, and then they relaxed.

Then they moved… upward, but her eyes never left his as her hands finally and slowly drew the flimsy T-shirt up and over her head. Then she dropped it on the floor beside her chair. Her breasts with their erect dark nipples standing stiff and proud. Nicki was shocked out of her mind. She couldn't believe she'd just done what she'd done. But she hadn't done it, she asked herself furiously – had she?

'No, Mr Davis,' Nicki said emphatically, but quietly. 'Mr Davis, I can't.'

'Yes,' I said quietly, confidently, 'you can, simply because that's what you really feel like doing right now. Isn't that true?'

'No, Mr Davis,' Nicki answered defiantly, but quietly, 'it isn't.' She felt herself getting angry. She hadn't done it, but she had. She didn't, but she did. What, she asked herself angrily, was going on? No, she wouldn't. She wouldn't. Not for anything. She just wouldn't. She couldn't!

'Yes,' I said quietly back to her, 'it is. And the feeling to stand up now and take off all your clothes is getting stronger by the second. You can feel that. And in a second or two you'll do just that.'

'No,' Nicki said defiantly. 'Mr Davis, I can't. Don't do this, please. I can't.' She realised then that she wanted to, but there was no way she was going to let herself. Then she wondered why she wanted to and remembered what he said; that her subconscious mind was stronger than her conscious mind and it was now overriding it with that superior strength, no matter what she wanted.

'I'm not the one doing it, Nicki – you are,' he answered calmly. 'And yes, you can and you will.'

Nicki realised he was right. She was the one doing it, but she wasn't – not really… but she was. Her anger and panic was growing by the second, and then she shocked herself well and truly by moving. She couldn't believe it. She was actually moving without her own consent to do so. She was already rising slowly from the chair before he had finished speaking. Her glowering, angry eyes never left his as she stood staring down at him. Her nipples and firm breasts quivered as the angry breath shook in her throat with each exhalation.

'No, Mr Davis,' Nicki insisted defiantly, then died inside as her fingers moved slowly for the button of her denim cut-off shorts. She tried to stop them. They hesitated, but then continued.

'Don't tell me,' I said gently. 'And don't get angry with me. It's your powerful subconscious mind you're talking to and dealing with, not me.'

'No,' Nicki denied again when her fingers released the button. 'No.' But her left hand took hold of the zipper and slowly began to slide it downwards while her other hand held her shorts. She could not believe what she was doing. Stripping off her clothes in front of her mother's friend's husband. Her embarrassment was felt from the top of her head to the tip of her toes, but still she kept doing what she didn't want to do.

'You're the one doing it.' He smiled victorious. 'Not me.'

Nicki watched as he dropped his gaze from hers and watched her hands. The zipper hand reached the bottom. Her fingers had released it and that hand hung limply by her side. The other hand trembled as it held the open front of her shorts between her fingers. She could see him waiting. She watched and she waited with him. Her gaze was boring holes in his head. Then it happened. The fingers belonging to the hand that held the shorts let go. Denim fell in a tiny heap around her ankles. Nicki could have died. She wanted to cover herself, but she didn't. She couldn't. She felt hot from top to bottom with shame, but was glad she had decided to wear those particular panties. She wondered then if he noticed her dark bush beneath the sheer panties. Of course he did, she reminded herself; he wasn't blind.

Slowly I let my gaze move upward from her shorts around her ankles, up over her shins and knees, up over her shapely thighs, up until it rested on her blue panties. My cock flexed wildly inside my pants at what I saw. The front of her panties was puffed out a little, filled with the bushy pubic hair that lay beneath the flimsy material of her dainty underwear. My cock flexed strongly again.

'No,' Nicki said defiantly. 'Mr Davis, please!' She felt her fingers wanting to do something she did not want to for anything in the world, but for the life of her she didn't seem to have any control over her own body. She couldn't believe it and was dying of shame and embarrassment.

He raised his gaze to hers. Nicki stared bloody murder down at him.

'The sooner they're off, the sooner you'll be as cool as

if you were in a cold room at the supermarket,' I said.

'No,' Nicki snapped angrily. 'Mr Davis, I can't. I can't!' Again she felt her fingers twitching, as if readying to do exactly as he said. She tried and tried to force them to cover herself, but they just would not obey her – not in the slightest. Then she nearly died. Her fingers began to tremble.

'Yes,' I grinned up at her, 'you can, and you will… do it now.'

Nicki was dying on her feet with shame and embarrassment. Her hands moved slowly to her waist. Her thumbs hooked in each side of the waistband and hesitated. Her mind screamed at her to run out of the house, even if she was in her underwear and topless, but her body did not move a muscle, other than the way he had told it to move. Her heart thumped and her temples beat a staccato pulse in her forehead that she felt in her groin. Nicki was aware she was becoming very wet, but she forced that thought from her mind. It wasn't her, she figured, and wondered at the same time. It wasn't – was it? Ripples of heat and tingling were running up over her lower belly and between her buttocks. She felt each cheek clench and then flex with a strong sensual sensation. She felt herself juicing like she did whenever she masturbated in her bed.

'Mr Davis,' Nicki begged him, 'please, I can't. Oh, please, I can't. I'm a… I'm a… I *can't*. Please, Mr Davis? Don't make me. I just can't. Please, Mr Davis?'

The idea of accepting exactly what was happening made me even more hard as my eyes glued themselves to her hidden Greek pussy. Her tone had taken on a pleading, begging note, as if I could control what she was doing, and not her. It seemed almost as if she believed she was helpless before the suggestions I had given her and that their fulfilment would be a happening reality, with me being the only one who could stop it from happening. Nicki shifted her weight from one foot to the other and back again, rocking gently from side to side. Her fingers and thumbs continued to tense and relax as they lightly gripped the waistband of her underwear. A power; Nicki believed I had a power over her that she could not overcome. It was amazing.

'Nicki,' I said, 'do you believe that what I have suggested to your subconscious mind you will do, whether you want to or not, simply because I suggested it?'

'Please, Mr Davis, but yes. Don't make me do it, please?' Nicki pleaded; she was and felt desperate.

'And do you believe that only I can stop your subconscious mind from making you do something you don't want to do consciously?' I asked, probing her momentary belief system.

'Oh, Mr Davis, please?' Nicki begged. 'Yes, but don't make me… please?'

'But you do want to follow that suggestion, don't you, Nicki?' I said. 'Be honest, or I can't help you.'

'Oh, Mr Davis, Please? Yes, you know I do. That's why I'm down to my knickers. Please… Mr Davis, please?' Nicki pleaded, embarrassed to the very core of her for having to admit it to him, but she did, only more so than she would normally ever tell him to his face.

Amazing. I was completely amazed. I had no idea a person's belief system could be so powerful when used against them.

'Mr Davis, please,' Nicki wailed as her fingers tensed and began to drag her panties slowly downwards. Her gaze lowered to see the top of her glossy dark curls being revealed to the man. Her face flushed from shame and embarrassment. Her buttocks clenched and unclenched

23

several times. Strong radiating pulses of raw sexuality were firing and torching up from between her thighs.

I allowed her to suffer at least until I could glimpse the top of her bushy black Greek forest. Then I put her out of her misery, momentarily.

'Okay,' I said, looking up over her gorgeous breasts and into her large tear-filled eyes, which pleaded with me for rescue from herself. 'I think your subconscious mind would find it less stressing to your conscious mind if it could make you feel relieved by releasing your panties and sitting down to relax for a while again.' Then I added, 'But with your thighs parted.'

'Mr Davis, please?' Nicki begged, her relief evaporating as fast as it had come when he said about the position of her knees.

'Would you rather be standing there buck naked?' I suggested.

'No,' Nicki admitted, pouting, then her hands slowly moved away from her knickers. She sighed deeply and then slowly sat down, watching her knees, one to the other and back again. Slowly they moved apart. Then they moved even wider until each calf was pressed firmly against the chair. She closed her eyes with raw shame, and blushed when she looked up and saw his gaze riveted on the very centre of her hidden black nest.

I was still amazed. My mind raced in forward planning, not really sure how to take advantage of the opportunity, but sure I was going to, somehow. I could see she was beginning to relax.

'See how much better you feel now?' I said. 'You were right; your subconscious mind is definitely following each and every suggestion I'm giving you, and very strongly, too. Wouldn't you say?'

Her eyes opened, but she did not look at him. Nicki

knew he was right, though. She did feel a little better. Not much, but a little. If only her legs were not so damn far apart. She felt like the smuttiest of sluts; like a real harlot; a common tart of the highest order.

'Yes,' Nicki said quietly, then added, 'Mr Davis, may I close my legs, please?'

'Yes,' I said, not really knowing why. 'You may.'

Nicki's knees clamped slowly together. Her lungs filled with air and she sighed, knowing she was visibly relaxing before his eyes. Then her gaze found his. It was different somehow. He smiled at her, recalling the strange feelings she'd had as he said she could close her knees. She felt like he was her master and she was his slave, or something. Then to her horror she felt herself moisten instantly and strongly.

I hardened even more as I watched her, and felt myself flex strongly again.

'I told you Greeks have the most powerful subconscious mind of all the races.' I smiled at her.

'Mr Davis,' Nicki said quietly. 'That was really embarrassing for me.' And she wasn't kidding. She was so relieved it as all over now. So relieved. Thank you, God, she prayed. Thank you.

I noticed Nicki seemed to have completely forgotten that her gorgeous tits were bare. She had made no attempt to cover them at all. Her arms lay loose and limp on her thighs. When she suddenly became aware of where my gaze was directed she looked quickly down at herself, but still her hands remained where they were.

'Mr Davis, please?' Nicki pleaded, indicating with her eyes that she be allowed to get dressed.

'You have lovely breasts,' I said, not really knowing why.

'Mr Davis, please?' she pleaded again, blushing bright

red from the neck up, as if wearing a scarlet necktie all of a sudden. Her nipples felt as if they were elongating in his gaze. Her buttocks heated again and her junction rippled in the same strong manner.

I sat back and relaxed with a sigh. This was going better than I had ever dreamed it would.

'So you realise now, Nicki, that your subconscious mind will allow you to follow any suggestion I give it, no matter what it might happen to be?' I cemented into her belief system and checked it at the same time.

She didn't look at me, but when she did answer after a few long seconds I was happy.

'Yes,' she answered quietly, her face lowered towards her breasts. He was right and she knew it.

'Why do you think it's so, Nicki?' I probed.

She didn't answer for about thirty seconds. I could almost see the wheels turning as her mind reached back for anything that might make a sensible answer to the question in her mind – anything other than she 'wanted' to.

'Because... because Greeks have... have... they have... strong minds,' Nicki murmured. 'And... I'm... Greek.' It was the only thing that came to her mind that made any sort of sense. Nothing made any sense anyway, but that was as close as it got.

'And proud of it,' I ended for her.

'I was.'

I smiled at her as she looked up, and it drew just the slightest of smiles from her as well. We just sat there then, me looking at her breasts and her eyes while she looked everywhere and anywhere, but at me.

'Your subconscious mind can not only make you "do" things,' I said.

'What do you mean?' Nicki asked after a few seconds,

finally looking directly and suspiciously at him. Her mind sensed it should panic, but she waited.

'Well, it can make you say things, too, like in telling the truth,' I told her.

Almost instantly Nicki blushed again, only more so and more quickly. My cock went bone rigid immediately in response to her reaction. She could have reached up at any time and covered her breasts, but still she had not. I became curious.

'You know why you haven't covered your breasts with your hands, Nicki, don't you?' I stated confidently, then added, 'And you know your strong subconscious Greek mind will make you tell me the truth when you answer, don't you?'

Nicki's gaze dropped to her breasts and hands instantly. Her arms and fingers tensed, but didn't move to cover her breasts. After a few seconds she replied; yes, she knew, but didn't want to admit it, even to herself.

'Yes,' Nicki answered softly, but added nothing more. What else could she say? Plenty, but she wasn't going to. She couldn't. She would die. She would just die.

'Well?' I asked, after waiting patiently.

She squirmed in the chair and looked around the room before finally answering, and my heart soared and my cock hardened and flexed powerfully once more.

'Because…' Nicki began hesitantly. 'Because… you haven't… you haven't… told me I can.' In saying that she became aware of a very strange sensation. It wasn't bad, but it was strange and strong… very strong. She felt like owned goods all of a sudden. And shocking her truly, the feelings and sensations did not feel all that bad. In fact, they felt good.

God, I was in heaven. She had completely accepted the suggestions into her conscious belief system that I

27

controlled her mind and actions. Her answer was the truth, according to the best of her momentary belief system.

'That's right,' was all I could think of to say right then. I wondered when it actually was that I had hypnotised her. I wanted to bottle the technique and make a fortune. 'You may put your top back on now and cover your breasts,' I said, not really knowing why. Maybe I wanted to enjoy my assumed power over her mind.

Nicki felt the relief rush from her head to her toes. She quickly reached for her T-shirt and slipped it down over her head. Then she took a deep breath and sighed, then visibly relaxed. Her gaze met his. She felt her confidence returning by the second, as well as her defiance.

Chapter Five

'So,' I said with a sigh and a smile. 'What do you think of that demonstration of the power of your own mind, Nicki?' I asked, then added, 'Knowing you can only tell the truth, the whole truth, and nothing but the truth.'

Nicki stared at him hard for many seconds before answering, and when she did the defiance and strength was now clearly in her gaze that held his, but she knew the words she would say when she answered.

'It works because... because...' she began, then found the truth with a small defeated sigh. 'Because... you can somehow... you can somehow control my... my subconscious mind and... and... make me.' She finished, hanging her head low.

I smiled softly, if that was possible. I didn't want to appear as if I was gloating over the truth of what she believed.

'Seems that way, doesn't it?' I confirmed to her mind.

'Yes,' Nicki replied after a few seconds, but she didn't look at him. Then she asked, 'Why are you doing this to me, Mr Davis?' She asked as she met his gaze head on with defiance and strength.

I looked at her directly and replied, 'Because I can. Can't I, Nicki?'

Nicki's spirit blazed immediately, knowing he was right, and she held his gaze for long moments before finally answering.

'Yes,' she said evenly, again that strange feeling of being someone's property, to do with as they liked, washed over her... and it was not unpleasant.

'That's right,' I cemented. 'I can. And that means I can do anything I want with you, if I really want to. Doesn't it?'

A full minute passed this time before Nicki answered, her gaze not leaving his the entire time.

'Yes,' she said. 'I guess so.' But in reality, she 'knew' so.

'That's right,' I cemented again. 'How does it feel to be my slave?'

Nicki's eyebrows arched almost to the top of her forehead and her mouth dropped open, but her eyes, her eyes just hardened as she answered.

'Your slave? Your slave?' she repeated. 'I'm not your slave.'

'Aren't you?' I asked, then said forcefully, 'Strip off completely, now. Right now. Do it now and be quick!'

'No, Mr Davis! Please?' Nicki heard herself beg, but her hands and fingers were already reaching for her T-shirt again. 'Please? Please? Don't do this. Please? Don't, Mr Davis. Don't, please!' Her mind panicked and raced with a barrage of chaotic thoughts that rushed everywhere and nowhere at the same time, accomplishing just as much ado about nothing. Her top was already covering her face on the way up over her head.

'Pull your top back down and don't strip,' I commanded her.

Nicki's hands froze, and then slowly pulled her T-shirt back down so that it hugged her breasts once more. Then she sighed and hung her head. She felt defeated – defeated by her own mind, and him, somehow.

'So,' I said, 'what are you?' I could see the inner turmoil going on between both her minds – what she had seen and what she believed, along with what made sense to her as proof of the seeming limitless power she believed I now somehow had over her.

'And when you do finally answer,' I said, 'you'll look me right in the eye and say it with feeling. You hear me? With feeling, knowing you really believe the truth of what you're saying, because you know you can't lie now.'

Another full minute passed silently in the lounge while she watched his gaze drill holes in her crotch. She could feel the intense heat there. Ashamed in knowing, Nicki realised she was juicing again, and very strongly this time. Frowns came and went on her forehead. Then they came and went some more. Her chin remained downcast to her chest while she thought.

'What are you?' I prompted.

Nicki answered and slowly raised her head; her face directly aimed at his.

'Your... your slave.' Nicki breathed quietly while holding his gaze, then dropped hers to her lap.

I dropped my gaze from her; my cock was preparing to riot within my trousers and go on a spending spree to shop till it dropped without me.

'Again,' I said strongly.

'Your... slave,' Nicki repeated softly, looking up briefly at him when she said it, but then dropping her gaze again after she'd done so. The words seemed to be coming more easily. Not much, but a bit. Again that feeling of being goods and chattel overwhelmed her with a feeling and sensations that she did not find unpleasant. In fact, she squirmed in the chair, feeling the liquid heat draining through to settle between her already overheated buttocks.

'Again,' I insisted.

'Your slave,' Nicki repeated a little more firmly, beginning to feel absolutely sexual.

'Say it in full,' I pressed. 'You are my slave.'

Nicki's eyes glared at him. Her buttocks flexed and her

31

female core beneath her dark bush tingled in such a way so as to almost take her breath away. The feeling sent shockwaves of ripples throughout her vagina.

'I… I am your… slave,' she said.

'Again, with feeling,' I said strongly.

'Mr Davis, please?' Nicki pleaded. Her hormones were racing… right away from their owner. She could feel it as a happening reality, right there in front of her mother's friend's husband.

I said nothing. I just looked at her – waiting. Then she sighed.

'I am your… slave,' Nicki said, but without the defiance. There seemed only acceptance now. She felt strange, very strange, well and truly embarrassed, but it was a nice type of strange.

'Again,' I said, not as strongly.

'I am your slave,' Nicki said, feeling comfortable with the words and not really knowing why. She felt as if something inside had been set free, but had no idea what that something might be.

'Again,' I said.

'I am your slave,' Nicki said, this time feeling something almost akin to pride. She could not believe it. Yes, pride. She could not believe it.

'You are my Greek slave,' I said.

'I am your… your Greek… slave,' Nicki said, again feeling that strange sense of pride that made her feel good without feeling guilty.

'Again,' I said. 'And look at me each and every time you say it.

'I am your… Greek slave,' Nicki heard herself say. And again that feeling was there, although she had no idea what she should be proud of.

'Say it as you believe it the truth you believe it to be, or call yourself a liar to yourself,' I said.

After a minute or two of clearly thinking about my statement she answered softly.

'I am your Greek slave, Mr Davis,' Nicki heard herself say, knowing she actually sounded as if she truly meant it.

'You really meant that one, didn't you, Nicki?' I probed.

After another long pause Nicki looked up at him, the defiance, but not the strength, now gone from her gaze. She felt as if she had found a new strength, but from where did it come? From where did she get it?

'Yes, Mr Davis,' Nicki answered. 'I do.' Then she sighed and relaxed back more deeply into the chair, somehow feeling as if now everything was going to be all right.

'In fact, Nicki,' I went on, 'you are my proud Greek slave. Isn't that the real truth of the matter, now that you've come to accept your own belief in the fact?'

Nicki's eyes had not left his while he'd been speaking.

'Yes,' she said without much delay. She knew it was true. It was true.

'What are you?' I asked, holding her eyes in mine.

'Your proud Greek slave,' Nicki replied, internalising that truth now as her own.

'In full, Nicki, with feeling,' I insisted.

Nicki took a deep breath and looked at him. He smiled at her in return.

'I am your proud Greek slave, Mr Davis,' Nicki heard herself say, evenly and truthfully.

'And how do you truthfully feel about that truthful fact, Nicki?' I asked.

Long minutes passed while we sat opposite each other and held each other's gaze. No defiance or anger passed between us or showed in her expression. We just looked at one another while she came to grips with and discovered her own truthful answer. I smiled at her once or twice – she tentatively returned my smile each time.

'Good,' Nicki finally heard herself quietly reply. And she did. She didn't know why, but she did, and she didn't feel guilty or ashamed or embarrassed any longer. She just felt good.

'Do you really believe that truth as you believe it to be, Nicki, knowing you couldn't lie to me now, even if you really wanted to?'

'Yes, Mr Davis,' Nicki answered almost immediately. 'I do.' Because she knew she did believe it. She just did... now.

I smiled at her. She returned my smile.

'You know, Nicki,' I said, 'I've never had a slave before. I actually feel very proud right at this moment. And I have your honesty to thank for that. Thank you,' I finished.

I could have sworn I saw Nicki's chest swell a little, but I couldn't be sure. She did smile though, and it was a truthful smile, an honest smile, which indicated to me her total acceptance of what had transpired between us.

And me? I was still completely blown away and amazed by the whole thing. I still wondered now and then how I actually did it. Now what? I wondered as we sat there smiling honestly at one another. She was my slave for no other reason than she believed she was. It was as simple as that; she believed she was. I concluded that that was what hypnosis was really about; a person's belief system and the influencing or control of it for other purposes than what the owner might want to believe if given free will and a choice in the matter. I was amazed. Where had this handy little tool been all my life?

'What do you think slaves should call their Master to show the proper respect, Nicki?' I asked her quietly, holding her eyes in mine.

Nicki genuinely thought about it for a while before answering him, and when she did she seemed pleased with the correctness of her answer.

'Maybe… Sir,' Nicki said. 'Or Master, I guess. It would depend on him.'

I said nothing. I just looked at her with what amounted to admiration for her genuine-felt honesty in her answer. I smiled warmly at her, which brought forth then the most affectionate and wonderful smile I think I've ever seen on the face of a female in all my life. It began at her eyes and radiated downward over her face, ending with giving me the warmest feeling from another human being I've ever had. I was actually beginning to feel quite strange, in a very strongly sensual and sexual way.

'What would… what would… you prefer?' Nicki suddenly heard herself ask softly, quietly, her big dark eyes feeling like liquid pools of sheer female femininity. She was completely surprised by the sound of her own voice asking.

I was stunned. Her face had honesty written all over it with her question. It had innocence, too. Her face had innocence. That was it – honesty and innocence.

'Which word do you think, as my slave, would suit your saying it such that it would roll off your lips like honest sweet honey every time you said it?' I replied.

Nicki thought for a moment, searching his face honestly for the answer to his question. Then she smiled. It felt like such a beautiful smile to her own awareness; a soft smile; a wonderful natural feminine smile.

'Sir, I think,' Nicki said, 'Master sounds a bit formal, maybe?'

I smiled at her.

'Yes,' I agreed. 'I think an honest slave should call her

Master "Sir", but only when they're alone and in private. A Master-slave relationship is one of mutual respect between both and the natural dominant and submissive positions of both. Okay, Sir it is then, Nicki, when we're in private.'

'Yes, Mr Davis… um, sorry, I mean, yes Sir.' Nicki answered finally with a sheepish grin, feeling strangely proud when she said the word, Sir – in a sexual kind of way. Yes, she thought – definitely sexual.

'And are you happy with that way of addressing me in private, Nicki?' I asked genuinely.

'Yes… Sir,' Nicki replied. Now she couldn't think of addressing him in any other way. It was as if he had been responsible for liberating something from deep inside her; something that maybe had been trying to get out; that had meant to be let out at this time in her life.

'Are you sure?' I prompted.

'Yes, Sir.' Nicki answered easily – and she was. Yes, she was.

'You make me feel very special and proud, Nicki,' I said earnestly.

Nicki's face seemed to beam suddenly, or maybe it was my imagination, but her smile wasn't. It was real. It was honest. And it was innocently truthful.

'Thank you, Sir,' Nicki said, unprompted by any question. She felt herself moisten again, this time in earnest and in abundance.

'Do you feel proud to have a Master now, Nicki?' I asked.

'Yes, Sir,' Nicki answered immediately. 'I do. I'd never even thought about it before, but… I do now.' Then added, 'Sir.' And the juices kept coming and kept right on flowing.

'That's okay, Nicki,' I told her. 'However it comes out naturally in each sentence – don't try and find a home for it by itself. Okay?'

'Yes, Sir.' Nicki smiled quickly at him. Both words sounded natural to her now.

Amazed wasn't really the word going through my mind as I sat there wondering what to do and where to go with Nicki next? It just wasn't.

'How do you feel about having a Master, Nicki?' I asked. 'Really feel?'

Nicki thought about it for at least a minute before answering him.

'To be honest, Sir,' she began, 'it feels different, but in a good way. I'd never thought about having one, but now that I do, it feels good.' She finished, aware of her own natural oils simmering between her thighs.

'Yes,' I said with a smile into her big dark Greek eyes, 'it does, doesn't it?'

'Yes, Sir, it does,' Nicki agreed, feeling her libido rising dramatically by the second.

I smiled with her as we both just sat there quietly enjoying each other's company, and, seemingly also enjoying the beginning of our new relationship as Master and slave.

'What do you think the role of a slave should be, Nicki?' I asked.

'To serve him as a slave, Sir.' Nicki finally answered after some thought and moistened strongly again, instantly. She was his slave.

'In what ways should she serve him as a slave, do you think?' I asked, trying to lead her belief system in the direction I wanted.

'Every way he wants, I guess, Sir.' Nicki replied, the smile leaving her face slowly as her juices began to boil now.

'What do you think the role of the slave's Master should be?' I asked.

'To look after his slave, Sir, I guess,' Nicki said after only a few seconds' delay. Her mind was recoiling from all the sensual images of being pleased coming to her mind and senses all at once.

'In every way?' I prompted.

'Yes, Sir.' Nicki answered softly, dropping her gaze from his.

'Do you think it would be disrespectful for the slave to disobey her Master, Nicki?' I asked.

'Yes, Sir,' Nicki answered, looking up into my face. 'It would be, I guess.'

'You only guess?' I asked.

'No, Sir – it would be,' Nicki said.

'Do you think a Master has the right to punish his slave if she disobeyed him and was disrespectful in doing so?' I asked her, testing her new belief system.

After about half a minute Nicki answered, her body juicing again at the thought of her breasts bound tightly with rope. Thoughts of her pussy being paddled with a hairbrush and of her backside being spanked by a strong hand, as well as being suspended naked to a rope on the ceiling, hanging to her tiptoes while being whipped didn't help her body's sensual tidal flow.

'Yes, Sir,' Nicki said, and lowered her gaze from his. She was going crazy with raw, unadulterated lust and wanted badly to touch herself.

'You wouldn't ever be disrespectful and cause me to have to punish you, as is my right as your Master, would you, Nicki?' I asked, sowing the seed.

'No, Sir,' Nicki said softly, quietly. And she had no intention of being disrespectful.

'Good girl,' I said with a smile. 'I know you'll be a good slave and make me even more proud of you than I feel right now. Is that what you want, too, Nicki? To feel proud?' I asked.

'Yes, Sir,' Nicki said quietly, and she could not stand it; she could imagine his penis thickening inside his trousers like a snake getting ready to strike… right between her thighs… deeply… very deep.

'And do you want me to be proud of you and your slavery to me, too?' I then asked.

'Yes, Sir,' Nicki answered softly, looking at him, his penis growing inside her mind to gigantic proportions as it lay fully embedded inside her, stretching her, expanding her, filling her, widening her.

'So there would never be any need for me to punish you or use your own mind against you again to get you to obey me as you should as my slave, would there?' I said.

'No, Sir,' Nicki said quietly, dropping her gaze from his as she recalled her earlier experience with her knickers. Maybe she should be bad, she thought. Punishment sounded hot right then. Everything sounded hot right then.

'Good girl,' I said. 'I'm even more proud of you now, Nicki,' I added honestly. 'I really am.'

Nicki looked up at him and smiled gently. Her face was clear and honest, but she said nothing. She thought plenty, but she said nothing. She couldn't. She was cooking from the inside out.

'Do you think a slave should wear something of her accepted slavery whenever she and her Master are in private, as a sign of her acceptance of him and respect for him as her Master?' I asked.

'Yes, Sir,' Nicki answered, after a few seconds' thought. She was going to go crazy at any second; she wanted him inside her. There – sliding in and out. Slipping in her oil.

'I think so, too,' I agreed. 'How do you feel about a collar around your neck?' I asked.

Nicki felt her eyebrows only rise a little, but they did rise. Then after a few seconds they lowered as she held his gaze.

'Can it be a soft one, Sir?' she asked, looking at his with those big innocent eyes, feeling her juices flow strongly again.

'Yes,' I consented. 'You can pick it out, if you like. Sort of like an engagement ring. Would you like to do that?'

'Yes, Sir,' Nicki replied immediately, and then added, 'but where... how do I...?'

'I'll tell you the names of several shops,' I told her. 'You'll visit all of them and check the different ranges for the exact type, style and colour of the slave collar you'd feel really proud to wear in private with me as a sign of your accepted slavery... to me. Can I trust you to do that task for yourself as soon as you can, if I pay you for it when you bring me the sales docket?'

'Yes, Sir, you can,' Nicki answered immediately, already imagining what kind of collar she wanted and feeling so sensual, so hot.

'Okay then,' I said, 'that's great. In fact, I think it's really exciting. I'll let you surprise me when we meet next in private by letting you buy it by yourself. Okay? Then you can give it to me and I'll collar you officially and we'll celebrate, sort of like an engagement party, only for a proud Master and his proud Greek slave. Are you happy with the idea of a formal collaring for you?'

'Yes, Sir,' Nicki beamed as she looked at him. Her eyes felt big and beautiful. She felt herself grin proudly. 'I am.'

'Good,' I said with a broad excited smile. 'It's settled then. I am your Master so chosen and accepted willingly by you, and you are my chosen proud Greek slave, and I willingly and proudly accept you, too.'

'Thank you, Sir!' Nicki beamed proudly.

'Thank you, too, Nicki,' I said. 'I'm sure we'll be very happy in our new relationship.'

'Yes, Sir,' she said softly. 'I do, too.' She inhaled her own sexual fragrance and nearly fainted. God, she needed to be taken right there, right then... by him... her Master. Nothing else would do.

'Good,' I said, sitting up straight in my chair and holding my breath. This was it. This was the time. This was the place. And she was the one. 'You may now undress slowly, sensually, willingly, happily, and completely, Nicki. Without shame, embarrassment or guilt of any kind. And when you've done so, you may undress me, your Master, and allow me to pleasure us both in any way I choose. And,' I added, 'you may do it... now.'

Nicki's eyes widened for a few seconds then settled down. She dropped her gaze from his and hung her head towards her chest for almost a full minute that seemed like an eternity before she raised it again. When she did her eyes felt like two big beautiful round discs of softness, of warmth, and of uncertainty. Then she collapsed mentally and physically into and inside of her own natural female slavery.

'Mr Dav... Master,' she said meekly, and then hesitated while holding his gaze. 'I'm... I'm a... I'm a... virgin.' She almost whispered, drowning in the milky depths of her unmistakable sea of sensuality. She smiled again, warmly, proudly, and honestly. Then he reached out and took her right hand in his right hand and squeezed it firmly, yet softly, and smiled.

'Not for much longer,' I said, with a twinkle in my own eyes.

Nicki felt her mental hymen tear. She dropped her gaze from his and sighed. She could hear it. Then slowly, she

41

raised her face and eyes once more to fix and focus directly on his and just look at him for long tense minutes. Then she spoke, or rather, she heard herself breathe.

'Yes, Sir.' Nicki heard herself whisper softly, finally. She felt her face changing before his eyes into the warmth of a woman and a female who knew and willingly accepted the fact that she was about to lose her virginity. She was about to become who she really was and now wanted to be… a female… a proud Greek female… in slavery… with her Master.

'Again,' I said with a comforting smile. 'With feeling this time.'

Nicki looked up at him, overwhelmed. Her eyes were misty as she smiled warmly. 'Yes, Sir,' she said firmly, proudly, femininely, positively. 'Yes, Sir…'

I could have cried right at that moment, as the emotion of the event seemed to well up and nearly overwhelm me. Slowly she rose from the chair to her feet, her eyes never leaving mine for a single second. Her clothes seemed to disappear before my eyes, yet I can't for the life of me recall seeing her take them off. I was lost in the sensual whirlpool of my new Mastership and my slave's beautiful and innocently sensual eyes. I rose then when she held her arms outstretched for me to do just that. As her hands reached for my shirt my gaze dropped and disappeared forever into the lush, sensual black Greek forest of virgin sexuality between her legs.

'Yes, Sir,' Nicki breathed into his face with a full sensual and hesitant smile as she stepped closer and unbuckled his trousers with trembling fingers, waiting for his snake to be freed from its lair and strike her good, once and for all, finally. 'Not for much longer.'

I drowned. She drowned. We drowned… in her slavery and mine… from that moment on… for better, for worse... until death did us part.

'Yes, Sir,' Nicki heard herself breathe again as her thighs trembled with anticipation and gravity allowed her warm virgin oil to begin flowing freely down her inner thighs from its natural Greek source. 'Not... for much longer...'

Chapter Six

'Welcome to new friends,' I toasted them all. I had suggested to Lauren that she invite Marcena and her three Greek daughters over for dinner on Friday night. We sat around the table eating. Lauren sat at one end of the table, with me at the other. Nicki, wearing a sexy velvet collar with a small D-ring attached in the front, sat on my left. Athena and Appolonia, the stunningly gorgeous twenty-year-old twins sat on my right. Marcena sat next to Nicki.

I'd been amazed when they had first come through the door. All of them were olive-skinned and beautiful, like their mother. Long thick dark hair adorned the classic Greek heads of all of them. Although dressed conservatively they looked very feminine sitting around the table, talking and laughing. But Nicki, who smiled shyly at me from time to time, looked absolutely lovely. She would casually check both ways to see if any of the others had noticed, each time she glanced my way.

'What beautiful neckwear, Nicki,' I smiled. That drew everyone's attention to her and her collar. She blushed openly and smiled, lowering her eyes immediately. Her hands came up to touch it softly.

'Yes,' Lauren said. 'It's lovely.'

'I've never seen it before,' Marcena said. 'When did you get it, Nicki? You don't normally go in for that type of look.'

Nicki continued to blush as she answered her mother, not looking directly at her. All of a sudden she felt all eyes upon her. 'Oh, It's just something that was on special the 'other day,' she replied, hoping they all would just go on with what they had been doing and not make a fuss. It had taken all of her courage to wear it.

'It's cool!' Appolonia beamed. 'I didn't see you wearing it before we left.' She'd never seen Nicki in anything remotely like it before, either.

Again Nicki fingered the soft velvet collar, looking everywhere but at her sister. She wished he hadn't drawn everybody's attention to the fact she was wearing it. In a way, she'd hoped no one would notice it at all, except him.

'I put it on in the car just as we arrived,' she replied.

'No wonder I didn't see it on you at home – it's great,' Athena said, knowing that if she had seen it she would have asked Nicki if she could borrow it sometime.

Marcena then turned to Lauren with a knowing grin. 'Kids will wear absolutely anything these days,' she said.

I watched Lauren nod and smile, reminding myself that I didn't like either of the two older women at all, right then.

'Yes,' Lauren answered. 'Thank goodness I don't have to put up with that aspect of them any more.'

Both women laughed then and continued chatting. Athena and Appolonia went back to sipping their wine and talking quietly between themselves, which left Nicki head down and silent and frequently lifting her gaze to glance at me. I smiled whenever I caught her eye. When I did she glared at me. I just smiled back at her each time, picturing her naked with those long Greek legs and fully bushed centre, wearing nothing but that sexy collar. My body surged in agreement with the sensual visualisation.

Dinner over, Lauren and Marcena began clearing the table and attending to the dishes.

'Why don't you put some different music on?' Lauren

45

said to me.

I nodded and rose from the table.

Nicki looked up, then rose from the table and casually walked into the lounge. He was at the music centre. Her heart raced. She wondered if he liked the collar that she'd picked out for herself. Her thoughts had been on nothing else after she'd left him previously. She'd gone and bought it as soon as the shop had opened on Monday morning, not bothering to try any other stores. She'd fallen in love with the collar and the wearing of it as soon as it went around her throat. Her body flushed almost instantly. The memories of what she had done with him on Saturday had come rushing back at the time to swamp her mind and awareness with a vengeance. Feeling very hot and bothered she then left the shop with the collar tucked snugly in her purse.

'It's beautiful,' I said quietly but enthusiastically to Nicki when she came up to stand beside me at the music stand. Head down and eyes lowered, she looked magnificent.

'Thank you, Mr Dav – thank you… Master,' Nicki said quietly, correcting herself. The waves of sensual heat came thick and fast at addressing him that way, as well as wearing the velvet collar around her throat. She was excited at having to keep their secret in front of everybody and knew she'd have to be careful she didn't let anything slip, like a knowing look.

I turned my head in the direction of the kitchen to listen to the noise of the women washing up. The lounge was around the corner from the dining area, but not by much. I reached out and touched the collar.

'Beautiful,' I whispered, feeling the warmth of her skin. She giggled softly, still gazing down at the carpet. Then she quickly looked around towards the kitchen. My hand deliberately moved from the collar around her throat and gently came to rest on her nearest breast.

'Oh,' she gasped quietly, startled. 'Mr Dav – I mean, Master, they'll see. Please don't do that here.' That would be all she needed, she thought frantically, and then checked behind her towards the kitchen again. She heard him chuckle quietly. No one was there. They were still washing up. His hand, however, had not moved from her breast, and began squeezing gently.

'Oh, Mr Dav – Master, please, they'll see.' Nicki pleaded with him in a hushed tone, in spite of the warmth spreading through her chest and between her legs. Then his hand moved slowly across to settle warmly and firmly onto her other breast. It squeezed, hard.

'Oh,' she whimpered softly between her teeth when I squeezed her breast again.

I checked the kitchen direction, standing there rolling her stiff little nipple between my fingers and thumb. It lay engorged beneath the thin covering of her dress, beneath which she wore no bra.

'Oh Master, don't… please?' She pleaded with me quietly and emphatically, becoming seriously aroused with the excitement as well as me touching her. My wants came first, I decided. This she had yet to learn. Slowly I released her nipple and breast from my grasp then dropped my hand to my side. I laughed quietly as she sighed heavily, obviously relieved that no one would catch her being touched now.

Nicki's body felt flushed and hot. The others would be sure to know she had been doing something if they were to come in, she thought in a panic. Thank goodness he'd stopped. But her breasts now felt cold from where the warmth of his hand had been on them. Her nipples ached from his kneading them between his fingers and thumb.

'Turn around so you can see when they come in,' I

said to her. She looked up at me suspiciously, her face flushed. I smiled. 'Do it,' I said quietly, commandingly.

Nicki didn't trust him now at all, but the strength in his tone told her it was not a polite request. She knew he was having fun at her expense, and in a way it was exciting and naughty, but it was too risky. Slowly she turned around to face the entrance to the lounge then glanced up at his face. When he smiled at her she felt weak in the knees. Such a warm smile; so strong, and it danced.

'Oh,' she gasped when my hand came to rest gently in the small of her back as she stood watching the entrance.

'Master, please,' Nicki pleaded quietly.

I ignored her protests and began to lower my hand smoothly over her dress towards the top of her buttocks. The thin material felt cool as my hand slid over it and downward towards the firm curve of her behind.

'Master, please,' Nicki begged him, but it wasn't doing any good. He was intent upon having his way with her no matter what. A strange sensation of rich textured warmth then entered her mind and body. She felt so controlled, so in his power over her that she had willingly given him.

I cupped her left buttock and squeezed firmly. 'Oh,' Nicki gasped. My cock surged in answer to her soft cry of alarm. Then I moved my hand slowly to her right buttock and weighed the firm flesh of her for a few seconds before squeezing it, too.

'Mast—'

'Be quiet,' I snapped at her.

Nicki shut her mouth instantly and let out the remainder of her breath with a soft sigh, terrified that someone would come through to the lounge at any moment. Her gaze never left the corner around which they would appear.

She blushed as his hand continued to move from one cheek of her bottom to the other, squeezing hard. It almost hurt, but not quite. It was, however, having an effect on her private person. She felt warm and quickly became aware of the familiar pooling of the sexual energies between her legs. Her breath trembled a little as she tried to control each exhalation.

My heart picked up the beat as I released her ass from my grip. Gently, I forced the edge of my hand between her buttocks as far as the thin material would allow.

'Mas—' Nicki began to protest, but shut up instantly when he suddenly grasped a handful of one buttock and squeezed very hard; then she grimaced with pain. He then released his forceful grip and went back to cupping and weighing each cheek.

I was revelling in the absolute and utter control I had over her. My body was as hard as granite. 'Remember what we said about reward and punishment?' I said to her, squeezing her ass. She gasped, but nodded her head. 'Your resistance is not pleasing. You will have to be punished when we're next alone.'

'Ow…' Nicki gasped again when he squeezed her bottom painfully with the word, 'punished'. Her heart raced. The pulse throbbed in her temples while another part of her, the female part, throbbed in its own natural way at his dominant handling of her private person, almost in view of her sisters and mother, not to mention his own wife.

The warmth between her legs was getting warmer and the blush that had begun was now in full bloom, like the first red roses of spring. It crept determinedly upward over her neck and face. She felt hot and bothered and prayed desperately that no one came into the lounge. The noise of dishes being washed and cutlery being moved around against the metal sink became her only moment by moment security.

'Oh.' She groaned quietly as he squeezed her bottom again, but he followed the pain he'd caused her with smooth sliding actions of his hand that pressed gently, but as far as they could between her buttocks.

Her mind suddenly filled with visions of his erect living length and girth in her mouth as it had been on the Saturday before. Its shiny smooth helmet had both entranced her and enthralled her at the same time. As if mesmerised by a Cobra in a basket she stared at it several times when not in her mouth; its head had glistened from her saliva. Then instinctively she squeezed her thighs tightly together as the rich taste of him flooded her memories, that very first taste. God, she thought, that first wonderful addictive taste of him was hers.

'Turn around,' she heard him say. Distracted and with her thoughts elsewhere she turned without thinking and faced the music centre.

'Oh...' Nicki gasped when his hand came to rest on her lower belly. Quickly she glanced back over he shoulder, then at him, her eyes glowering yet excited. He pressed a little lower.

'Oh please, Master... no,' she pleaded, but he pressed a little lower still, bringing another quiet gasp from her lips. He was feeling the firm top of her mound, but the tautness of her dress prevented him pressing any lower.

Her senses spun from a mixture of fear and excitement both. His hand was almost there. He kept up a steady pressure just above the line of her pubic hair. She closed her eyes, praying none of the others would come into the lounge. She wished she wasn't wearing that particular dress, and then he could have reached further down... down there.

'Ohhh,' she sighed softly.

I knew it wasn't a sigh of protest and smiled at her

situation. Gently she leaned her weight against the pressure of my hand. Then I knew it would be only seconds before we'd no longer be alone.

'Go and sit down,' I said quickly, quietly. She spun around instantly and walked to the nearest chair, sitting down and smoothing her hair, looking a little hot and flustered. She looked gorgeous in the collar. My body rocked and rolled within my trousers, wanting her. But I knew it would take all of my self-control to take her the way I wanted to, savouring the loss of her cherry slowly, deflowering her deliciously innocent Greek virginity at my leisure and pleasure until I had completed her as my first fully fledged non-virgin female slave.

Nicki breathed a deep sigh of relief as she settled into the chair only seconds before Athena and Appolonia came into the lounge. The room was subdued in lighting, compared to the brightness of the kitchen and she was glad. They would have seen her blushing for sure, otherwise. Her twin sisters sat down across from her and continued chatting without even looking her way, apart from a few quick smiles.

Another wave of relief washed over her from head to toe. Her fingers played with the small silver D-ring on the collar around her throat. It was meant for a leash and she knew it, had pictured it, being led and she following obediently.

When the sound of her mother's familiar voice brought her mind and senses back to the reality of the moment she looked up, still very hot and bothered. And now he was going to punish her, she remembered with a flush of excitement and dread.

'Oh,' she gasped quietly, startled. His hand gently rested on her shoulder in passing. He was staring directly into her eyes. Quickly she checked her sisters, but they were still engaged in their own animated discussion. Her gaze quickly went back up to his. She could smell his masculine scent.

'No touching,' I said seriously to her. Her eyes widened and I smiled, wondering if she wondered if her new master could actually read her mind. Even in the dim lighting I could see she was blushing.

Chapter Seven

The next day, Saturday morning, I awoke and stretched like a big lazy cat around seven-thirty. Winners are grinners, I thought. Lauren had already gone. She and Marcena had arranged to go shopping together as a way of getting to know each other better. I went down to the kitchen and made myself some bacon and eggs, and while eating them, reminded myself that I didn't like my own cooking. I thought about all that had happened since having the experience with the hypnotherapist, still amazed that I had actually coaxed Nicki to accept me as her master. Then I began to think seriously about her, and about her sisters. They were both as exceptionally gorgeous as she was, although a little older.

The thought of her wearing her slave collar came back to me. The visualisation filled my sensory awareness with a deep stirring between my legs, although I had to admit that the most powerful sensual feelings I had were always associated with the knowledge of the absolute control I now seemed to have over her. To have that same level of control over her twin sisters as well seemed such a stretch of good luck that I couldn't imagine it being a happening thing. Nevertheless, I intended to work on it. At the moment I wanted to concentrate on Nicki and her slavery to me. Baby steps, I smiled to myself… baby steps.

The doorbell rang.

I rose from my chair, drawn to the lingering sound like a moth to a flame, like a bee to the queen of his hive.

'Hello, Master,' Nicki beamed.

I smiled and stood aside and allowed her to pass by me. Her perfume was intoxicating at that early hour of the day. My groin hardened in anticipation of whatever the day might bring. She was not wearing her collar.

'How's my beautiful Greek slave today?' I asked, following her into the lounge, where she sat down. I frowned.

'Great,' Nicki said, placing her bag down by the side of the chair. She watched him sit down, wondering about the stern look on his face. He stared at her while she drowned in his strong male gaze.

'Who is the master here, Nicki?' I asked, watching her eyes widen.

'You are, Master,' Nicki replied, wondering why he had asked her that.

'Did you ask to sit down?' I asked, determined to set the rules right from the start.

Nicki looked away then quickly back at him, and then slowly got up out of the chair.

'Can I sit down, Master?' she asked him softly.

'No, you may not,' I said. 'There's a little matter of your punishment from the other evening to take care of first, as well as something called respect.'

Nicki had been rebuked and she knew it. That wasn't the way she had planned to start her day. She awoke early, excited and eager. Now she was in trouble before her day with him had even begun. 'Yes,' she said quietly, her eyes downcast.

'Yes, what?'

'Yes... Master,' Nicki said, blushing from embarrassment. She cursed herself for forgetting. She would have to be careful and always remember.

'Here is your punishment,' I said, thickening between my legs. 'You can choose. Either I don't talk to you all day or you accept whatever discipline I decide for you.'

'I don't want to go all day without talking to you,' she answered quickly, then reminded herself, 'Master.'

Music to my ears, I thought. That word was definitely music to my ears. 'Then I'll spank you as your first punishment,' I told her.

Nicki's eyes widened. Spank her? Her gaze darted directly to his face. Spank her? Even her mother had never spanked her. None of them had been spanked.

'Spank me?' she heard herself ask. Her heart raced. She could almost hear it beat wildly inside her chest. She stood with her hands clasped together in front of her. She stood facing him and staring at the carpet.

'Do you accept your punishment?' I asked, revelling in my power over her.

'Yes, Master,' Nicki answered apprehensively.

'Good girl. Step over here between my knees.'

Nicki's pulse began to throb as she stepped forward. She looked down at him looking up at her. His face was not smiling. Then she watched his gaze leave her eyes and move slowly downwards over her body as if he was inspecting her. She blushed and felt hot. Her mind was a mixture of fear and excitement both. Her breath quavered as it left her lungs.

I was on eye level with her untouched Greek virginity and I was hard. She wore a blue tank top with no bra underneath. Her breasts filled out the top sensually, the material ending mere inches below the underside of them. Her nipples were already erect, studding beneath the soft cotton top. Between the bottom of it and the beginning of her cut-off jeans lay nothing but tanned bare skin, centred by the sexiest looking navel I had ever seen. I had an urgent need to sink my tongue into it as she stood in front of me, and so close. Her tummy was flat, concave even, with only the slightest hint of rounding down towards her lower belly inside the shorts. From the frayed cut-off bottoms extended her shapely tanned legs.

I thought she was perfect… absolutely perfect.

She held her hands clasped loosely in front of her.

'Hands to your sides, Nicki,' I said without smiling. She moved them.

'Oh,' Nicki gasped when he slowly reached forward and unclasped the button on the waist of her shorts. Then his fingers slowly lowered the zipper and let go. They fell in a heap around her ankles, and she drew in a quick breath.

The sight of her in that way hardened me even more. Now I was even closer to her precious Greek virginity than I had been, separated only by the flimsy barricade of her blue underwear. My pole flexed demandingly. My gaze zeroed in on that blue V between her tanned thighs. For the moment her underwear hid the lushness of her Mediterranean carpet, but her lower belly gently rounding towards the waistband of her dainties was incredibly stirring.

'Do… do you really have to spank me, Master?' Nicki asked, enjoying the way he was gazing at her, but horrified at the prospect of being smacked like a baby. Tears began to well in her eyes and brimmed threateningly as she began to accept his seriousness.

I managed to tear my gaze away from enjoying the wondrous mystery of her Greek V. My eyes found hers shiny and brimming with her uncertainty of what was going to happen next. I smiled warmly.

'If I didn't care about your slave training, Nicki,' I told her, 'I wouldn't bother disciplining you at all. But somebody has to be the very best slave for me, so why not you? Would you rather me find another slave and care about her instead?'

Nicki felt as if she'd been stabbed. Her tears rolled suddenly down her cheeks, caused by just the thought of him not wanting her as his slave. 'No,' she said softly.

'Well,' I said, my heart reaching out for her self-inflicted anguish, 'do you want me to care for you to be the very best slave for me that you can be with your discipline training?'

Nicki's tears ceased. Squaring her shoulders she kept her gaze on his. She had come to him as his slave, she concluded. Who would teach her to be a good slave for him if not him? She wasn't there to cry like a baby girl.

'The time for tears can pass now, Nicki,' I told her firmly. 'They belong to yesterday. In order to help you and your future with me as my slave, discipline is a necessary part of your training.'

'Yes,' Nicki answered quietly. Her eyes looked at the one she had chosen to call her master, the one who was going to help her to be the very best slave she could be for him. The least she could do was stop snivelling like a child.

'And in that way I'll help you to see that you are not your emotions, that you are not your thoughts, and that you are not your physical sensations.'

'Yes,' Nicki heard herself reply. She was a little frightened by the authoritative tone he was taking with her.

'Good,' I said. 'Turn around,' I instructed her quietly but firmly. Slowly she turned and faced the other way. Her panty-covered bottom taunted me. I felt as if I was in a dream. My groin was harder than I'd felt it in a long time and her shapely buttocks dared me to explore their deeper nether source of mysteries, barely hidden beneath the almost transparent blue material that covered them like a second skin. The deep dark valley between them showed clearly as the happening place to be right then. It took all of my self-discipline not to take up that dare. I sighed contentedly. She belonged to me.

'Lie down over my lap,' I instructed her, leaving her panties in place, in spite of the urgent yearning between my legs.

'Oh,' Nicki gasped softly. 'Yes,' she said, and then lay down over his lap, such that she was across it, knowing her bottom lay right beneath his eyes. She blushed. It was almost too much embarrassment for her to take.

'Now, Nicki,' I began, deliberately flexing beneath her belly. 'Do you feel that any solid relationship of sharing and caring should have more than one boss?'

'No,' Nicki heard herself sigh. She was blushing, lying over him. His hard lump pressed firmly against her mons.

'And do you feel the stronger one should be the one in charge of everything?'

'Yes,' she sighed. Someone had to be in charge. She felt his body move. Silently she gasped, and then closed her eyes as a deep wave of pleasure and excitement ran up and down her spine.

'And do you feel that a demonstration of his being in charge should be given of the same strength that will protect her and care for her?'

'Yes,' Nicki heard herself say without hesitation. It was all very puzzling, but she felt so excited and aroused. If she wasn't worried about him spanking her, she could just orgasm right there on his lap with his hard bulge poking her. She recalled what it looked like in the flesh, standing. She felt hot.

'Do you feel that we have such a relationship?' I asked her, aware of my balls beginning to ache from so much sexual tension and so little relief.

'Yes,' Nicki answered immediately. She knew they did, had somehow felt it from the word go.

'Good. And do you feel it's only right that you should want to have such a demonstration then, so you know that I care?'

'Yes,' Nicki replied quietly, breathing out. But she feared being smacked on the bottom. Her tension in all areas mounted, telling her so in each hesitating breath as it flowed outward over her dry lips.

'Good,' I said, raising my right hand. I stared at her firm buttocks. 'Then enjoy your demonstration of my caring…'

Nicki cried out suddenly as his hand smacked down hard, several times across her right buttock. She jumped and squirmed in stinging pain, twisting and groaning beneath him, but apart from her initial outcry of alarm she never uttered another word. Instead, she fought to hold in the blazing agony.

Her world then continued to explode in a frenzied sea of pain and shock as he smacked her buttocks without stopping. She wanted to scream out, but his hand was coming too fast. Forcing herself down she desperately attempted to get away from the blazing heat in her throbbing backside, only to be met by that bulge pressing just as hard back up into her. Again and again she clenched her fists, holding in the pain.

With the delivery of the last smack I stared down at her sheer blue panty-clad ass. The right cheek was as red as a beetroot. I trembled, feeling my cock pressing up against her belly as she lay across my lap, gasping and sniffing quietly.

'Now do you know who's in charge of our relationship?' I asked her, my breath shaking from the effort of her rapid spanking.

'Yes,' Nicki sniffed. He was in charge. Of that she had no doubts whatsoever, but surprisingly, she was not as displeased with the spanking as she thought she might have been.

'Who?' I asked.

'You are… Master.'

'That's right. And would you like to feel how the strength that just spanked you will care for you when you need caring for?' I said.

'Yes,' she sniffed quietly.

I rested my left hand across her tender rump while the fingers of my right began to explore the forced damp patch of warmth deep between her thighs.

'Ohhh,' Nicki gasped when his fingers slid back and forth over the panty-covered entrance to her slick Greek cavern. Her eyes closed and she clenched her fists. Then she felt him again, pressing her panties deep between her two cheeks.

'Ohhhh.' She gasped more loudly as his hand slowly worked its way deep between her buttocks. It pressed gently against her nether necklace. Then, as she squirmed and revelled in the incredible fingering between her legs and buttocks in that unusual way, he held her and manipulated both orifices of her body until she could take it no longer.

'Oohh, God,' she moaned, knowing she was going to come. Flushed and embarrassed, but not caring, she ground her hips down on his lap, pushing her buttocks backward against the sliding fingers and single pressing thumb as her loins began to flame.

'Aaagh!' she suddenly cried in blazing pain as his hand crashed down hard and fast several times across her left buttock. She jumped and squirmed, twisting and groaning beneath him and this time she sobbed. All sexual tension had vanished instantly. Her fists clenched again, holding in the pain.

Her dreamy world then exploded in another unexpected and frenzied sea of pain and shock. His hand blazed down across her left buttock without stopping. She wanted to scream out, but the smacks came too fast. Desperately she forced herself down against his bulge, attempting to get away from the pain and stinging heat in the throbbing left cheek, only to be met again by that hard lump pressing up into her lower belly. Her fingernails dug painfully into her palms, so tightly were her fists clenched.

With the delivery of the last smack I stared down at her sheer blue bottom. Beneath her underwear I could see that the left cheek was now as red as the right, both now like two crimson peaches that trembled as I stared at them. Still my cock pressed up against her belly as she lay across my lap, groaning and sniffing quietly.

'Are you sure you know now who's in charge of our relationship?' I asked, my breath heavy from the effort of her second rapid spanking.

'Y-yes,' Nicki sniffed emphatically. She now had no doubts whatsoever, and surprisingly, she was still not as displeased with the spanking as she thought she might have been.

'Aaagh!' She jumped, startled once more as her bottom exploded again in a fiery fury of pain. But this time the smacks proceeded steadily, heavily, and with rhythm. The pain began to turn pink in her mind's eye, then red, until finally she could no longer hold in the deepest pain of enduring the stinging hurt and she cracked, opening her fists and spreading her fingers wide.

The tears drained outward from her heart. And with the release of all that pain arrived a feeling so strange as his hand thundered down repeatedly and relentlessly on her poor bottom. The pain was suddenly no longer there. It was leaving, and not just the pain of his spanking. The pain of her life was leaving, too. The only momentary awareness was of the tears of her life's hurt flowing freely for the very first time; a feeling of being free, of being given permission to cry, to let out all the times when she'd wanted to cry throughout her life, but did not. And now she did, openly, honestly and without restraint until finally there were no more tears left to cry. Only then did the firm hand striking her bottom cease its powerful downward strokes.

I stilled my hand on her trembling buttocks and then began to stroke her and nurture her, rocking her on my lap like a baby until her heartfelt sobs had gradually turned to whimpers, and then to occasional sniffs.

'Who?' I asked.

'You are, Master,' Nicki said hesitantly, feeling as if a heavy weight had been lifted from her shoulders.

'That's right. Would you like to feel how the strength that just spanked you would care for you when you need caring for?'

Aware now of the deepening heat throbbing over her entire bottom, Nicki nodded, but she didn't answer. Resting his left hand across her tender rump, the fingers of his right began once again to explore the damp warmth between her thighs.

'Ohhh,' she gasped. Her eyes closed. She clenched her fists again, readying for the next painful onslaught and again felt his hand pressing her panties deep between her buttocks.

'Ohhhh,' she gasped more loudly as his thumb slowly worked its way deep. Then it pressed gently on her rear rim.

'Oh!' she gasped and began to squirm, revelling once

more in the incredible fingering between her legs and buttocks in that unusual way. Firmly he held her lower back down and manipulated the entrances to both orifices of her body until once again she could take it no longer.

'Oh,' she moaned, grinding her hips down on his lap. Again she pushed her buttocks back against the sliding fingers and single pressing thumb. She felt it coming, the rising tide and the approaching thundering wave. Her body stiffened and tensed to welcome it.

'Ohhhnnnnnn…' she groaned deeply, her climax almost swamping her senseless while he held her that way.

I allowed her a few minutes to settle, then spoke, but it was not what I wanted to say.

'Your punishment is finished,' I said. 'Get up now, but leave your shorts off and take your underwear off as well. You'll clean the house naked from the waist down just as a reminder, and also so I can enjoy the sensual sight of you. But get out of line and you'll be punished again. Do you understand?'

'Yes, Master,' Nicki answered softly, awkwardly getting up off his lap and standing. Slowly, blushing, she slid her sheer blue panties downward over her throbbing backside and thighs. Stepping out of them she placed them in her bag, acutely self-conscious of her bare bottom and her lush bush that was now fully visible to him.

I sat back in the comfort of my leather chair, holding fast to the sight of her tight red bottom. Turning, she walked slowly towards the vacuum cleaner. Her buttocks were bright red, and I loved them dearly. There was something about the sight of those scarlet cheeks that caused me to grip myself firmly as she went about the housecleaning, and as I did so I dreamed about the future I wanted to have with her as my slave.

I watched her busily working the vacuum cleaner into

a mechanical sweat and from time to time she looked at me and smiled shyly. I smiled back, my smile broadening whenever I saw her tight red buttocks quivering as she pushed the mechanical cleaner. I had held that Greek butt captive in my hands, I thought, pleased and aroused at the same time. Glancing down, my watch told me the time and I sighed at the idyllic way I was spending my day as a natural male.

My body was so hard, every fibre of my male being demanded that I bend her over the nearest chair, then rapidly deprive her of her tantalising Greek fruit. But I'd already decided in my mind's imagination that I'd savour that wonderful moment, as well as the lead up to it, by simply enjoying the sensual sight of her for as long as I wanted to.

The piercing of her inner backstop wasn't a matter of if, but simply when. It was then that I decided I'd encourage Lauren to spend as much time with Marcena as possible. That would get her out of my hair and give me more time and opportunity with Nicki. In the meantime I was enjoying myself in so many natural ways that Lauren had never allowed me to, simply by seeing Nicki, as she was, a natural female who wanted to be no other way for me. It was wonderful. I smiled at her again when she peeped shyly at me.

Nicki took a really deep breath and sighed contentedly. Smiling at him every now and then, she pushed and pulled the vacuum cleaner back and forth over the carpet. Her backside throbbed as she worked diligently, but the pain was a different pain. She didn't know why, but she felt great and wondered if she would always feel that way after he punished her. She wanted to be the best slave she could be for him. That was all that mattered.

Pushing the vacuum cleaner in a different direction, she

glanced across and smiled again. He smiled back. Thrilling to his attention she worked harder, aware of her state of dress – or undress, as the case was right then. Again she noticed the deep throbbing warmth between her legs and buttocks. It felt good. Her body felt relaxed, but hot. Smiling to herself, she worked the cleaner harder.

She had now experienced a first with three new things in her life; a real orgasm induced by a man, a solid spanking, and now she was doing the housecleaning naked from her hips to her toes, in front of a man in his own house, aware that his wife could walk through the door at any moment. But what made it so highly erotic was that he was watching her do it, and all on a Saturday morning. She felt nervous, aroused and excited, and she felt sore on her bottom. She also felt deliciously and embarrassingly wet.

'Nicki!' I shouted at her from across the room and above the din of the cleaner. She stepped the motor off and came over to me. The sight of her dark hair caused my body to spring instantly to life again.

'Where is your collar?' I asked when she stood before me, looking at me from beneath her raised eyebrows.

Nicki reached down beside the chair, quickly delving inside her shoulder bag. She brought out the sexy velvet collar with its little D-ring attached that felt absolutely erotic in her hands. She smiled at him.

I held out my hand for her to pass it to me. I had planned a surprise, one that I had promised her, one that I was sure she had forgotten about.

'Kneel before me,' I told her firmly.

Nicki's heart skipped a beat. Slowly she sank to her knees, her eyes holding his gaze all the way down.

'I'm going to collar you, Nicki,' I told her, 'as my personal Greek virgin slave. Are you sure that's really what you want?'

Nicki's heart swelled and almost burst. She thought he had forgotten. Her emotions roller-coasted, her eyes misted, but she didn't speak. She was overcome with the sudden and unexpected heartfelt emotion of the moment and could only nod as she gazed up at his face.

'Repeat after me,' I said. 'I, Nicki, do accept this collar as an expression of my master's ownership of me.'

Nicki repeated his words perfectly, but slowly. It was as if he was talking in slow motion. Each word contained such strength, such control, and such ownership.

'And I do so freely and fully,' I said next.

Nicki repeated his words with feeling, her emotions mounting.

'I agree to honor our relationship above all others,' I stated.

Nicki felt her eyes brimming with tears, but she repeated every last, loving, bonding word.

'I will always seek to fulfil his every desire, for whatever he desires in the moment.'

Again Nicki heard herself say the words she knew she was committing to, feeling as if she were getting married. The tears finally overflowed her rims and cascaded down over the smooth skin of her cheeks.

'I will wear this collar with pride, knowing that my master cares for me, respects me, and holds me above all other women.'

Nicki said the words, felt them, and internalised them into her very female soul.

'I promise to always communicate openly and honestly with my master, and never keep anything from him.'

The words flew directly into her young Greek virgin heart. She repeated them through her full, deep pink lips and the lump in her throat, while she watched him gazing down at her. Her emotions tumbled from dizzy heights to bottomless pits and then back up again.

'I do hereby surrender control of my body and my submissive soul for any and all purposes, as my master sees fit.'

Nicki's mind floated on a sea of wonderment. In her mind and imagination the world listened and watched while she took her vows of slavery and repeated her bonding oath to him.

'I will strive to be the very best female I can be for my master and will not disrespect him.'

Nicki's lips said the words; her body imbibed them in her own female alcohol and her fate was sealed forever, according to her own free will, while her tears ran freely down her face.

'I will love him in silence and in his absence with my female soul.'

Nicki could hardly speak, such was the emotional turmoil going on inside her mind and heart, but she did, word by powerfully bonding word.

'I promise to keep myself physically and emotionally healthy and always have a happy heart.'

Nicki's heart wasn't just happy, it was ecstatic, but she said the lesser words, nevertheless, then cried silently a little more.

'And with freely given consent I accept my role as a natural female submissive slave to my master from this day forward.'

Nicki's heart was fit to burst with suppressed emotion. She wished she were wearing a white bridal gown with a long train. She stumbled through the words.

'Until such a time as I am released by him or no longer wanted.'

With those words Nicki hung her head and nodded,

weeping silently at the thought of him releasing her or not wanting her as his slave. The powerful words cracked the dam walls of her emotional dyke as she cried openly like a baby. Then she felt his strong hands on her head, then on her shoulders and then under her arms. He lifted her to her feet to stand before him as he stood. She finally said the words about him releasing her, but she never wanted to say or think about them again.

'I accept you, Nicki,' I said, the lump in my throat threatening to prevent one more single word.

'I accept you, too, Master,' Nicki sobbed softly.

I placed my fingertips under her chin and gently raised her tearstained face to mine. Then I kissed her tenderly and fully on her slightly parted lips.

'Ohmmm...' Nicki moaned and sobbed beneath the strong warmth of his settling kiss. Her tongue danced with his while her heart fluttered and then soared in the heavens of her collaring, her formal bonding to him. Then slowly, he broke the kiss and smiled at her.

'My lovely little Greek virgin slave,' I said quietly, surprisingly, with real love in my voice.

'Oh, Master,' Nicki sobbed and then burst out crying again while he held her safe in his arms that tightened around her back and shoulders.

'Your Greek virginity is mine, Nicki,' I told her quietly, but firmly. 'You know that, don't you?'

Nicki couldn't speak, but she nodded. Her mind was so full of her swelling heart it could not string the words together to make thoughts. Instead, her answer was to wrap her arms around his waist and hug him tightly. She wanted him to have it and no other, remembering his eyes when she had last glanced at him. They'd danced and shone with his own unshed tears.

Yes, she knew, I thought as her arms squeezed me

tightly. My own eyes had misted for reasons I wasn't too sure I knew or even wanted to admit to myself right then, but she knew. I didn't need to hear the words.

Chapter Eight

I loved the beach. The white grassy sand dunes rose sharply approximately twelve feet high on either side. Between them a smooth hidden strip of bright golden sand edged them both, also some twelve feet wide and long. It emptied out between the two dunes and turned then opened up onto the main sandy beach and the ocean's shore of many crustacean shells. Its hidden location was perfect. It was why I was there.

Nicki lay beside me and was reading a book. This time I brought her with me, instead of leaving her in the house to do the cleaning. Gazing at her I could imagine her shapely legs, her firm female loins, flat muscled stomach and full young breasts absorbing the seeping lazy heat as it simmered and drew upward and away home on its way back to the mother sun. I could almost visualise it passing through her female flesh, bones and tissue, relaxing them, soothing them, re-energising them, and replenishing them as it always seemed to do me. I loved the beach and my little hideaway.

One week had passed since collaring her. It had been a week of mixed emotions for me; mixed in a way that, for once, when Lauren had actually approached me for sex I rejected her. She hadn't liked it, but I didn't care. It had always been the same between us. Whenever her natural female itch needed scratching I was always there, ready, willing and able, like a faithful dog.

I always had the feeling of being used and had always felt affection-deprived. I'd told her once of my feelings on the matter and she laughed, saying I was suffering from the Poor Me syndrome. Something inside me had switched off toward her after that. I didn't know what, only that I never felt the same way about her again. So, I had simply focussed on my writing and my fishing, and coming to my little hideaway whenever I could, which was mostly on a Saturday, and sometimes I didn't even fish. I just went there to be.

Slowly I watched her roll over onto her back and stretch like a lazy cat. She wore a simple two-piece bikini, which I'd bought for her at a store along the way. She'd been thrilled and excited when I met her at the door and told her of my plans. I sighed and stirred then when I watched her part her legs slightly to expose her body totally to the exploring fingers of the warm sun's curiosity.

Her hand came up to her face to shield her eyes with the book she'd been reading. Then she reached out with her other hand and dragged her carry-bag under her head, using it as a pillow while she settled her neck and shoulders upon it. She reopened the book to begin reading again. I immediately felt the warmth of the incredibly sensual sight of her between my legs and moaned silently to myself.

Nicki sighed deeply as she felt the luxuriating direct heat from the sun's warm morning fingers. They felt their way through her bikini and into her naked flesh itself. In particular she felt that direct heat through the dark nipples of her breasts and the black pubic hair that hid her shapely female folds, gentle hills and deep moist valleys from the world's view in the little sandy cove he had brought her to.

She felt extreme warmth in those particular areas of her body that lay covered by the swimsuit he bought her. It had been such a surprise. Her warm sex felt as if it had begun to deep-fry in its own natural virgin oil. That feeling was relaxing her even more deeply, such that she closed the book and put on her shades, then relaxed fully and allowed nature to do its perfect work in warming, relaxing, and tanning her body to absolute perfection. She loved the beach, but didn't get to go very often by herself because of her mother's suspicious nature. Mostly she went with her sisters.

Her mind wandered in and out of the warmth of her lazily relaxed and dreamy state of being. As it did so her awareness drifted in and out of many different altered states associated with her waking daydreams of him having power over her and controlling her.

Those thoughts had been responsible for many occasions of self-pleasuring throughout the long week while waiting excitedly to see him again, to be with him again. She had also been having dreams, sensual dreams of him, her master, visualising often in her imagination his strong masculine dominance and control of her in his erotic fantasies.

Lying there beneath the rising morning sun, at times she sensed that her awareness was simply not aware of anything at all as the penetrating warmth of the sun's heat invaded her relaxed flesh from above and below. She was only aware of lying beside her master.

The sun's absorbing rays seemed to meet in the middle of her body, melting away whatever thoughts or concerns she might have had. But right then she was simply not aware of anything at all, except warmth, peace, and contented quiet. The sound of the faraway seagulls scrapping for food somewhere off towards the horizon, way out over the deep blue sea, caught her momentary attention. Then she heard a long sigh from her master, who was right beside her, exactly where she wanted him, exactly where she knew he wanted to be.

'Nice private beach, Nicki?' she heard him say. The rich sound of his voice entering her lazy awareness caught her between two very real worlds, one of sleeping, the other of waking. She knew she wasn't really in either, at that moment. For a second or two she thought she must have been dreaming.

'You need to even your tan,' I said to her as she stirred. 'Take off your top and give it to me.' I felt the rush of power and control over her as soon as the words left my mouth. Then I felt the thickening and the lengthening.

Nicki was suddenly fully aware again, startled by his instructions for her to comply on a public beach in broad daylight. She sat upright, her arms quickly moving to cover her bikini-clad breasts. Her knees drew immediately upward and closed tightly together. She quickly looked left and right, and then at his face, knowing his eyes danced intensely behind his dark shades. Back to the sun his shape was outlined, silhouetted against the rising corona.

She loved the intensity of him. With her free hand then she hesitantly removed her bikini top, her gaze darting all about her before finally settling back into his serious face. She hoped that if anyone came along he would tell him or her to get lost in a hurry.

'Good girl,' I smiled, lowering the sunglasses from my eyes. My gaze was rewarded with such a vision of sensual and sexual loveliness, the like of which I don't believe I had ever seen before. Still looking around in all directions she handed her bikini top to me. My groin flexed strongly with power, with fondness towards her, and from the sight of her gorgeous breasts with their brown stud nipples.

Nicki had never actively sought men as sexual companions, but she now felt herself respond with increased warmth, and knew it wasn't from the morning rays of the sun. Maybe this is where it would happen? Oh no, she gasped silently, hoping he wouldn't choose a public beach in the sand for her virginal deflowering.

'Lie back down,' I said. 'And leave your arms by your sides.' As she did so my eyes couldn't help but travel the full length and shapely form of her. I yearned to see her absolutely and completely naked in public. Her athletic frame lay proudly facing me while I stared down at her. I reached for her.

'Oh,' Nicki gasped softly when he placed his right hand firmly on her left breast. His skin was warm. Her nipple erected further and said hello to his pinching touch. Then he moved his hand down to the inside of her right knee and pushed it firmly, widening them slightly apart.

'Master,' she gasped, attempting to sit up and look around for anybody who might be walking past the entrance to the little dune hideaway, but he gently pushed her back down. She was terrified and embarrassed. 'But... but somebody might come along.'

'Sunglasses off,' I told her, and then watched her hesitantly remove them. I smiled at her protests, but firmly held her pressed down into her towel. I loved her classic Greek features.

She had smouldering almond-shaped eyes, and they were even more attractive when worried or angry. Her black hair fell flowing like a dark waterfall to her naked shoulders.

Nicki lay with her arms stiffly by her sides, her fists clenched with the tension she felt. Her eyes darted left and right, then down at her bare breasts. Erect nipples graced and tipped both sensuously; each breast rose firmly yet softly upward. Trying to relieve her tension she looked down at her overall shape. It was hourglass, she thought proudly, but femininely so.

My gaze dropped from her superb breasts to her groin. I smiled, imagining her brewing virgin oil deep-frying her sex in the morning sun on a slow sizzle. Then I wondered what her olive-skinned Greek pussy would look like and taste like if shaven. Not a matter of if, I decided right then, but when.

Nicki stared down at herself, not consciously aware that she was doing it. Her gaze and focussed awareness was taken fully and completely by sensual surprise as she studied the sensuous high-cut V of her bikini bottoms. She felt herself blushing in the warmth of the morning sun.

'Take off your bikini pants and hand them to me,' I said to her, not being able to stand it any longer. She was my slave. I wanted to enjoy her virginal Greek sensuality publicly and to the hilt.

'Oh no, Master, please?' Nicki gasped and pleaded. She was horrified at the thought. He couldn't ask her to do that, not there on the public beach on a Saturday morning! She thought frantically, but inside she felt that the whole situation exuded an exciting and dangerous sensuality – a special beauty, somehow, and in him a quiet and powerful male strength as he waited for her to do his bidding.

Once again she tried to sit up, but gently he held her down on her back. Her thoughts were chaotic, her mind frantic with fear of her fully naked public exposure.

'Are you deaf, Nicki?' I asked her, feeling the frown of her resistance begin to interfere with my enjoyment of the moment. 'It was not a request.'

Nicki's focus then suddenly seemed to fill with the awareness of the dark hair that covered her soft sex, beneath which the lips now felt full of sexual arousal. They felt touchable, kissable, lickable and suckable.

'Oh,' she moaned silently as she felt once again all hot and bothered. Acutely embarrassed at doing that which he had told her to do her gaze focussed on her own body. She couldn't seem to tear it away.

Hesitantly, her hands reached slowly downward, hooking her thumbs into each side of her bikini bottoms. Her wide-eyed gaze darted left and right. She wanted to stop returning to stare at the junction of her thighs and raise her head to look into the eyes of the man who had told her to become utterly naked on a public beach. But she was suddenly afraid he would see how embarrassed she was and maybe read in her face the lewd thoughts she'd just been thinking. Quickly she glanced at him, then back to her bikini panties. He was looking at her, there.

'I can look, Nicki,' I said to her, knowing how embarrassed and frightened she was of being caught exposed and naked on a public beach. 'I like looking at you, down there.' And with that said I watched her slowly slide the decorative bottom half of her bikini down over her thighs and knees, until eventually she handed them to me.

'Please, Master?' Nicki begged him. 'What if someone comes?'

I took the bikini bottoms and placed them with the top on the opposite side of my towel, then stared into her eyes.

'Settle down and relax,' I said firmly to her, my gaze riveting squarely back on her dark Greek junction. My groin reared and backed into my belly, like a Boa Constrictor preparing to lunge and crush its helpless victim.

On an impulse I decided to take her mind off herself and stood up, then stepped over her legs on either side, just above her knees, where her naked and olive-skinned sex lay embedded between two shapely thighs. Quickly and suddenly I dropped my shorts to my ankles and stood naked before her as she lay on her back looking up at my standing part.

'Oh,' Nicki gasped, then blushed even more so; waves of sensual heat washed down from her head to her toes, heating her own natural virgin oil even more. '*Master*,' she implored him, but all she could see was the full and swollen muscle of his male's sensual sex, and the heavy down-covered sac hanging beneath it. Her gaze darted anxiously from side to side, but quickly returned to him.

Her sex lips quivered deliciously at the raw sight of him standing over her and fully aroused like that. She thought she could see a slight glistening sheen at the very tip of his swollen helmet and found she stared hard, even through her extreme embarrassment, to see if she was right.

Her eyes darted left and right again, not believing what she was doing, what they were doing on a public beach, and in full view of anybody who happened to come along.

'Sit up,' I said firmly to her, my balls beginning to ache with anticipation at filling her tightly virginal cunt with living life in the very near future. I could see she was no longer thinking about passers-by.

'Oh,' Nicki gasped as she slowly raised herself to a sitting position, drawing up her legs and crossing them at the ankles, her back straight, her arms straight and her hands in the sand behind her. As her torso rose her gaze zeroed in between his legs again and focussed upon the centre of her whole world at that moment. It quivered.

'Oh, Master,' she gasped. Her mind began to feel numb. She couldn't think, her present awareness mesmerised by the incredibly magnetising and sexual sight of that part of him standing full and tall, right in front of her face. Her awareness and senses were being drawn slowly towards that length and girth adorning his strong loins like a moth to a flame, as if by natural magic.

Her mouth was suddenly as dry as the Sahara. Her tongue snaked out in an attempt to moisten her parched lips, and they remained slightly parted even after her tongue had done its work. Nothing existed in her immediate awareness now, but that which consumed the utter essence of her extreme female focus. The concerns about someone seeing her completely naked on a public beach were now of absolutely no relevance whatsoever.

I stared down at the top of her dark head, knowing where her gaze was centred. I wanted those succulent lips around my balls, gently sucking. I wanted my rigid living pole in her mouth, and I wanted so badly right then to taste her warm virgin Greek oil that it was driving me crazy. Her tongue once again flitted nervously around her lips, moistening them. I flexed strongly before her eyes at the mere thought of firmly pressing my tongue deeply into that juicy Mediterranean slit.

'Oh,' Nicki gasped softly when the object of her attention suddenly and strongly pulsed only inches from her face, her lips, her mouth and her tongue. She suddenly felt very small, as if a bronzed naked Gladiator stood over her, controlling her, forcing her to feel strange and powerful sensations between her legs and in her breasts. Her mind was still, her focus steady. And between her warm thighs her imagination already had him, there. Then she thought briefly of where they were, on a beach, where anyone could see if they came along. She quickly looked around again, fearing discovery by a passer-by.

'Keep looking at me,' she heard her master's strong voice tell her. It came like an order, but she noticed only the power of the unspoken and expected obedience behind the words. Then he moved a little, his feet sifting through the warm sand, bringing his living loins almost against her lips. Her eyes almost blurred, such was her point of focus on the engorged living upright trunk of her master. It was there… right there.

'Oh, Master,' she heard herself gasp, but not loudly. Then she panicked again. 'Please… somebody might come…'

She then gasped unconsciously at the sudden and close proximity of that by which she had been so entranced. It once again pulsed in front of her eyes. Its glistening tip quivered. Her breathing became short and trembling pants, which hesitated as they flowed out over her lips. And with each breath inward she could now smell her master's male only an inch from her face.

The unique shape of its arrow form intrigued her imagination, its aroma strongly male and powerfully intoxicating. Her nostrils flared as she breathed him in. It was sublimely heady, like a potent and fermented wine.

Her senses swooned. Her mouth opened more, her tongue lying ready behind her teeth, like a pink snake ready to strike out into battle for the natural sustenance it needed right then. And all the while, unnoticed in her state of fixation, her own sex drained her warm and wasted virgin Greek oil from her body into her beach towel.

My heart pounded against my ribs while my pulse raced. My temples thumped and the blood surged around my body like heavy tidal seas crashing onto the shore in a thunderstorm. Gazing down upon her in my rapidly rising heat of the moment I stood over her. The dark nipples of her breasts had thickened and stiffened while I imagined the pink lips of her unseen virgin slit swollen with pure sexual arousal and deliberately imagined intent.

'Don't touch me until I tell you to,' I told her, and began to move my hips in miniscule circular thrusting motions before her face.

'Oh, Master,' Nicki moaned in sexual agony, wanting him with her lips, her mouth, and her virgin body. Her master's dominant voice commanded her and she obeyed, but with difficulty. She wanted him to spear her now, not wait any longer. The object of her total focus of attention was now rhythmically moving. It swayed as he moved, like a snake in a basket, as if alive.

Again she quickly looked left and right about her, not believing what was happening on a public beach, not believing what she wanted to do, what she knew she would do, at any second.

'Oh, Master,' she groaned with a fever that only another virgin female in urgent mating heat could possibly understand. His strong loins then repeated the movement, but added gentle up and down thrusting actions. The thick pole grazed lightly across her open mouth and lips, like a lollipop, with soft butterfly kisses again and again, but not exactly touching.

'Oh,' she moaned softly. Her mind felt faint. She was in another world and being strongly drawn towards that swollen brown length in the very centre of it. Her heated virgin oil began to pool more rapidly between her thighs and seep into the towel.

Her eyes no longer saw clearly, and instead riveted on the smooth girder of flesh and blood, which trembled and swayed, dipped and then rose within breathing distance of her mouth. Her master's living male essence was there – right there.

'Don't touch,' I said firmly, even though it was not what I wanted, and it took every ounce of self-discipline to say it when all I wanted to do was bury it so deeply inside her mouth and throat.

Nicki began to rock gently on her buttocks. It was an instinctive reaction, one she had not chosen to do, a way of relieving her inner tension.

She pursed her lips to reach for that which she so badly yearned for. She wanted to have it and to hold it for real again in her mouth and between her lips, and on her tongue. It glistened, leaking silver at its shining bulbous tip, taunting her. It dared her to sip and taste, to savour and swallow like a fine blend of the most precious intoxicant. She wanted to know the first living drop of him for the day, of his arousal at being with her, his committed slave. She longed to taste him, sexually, intimately, and then drink from his male tap, deeply and fully until his keg was dry.

Her heart raced as her tongue began to peep from between her lips, almost tapping his heady beverage. Her own sexual energy climbed unnoticed, higher and higher within her sensual mind and between her legs, while her empty Greek sheath still wept its virgin teardrops into the towel upon which she sat.

I felt I was sinking into a bottomless pit of absolutely new and different sexuality from which there would be no wanted or desired return. And now I wanted to fall into that sensual sexual pit with her.

'Not yet,' I gasped, barely under control, but I yearned, I needed, I longed for, I ached for, I burned for, and I desired for those virgin Greek lips to close about me, to cocoon me. 'Only when I tell you to,' I reinforced strongly lest her virginal weakness spoil the passing memories of my sensual enjoyment of being with her in the moment for as long as heaven would allow me to be. Placing my hands on my hips I cruelly dug my fingers into my own flesh to help with my control.

'Oh Master, please,' Nicki implored him, begging. She was going out of her mind with sensual and sexual delirium. Her inner flames rose higher still, and her natural virgin Greek oil leaked from her trembling crease like snow

81

melting in the early spring. Thoughts of his absolute and utter control and dominance over her, even on a public beach, consumed her mind.

Resistance of any kind, no matter how justified, had long since vanished. She wanted to enslave herself to and impale her body on that stiff spear. She yearned to submit her female soul, to drink thirstily from his unseen keg of male life and being until sated. Only then would she be complete as a female in need. Her senses strained for the as yet unattainable.

Her mind spun with fevered and heated carnal thoughts. She felt wild with wanton abandon. She felt sluttish and feral with lust and desire for what she was surely going to be allowed to do, at any moment.

I watched agonisingly as Nicki's rocking motion quickened while her breathing turned to rapid moans and panting. I had no idea how much longer I could continue swaying like that before her face without yielding to the natural nature of us both, but I wanted the feeling I was feeling to last for eternity. I could feel the living breath of her virgin heat on my spar.

Unknowingly, Nicki's clenching Greek cleft continued to trickle freely from her covetous female heart. Her lurid imagination filled her mouth and throat with the taste of that delicious male honey and brown glistening flesh. She wanted it, needed it in her mouth and between her lips, down her throat and filling her deepest female belly. The powerfully sexual smell of his sap and his sweetened musky heat was stifling her, filling her lungs and her body itself. Her nostrils flared again, breathing the living life of him into her being.

'Oh Master, please.' She begged shamelessly, gasping and groaning with her compelling lust and desire. And then she moaned again without knowing it while her sexual tension rose inside her mind and loins.

Then, without glancing up at him for his permission she reached out hesitantly with her tongue, not knowing she was wetting her towel with seeping virgin oil. She wanted him. She wanted it. She needed it now, right now, or she was surely going to burst. Now she didn't care about where they were or who might come along. She simply didn't care at all.

'Now,' came the welcome commanding order from her master she had been yearning to hear. With an urgent cry of release her hand rose and her face homed true.

'Ohhh mmmm...' Nicki moaned with a loud gasping breath. Her head moved forward; her mouth opened and her tongue extended, dropping low in anticipation of its fleshy male-tasting upward travel, leaving the best until last. She aimed for his balls, and then licked him slowly with the flat of her tongue, all the way up to his glistening tip.

'Oh, shit!' I exclaimed breathlessly, feeling the absolute heat and hungry firmness of her tongue as she dragged the flat of it again and again upward along the very stem of me.

Nicki's sexual energy quickly reached its highest tension, like a taut bowstring that waited only for its arrow, its natural perfect shaft to skewer her right where it counted. Her lips and mouth closed wholly and completely over her master's sweet-smelling, strong-tasting sex, making the perfect female seal. As she savoured his warm semen his strong hands instantly closed around the back of her head and pulled her into and over that which she had been so strongly burning for.

She gagged, instinctively flaring her nostrils to breathe; such was the fullness now stuffed deep into her mouth and throat. Then he relaxed the pressure of his hands on her head and once more the flat of her tongue drew upward through the warm furred valley of his sac. She licked and suckled his heavy balls, then his length and girth again. Her taste buds absorbed the pure samplings of her master's deepest living male. Then she suddenly felt him tense and bend at the knees and she knew, she just knew. His hands tightened once more around the back of her head and neck, his fingers clamped in her hair.

'Ohhh, shit!' I groaned, finally letting nature have its glorious way with my body and its liquid contents. I emptied like a burst balloon and bent at the knees, thrusting deep inside her wonderful warm Greek virgin mouth.

Nicki groaned and whimpered tearfully with his living cock in her mouth. Her own sexual tension then suddenly let go with an inner explosion that almost debilitated her mind, along with her body. She sucked and swallowed again and again.

Her hands lifted to her master's clenching buttocks, pulling him harder, deeper; clasping each cheek tightly. Her fingers squeezed and kneaded the muscled flesh while her own blistering orgasm pleasured her senseless. It wracked her spine from top to bottom as she sat cross-legged and trembling beneath his balls with the heel she'd been rocking against wedged to her oily slit.

Her mind clouded. She felt faint. Her immediate awareness of anyone or anything vanished while her nostrils flared to breathe. Her lungs heaved with her panting and muffled sighs as she held him inside her mouth and throat and tried to suck him dry while she teetered on the edge of fainting. And she continued to suck and swallow, drawing deeply from the surging tap of his endless keg as she whimpered softly between his feet.

'Oh, yes,' I gasped. My body then gave utterly to the moment in her instinctive and glorious handling of me.

Buried inside the heated depths of her throat, sliding in and out I floated in a sea of rapture and pure sweet ecstasy as my intense climax consumed me from head to toe.

And I held her, sharing it through her with me. She convulsed against me, my hands holding her impaled on my tap while I drained the bottom of the barrel for her. Again and again my hands pulled her fully against and into me while thrusting inside her mouth and throat.

Nicki's mind and senses soared at her fiery orgasmic peak, completely losing her awareness and not knowing it, and not caring. Her sexual tension reached incredible heights. Whatever remained of her conscious awareness had now narrowed to the finest of fine pinpoints. Her hand then dropped instinctively between her crossed legs, and she shifted her heel to make room for its deliberate mission.

On the brink of a sexual frenzy, at the first touch of herself she exploded again between her legs and buttocks. Strong hands held her as she rocked and sucked against that which she still held in her mouth. Her other hand clenched his buttocks, holding him close in her urgent throes while unknowingly she cried the first real tears of her slavery.

For the first time then she began to drift upward towards heaven's seventh heaven, and by the time her dimming awareness had become aware of where she was and what she was doing, several debilitating and wonderful climactic minutes had passed. And then she sensed it was over for them both.

I knew that time had been standing still for us both, aware seemingly that the earth had stopped revolving while I softened inside her suckling mouth. My conscious awareness of where we had been together slowly began to fly away. A moment frozen, captured and trapped in a time of dominance and control that now no longer existed for me. And as my tension left my mind and body in one great rush on the orders of my male feeling mind my thinking mind followed, and followed obediently.

'Ohhh…' I sighed as a satisfied male and opened my eyes, looking down at the limp Greek virgin I still held tightly against my groin.

Nicki's lights of total awareness were almost out. She felt him holding her tightly. And it was while he held her and she rocked gently back and forth in her settling afterglow that she then felt herself falling. Her senses spun backwards into a deep and dark hole in the centre of a never-ending universe.

Over and over, down and down in a pleasurable spiral of peace and quiet, of absolute final tranquillity did her mind and senses tumble, resting in her master's strong, safe hands. Then her dimming awareness felt something firm and soft beneath her back and neck. Vaguely she wondered what it was, but then settled peacefully into the calming depths with a sigh, in a quiet sea of undulating sexual warmth. A part of her dimming awareness then sensed her legs being gently lifted apart, but her conscious awareness and chosen thoughts had long since vacated the scene. They were simply no longer interested.

She had been shocked and frightened by being ordered naked on a public beach. Then her free will had been bypassed with the sheer unexpectedness and sexual force of his male power and physical dominance over her and between her legs, and she between his.

Now she lay quietly subdued, flat on her back on her towel on the warm sand. Her feeling mind took over the running of things for a little while, so she could consciously take time out from a situation that had never before been visited upon her young and sometimes lonely virgin life before.

I smiled and thought of the fifty-yard walk back to the car. Then I smiled even more widely; knowing it was only the dance of time that separated her eventual completion from not being so. Next time for sure, I silently promised my beautiful semi-conscious Greek virgin... next time, for sure.

'Nicki,' I called gently, while shaking her shoulder a little. She stirred. I decided not to let her sleep in the sun any longer. The rays were developing a bite to them. Her eyes opened and blinked a few times, then she stretched and then smiled at me. It melted my heart. Immediately I thought of waking up to that beautiful female smile every morning for the rest of my life.

'Time to go,' I said with a smile, then added, 'devil woman.'

'Mmmmm,' Nicki moaned, then grinned with another stretch. The feeling and mental image of her stretching like that while lying completely naked on a towel on a public beach gave her definite thoughts of trying to delay their departure for the inevitable.

I handed her the velvet collar I had retrieved from her carry-bag. 'Put it on,' I told her. She reached out and took it from me, then fastened it proudly around her throat. Then she reached out to me again. I knew what for, but gave her my surprise instead, bringing out the link chain leash from behind my back and placing the clip end in her palm.

Nicki's lazy smile faded and her eyes widened. I knew she had been reaching for her bikini, not her collar. Her forehead furrowed and questioned, supporting the obvious query in her gaze, but she said nothing. She looked down at the clip in her palm, then back at me, then back at the clip again, and then back up at me.

She sighed when I frowned, then secured the locking clip through the small D-ring at the front of her collar. Then she closed her palm around the chain at her throat and slowly ran it through her hand, watching as I fastened the loop of the leash over my wrist and grasped it lightly between my fingers.

Her eyes again asked me where her swimsuit was. It was a good walk through the soft sand to where I'd parked the car. Her bikini didn't cover much, but at least it kept her virginal modesty protected from prying eyes. I smiled devilishly, knowing we'd pass behind the dunes and out of the eyes of anybody who might be walking along the main beach.

'Stand up, now,' I said, smiling, and then the thought of what I was going to do, going to make her do, began to arouse me. The questioning frown reappeared on her brow, and her eyes backed it up with the equivalent look.

'Stand up,' I said, a little more firmly.

Nicki's gaze darted left and right, searching for anybody or anything. Something was not quite right. The penny had still not dropped, but it was getting close.

'Can I have my bikini, Master?' she asked, concerned.

I smiled. 'No,' I answered, 'you may not. Now stand up or I'll punish you right here on the beach.'

'Oh,' Nicki gasped, her eyes quickly darting left and right again as she brought her knees up in sitting.

'Up,' I commanded firmly, realising then that the woman in her still had a lot of fighting spirit left to quell.

'Master?' Nicki pleaded. She wasn't sure what it was he had in mind, but she was sure she wasn't going to like it. She began to get just a little annoyed, and she began to panic.

'Up,' I repeated.

'Master!' Nicki exclaimed when the penny finally fell into the slot. 'No, you can't!' She felt herself becoming hot and bothered, knowing she was blushing with humiliation and embarrassment. He couldn't be serious. Leading her to the car across the beach in front of everybody?

'Yes,' I told her without a smile on my face, 'I can, because I'm your master. Isn't that true?'

Once more Nicki's eyes darted left and right and then back up to his face. Her terrified gaze implored him not to do it, but he was immune. The pleasure of leading his slave through the sand as if he'd just captured her was obviously what he had in mind.

'Isn't that true?' I repeated, a little more firmly.

Nicki lowered her gaze from his. 'Yes,' she said finally, not entirely defeated. God, she was going to be so embarrassed, knowing there wasn't a thing she could do to stop him.

'Yes, what?' I corrected.

'Yes, Master,' she said petulantly.

'Up,' I said evenly, beginning to lose my patience. Then I did and changed my mind. 'No, get over on your hands and knees,' I snapped at her sharply. 'Now!'

'Oh,' Nicki gasped, startled. 'No Master, please.' But she quickly did as she was told and turned over to position herself on all fours.

'Be quiet,' I snapped again, then stepped beside her left flank. Holding the leash to her throat I dipped and swept down the flat of my free hand squarely and firmly across her bare buttock.

'Oooww!' Nicki shrieked as the pain shot straight to her brain, but before she could think another thought her other buttock exploded in pain with the delivery of a second hard smack. She howled again in humiliated embarrassment and agony at being spanked on a public beach. The tears flowed from her eyes and her heart raced.

'Up!' I barked. 'Or do you want more of the same?' I watched her quickly jump to her feet. Her hands vigorously rubbed her bottom, while she stood head down and sobbing.

'Who is the master here?' I snapped at her.

Nicki didn't look up, but after almost a full minute she answered, 'You, Master.'

'That's right,' I said quietly, menacingly. 'Now pick up your bag.'

Nicki's utter humiliation and embarrassment had never known such dizzy heights and bottomless pits. She was about to be led naked like an animal on a leash across fifty yards of public sandy beach. Her eyes raced and scanned all around her as she bent forward and picked up the bag. Then he started walking away from her.

'Master, please,' she begged, suddenly having to hurry to catch up when the leash ran out of slack and tugged firmly on the D-ring of her collar. She felt the commanding force of its attachment to his wrist. The humiliation she felt was like no other, although she had yet to see anyone on the beach ahead. Stumbling quickly through the soft sand she hurried to keep up with his long strides. She protested but he ignored her, walking just fast enough to always keep most of the slack out of the leash attached to her collar. It was almost always taut.

She cried out, stumbling and falling to her knees. The leash jerked the collar around her throat. Then she began to cry. She looked up, pleading with her eyes as he stopped and turned to look at her. Gazing up at him her eyes darted left and right again, before returning to his face.

'Please, don't do this,' she begged him.

I wondered why she hadn't noticed we were not leaving

by the way we had come. We were walking through the soft sand behind the dunes, rather than the hard tidal sand in front of them where the people were. My heart reached out to her in her distress, but there could only be one captain.

'Get up,' I snapped harshly. 'Now.' Then I turned and began to walk away.

Nicki cried aloud, struggling quickly to her feet in the sand. The leash then tugged firmly on her collar and she stumbled forward, quickly catching up with him again. Her heart fluttered and her pulse raced. She was being led like a bitch on the beach, as if being taken out for a walk. Her tearful eyes frantically scanned ahead, but all she could see were the dunes and sand and the trees surrounding the car park to her right.

I felt like a captain, a sea pirate, leading her along, always keeping the chain leash just short of being taut. I jerked her constantly by the neck to keep up with me. My groin was hard. Each time I looked quickly back at her struggling through the soft sand my gaze zeroed directly in on her black bush. Her lush pubic shroud of virginity seemed darker for some reason, and seeing her at the end of my leash was having the most profound sexual effect on me. I felt proud, in a strange sexual kind of way. She was my goods, my chattel, and my slave.

I slowed then in my stride and stopped walking altogether, realising that something was happening to me. I was changing and I knew it. It wasn't the hypnosis or the fact that I could control and dominate her. It was having her as my slave, and her wanting me as her master. The emotion of that realising moment welled up in my heart, my throat and my mind as she caught up with me and stood still, puffing sweetly.

Slowly I turned around to face the realisation of my

living moment, knowing I had crossed a threshold of some sort in my life, a turning point, a crossroad, and I had turned the corner. She stood about a foot away from me.

Her mouth was open. She breathed deeply; panting, her pretty Greek face lined with glistening beads that sparkled in the sun. Her chest and neck were flushed from the effort of keeping up, and perhaps the embarrassment of being made do so on a leash attached to her throat whilst completely naked. Her lustrous black hair was tousled in disarray and clung to her right cheek.

'Jesus,' I sighed through clenched teeth, gazing directly into her eyes. The emotion of the moment settled squarely in my throat. 'You have no idea how hot you make me for you,' I said seriously. 'I am so proud to call you my slave.'

Her eyes widened instantly, and then widened even further when I said quietly, but intensely, and without thinking, 'I love you, Nicki.'

Then I turned and walked quickly until the slack disappeared from the link chain leash and tugged firmly at the collar around her throat once again. I stopped only when I reached the car. We had not seen one other living human soul on our first inaugural and formal walk as master and slave in public for the entire world to see, although we had passed a foraging dog wandering the beach.

I was sexually aroused and I was hot for her, to take her precious Greek virginity from her, to have her and to hold her for as long as we both lived. There was no doubt about that whatsoever. And I felt like leading her straight back to my private hideaway and doing the final deflowering deed once and for all on a towel in the hot sand.

Nicki had been shocked at the suddenness of his

statement, and at the shining unshed tears of honesty in his eyes when he'd spoken. Her gaze had misted instantly when he'd said the words he had. And in that one single moment of timeless time her embarrassment and shame at being led like a captured animal along a public beach had vanished. All she had seen was her master who really was proud of her, and who for the very first time had just told his slave that he loved her.

From his eyes and the look on his face when he'd spoken she knew he meant it. She became instantly aware of the collar around her throat, of the weight of the chain leash attached to it with the other end attached to her master's wrist. And she had become aware of the weight of his love for her. Her heart swelled as she realised also the weight of her love for him. As she'd hurried to catch up and then keep up when the firm tugs on the leash brought her thoughts back to the moment, the stinging heartfelt tears of her slave joy ran freely and unstoppably down her cheeks.

'Oh, Master,' she cried, throwing her arms about him and hugging him fiercely when he turned to face her after stopping beside his car. She felt as if she owned him, as well as the other way around. Burying her face into his warm shoulder she felt his strong arms immediately encircle her, wrapping her tightly against him in his protection. She felt safe and warm and loved, and she felt like his goods, his chattel, and his property.

The feeling of being owned by him right then suddenly became the most important, the most precious thing in the world to her. For the first time in her life she belonged to someone, she really belonged to someone, her master, him. And he belonged to her.

Quietly, she stood completely naked beside his car at the edge of the secluded car park and sobbed honestly into his shoulder, while he continued to hug her lovingly. It was the happiest moment she had ever known in her entire life.

I tried to speak as I held Nicki close to me. I knew the fine words I wanted to say, but none would come. Gently, I unclipped the leash from her collar and gave her back the bag that held her clothes, as well as her bikini. Then I held her at arm's length and gazed at her eyes, her breasts, her belly, and her lush Greek virgin pubes one last time for the day. She was beautiful. God, but she was beautiful.

'Get dressed now, sweetheart,' I said, the lump in my throat still obvious to me.

'Yes, Master,' she answered softly, stepping away from my reach and taking her bag. Then she raised her tear-filled eyes and gazed at me. And that once in a lifetime, never seen before look, to me, was beyond priceless. It was simply beyond priceless.

Chapter Nine

I smiled at Nicki as she sat looking shyly at me from her chair opposite. Another long week had passed since our day at the beach. We sat sipping a cold drink before she began her housecleaning. I hadn't yet decided if I was going to allow her to continue with it once she started, but that was her plan, at least. I'd spent the week in a strange mood, even for me, wanting a smoke several times, but somehow I'd managed to control the urge. It had been a time of reflection, and looking to the future as well. By mid-week I'd reached the stage of feeling miserably sorry for myself after contemplating all the years I'd been married and allowed Lauren to cause me to live my life as a man and not a natural male.

Now I couldn't see why I'd put up with Lauren's grudge fucks and lack of affection for so long. Thinking about Nicki, however, and the way I felt whenever I even thought about her or of being with her gradually rid those depressing feelings from my mind by week's end. I'd also researched male dominance and female submissiveness on the Internet, and thought I'd learned quite a lot for someone who plied his trade as only a writer and a journalist.

By the end of the week I was convinced I'd wasted many years of my life, but I did not intend to waste another single living moment of it living as a man, not one. I was a natural dominant male now and that was how I wanted to spend the rest of my life, and I intended to do just that.

'Why are so many relationships unhappy, Master?' Nicki

asked idly. It was so good to be with him again, in his presence and close to him. She hadn't felt balanced since she'd seen him last, when he led her back to the car from the beach on a leash, naked. She was ecstatic with her life now and the way it was going, but her week had seemed so drawn out, so long.

It seemed to take forever to pass. Every day all her thoughts had centred on the Saturday just passed, and on the words he'd said to her, those beautiful tender words she had never heard from another male human being, let alone a man. She had relived every single moment in minute detail, no matter where she had been or what she had been doing. Her master had been in her mind and her body's sensual awareness non-stop, all week long.

'Are you unhappy?' I asked her, smiling; she looked distracted or deep in thought.

'No, Master,' she protested immediately. 'I guess I was – I was comparing how I feel to others, maybe?'

'Then you're happy with our relationship, such that it is?' I asked, curious about her train of thought.

'Oh yes, Master,' Nicki beamed, believing it with all her young heart. 'It's wonderful!'

'Do you think it's an unusual relationship?' I asked, probing a little more.

Nicki smiled shyly. 'Maybe…' she replied softly, looking up at him from beneath her eyebrows. 'But only compared to the normal, and they're mostly unhappy from what I've seen. So I guess the unusual is more happy than the usual, in that case.'

I smiled. My little Greek slave was not just a pretty face. 'Do you feel disrespected as a female, by or in the way I dominate you?' I asked.

'No, Master,' Nicki answered softly, knowing it to be true.

'Even when I punish you?'

Nicki's backside recalled instantly the throbbing hotness she'd felt in her buttocks from the several spankings she had received so far. She blushed, and felt a little warm again there because of it. 'No, Master,' she replied, dropping her gaze, embarrassed.

I chuckled, seeing the crimson colour begin at her neck and then reach upward over her throat to her face.

'What about when I humiliate you as a form of punishment or training?' I asked her.

Nicki felt herself blush afresh, immediately recalling her walk along the beach, completely naked and tied to a leash. She had felt humiliated at first, but not now. And being spanked on a public beach had definitely humiliated her, but now, that too seemed unimportant in the overall scheme of her personal happiness in him wanting her for his slave and she wanting to be so. Picturing herself naked and on all fours, kneeling on her towel while leashed to him as he spanked her, slowly but surely brought a fresh blush to her face.

'No, Master,' she said softly, knowing that short, one word answer to be true as well. The warmth from the blushing had spread now to between her legs, but for different reasons.

'Thinking men and women are almost doomed from the start,' I said. 'As far as their happiness in a relationship goes.'

'Why?' Nicki asked, curious.

'Why what?' I frowned immediately.

'I'm sorry… why, Master?' Nicki immediately corrected herself, hoping he wouldn't spank her just for that, but not really sure that he wouldn't. He smiled. She felt immediately relieved.

'Since men and women think as opposed to feel,

whatever they've each learned will be interpreted differently to the way the other has learned it, even about the same or similar things. Therefore they'll have nothing in common regarding it.'

'Hmmm,' Nicki pondered.

'But as males and females, we have everything in common, naturally, and we didn't have to learn them, they came with us at birth, as a complete feeling package. We all knew how to feel when we were born, so we have that in common automatically, as natural males and females.'

'Yes, I see that,' Nicki said seriously. And she did, in a way, but she knew she was still putting it all together.

I decided to let her off for the interest she was showing, while I crystallised my thoughts on the topic, just by talking aloud.

'I believe that we were meant to live our lives by acting upon our feelings,' I said. 'Then supporting those natural feelings, whatever they may be, with our learned thoughts, not the other way round.'

'I've never thought of it that way before,' Nicki said honestly, and wondered why.

I smiled. Neither had I, until recently. But I did now.

'Not many do,' I said. 'But if we did we'd soon know who should be in charge of our actions on a daily basis. Most men and women don't cope, even on a good-hair day. But males and females cope always, even on a bad-hair day, because they feel good about themselves, without feeling guilty or ashamed. Men and women always feel guilty, that's why they're not happy, mostly, even on a good day. But males and females are always happy, even when their day is not going as planned.'

Nicki felt the adoration toward him right then in the very bottom of her soul. He really understood things.

Everything he'd said now made sense to her, almost.

I knew then that all the money in the world could not buy the feelings that went with the look Nicki was giving me right then. I felt like the most important person in her world at that moment.

'It's men and women that fight and argue and don't get on,' I continued thoughtfully, feeling as if I was on a philosophical roll of some kind. 'Males and females don't do that, simply because they're too busy feeling good about themselves and whatever they're doing at the time, which will always be whatever feels right, toward their partner as well as themselves. They don't think first, they feel first, and then they act. A natural male would simply not do anything that did not feel right at the time, and that includes imposing his free will upon his female, or another for that matter.'

Nicki's eyebrows raised and she smiled. 'But when you spanked me and led me naked along the beach, wasn't that imposing your free will on mine?'

I frowned.

'Master,' Nicki added quickly, cursing herself silently. She had a feeling her bottom would be red again if she kept that up.

She was learning. That's all I wanted from her. 'No, it couldn't have been,' I said. 'If it didn't feel right I wouldn't have done it. It's really that simple. And now, when you look back on it, did I really do anything you don't now believe was right for you?'

Nicki thought only for a moment, knowing she had been naughty and deserved the punishment.

'No, Master,' she replied softly, feeling the cheeks of her bottom begin to warm.

'That's what I mean,' I continued. 'A natural male or a natural female just wouldn't do anything that didn't feel right in the big picture. To each of their little pictures at the time it might not seem so. But in the big picture, nature always looks after her own. Natural males and females are nature's own children, I believe, always a perfect balance in the big picture, while the little pictures are always, and meant to be, just learning curves that draw the couple closer together.'

Nicki felt that same look of undying adoration on her face as she gazed at him, her master. He was right. Nature was perfect. She just hadn't thought about it from that perspective before.

'So, if everybody followed their feelings instead of their thoughts, they'd be living as natural males and females?' Nicki asked, putting it all together as a big picture in her thoughts.

'Naturally happy males and females,' I added, forgiving her again for her repeated misdemeanour. 'Even on a bad-hair day.'

'And they wouldn't impose their free will on their partner, just because they wanted to?' Nicki asked, further clarifying the concept of the difference between men and women, males and females.

I smiled and wondered how long it would be before it felt right to spank her bottom again. At the moment it did not feel right.

'Men and women want,' I told her. 'Males and females need. A male wouldn't want to do that. The man in him might, but if he were male-dominant in his personality he would act on his feelings, rather than his wants. If he were man-dominant in his personality he would act on his wants and hurt someone in some way. He would realise that it felt wrong, but his man-dominant personality would do it anyway, because it was what he wanted. When the wants of men and women get in the road of the needs of their male or female partner, there will always be hurt or arguments or dissatisfaction.'

'No wonder so many couples are unhappy,' Nicki concluded thoughtfully, feeling everything he'd told her had just fallen into place.

I nodded, trusting in nature. It was only a matter of time before her ass was grass.

'No, not couples,' I corrected her. 'Men and women, and it's because their personalities are thinking man or woman-dominant. Males and females simply have nothing to fight about. They only want to give, in one way or another, but they give naturally in different ways, according to their gender. This is the only thing each has to learn about the other. A feeling of sadness or happiness, of lust or desire, is felt the same way by both of them. There's no difference in interpretation, thanks to nature and their own natural human natures.'

'What if they misunderstood their partner?' Nicki asked, curious and not quite clear on that point.

Not a matter of if, but when. Not if, but when.

'There's no chance of it being misinterpreted,' I said. 'Because the feelings they acted upon would have originated with and from nature, their human nature, so they would have felt right and been right at the time in the big picture of nature, as the final balance.

'And it's the same for both,' I added. 'That way, any feeling of happiness derived from their actions toward one another would result in happiness of a long-term nature, compared to the achievements of the wants by thinking men and women, which if actually achieved, are usually only short-term happiness at best.'

'That's amazing,' Nicki said, full of admiration for her master. He was her father figure also, she concluded, as she gazed warmly at him. 'How do you know all this stuff?'

'I was an unhappy man for a long time,' I said bitterly. What was amazing, I thought, was that it still did not feel right to spank her for forgetting her slave manners whenever she addressed me, but the look she gave me was worth the restraint. An easy silence then fell over us for several minutes while we just sat gazing into each other's eyes, like a pair of teenagers in the throes of puppy love. I felt like all things to her right at that moment. I felt important to someone. I hadn't felt that way in a long time, even toward myself, and I realised something I thought was important, that I needed to be needed in order to be the male I wanted to be. Then I wondered whether her father would have approved of my spanking her, let alone the age difference between us.

'There's also no age difference between males and females,' I told her on a sudden thought. 'Nor attraction differences. All males past puberty are attracted to all females past puberty. That's nature's way, in order for any natural breeding species to reproduce and survive. That's nature's sole responsibility.

'That's why you'll sometimes see older males with younger females, or vice versa,' I continued. 'But they all have one thing in common when you notice it. They're all happy with each other. They don't think about or care about those natural differences in size, height, weight or shape. They just feel a natural attraction and act. Looks don't matter, or are not a major part of the initial attraction, at any rate. The attraction is simply that one is a male and one is a female.'

'Hmmm,' Nicki pondered thoughtfully, thinking about her master and herself. 'That means that the whole world should be attracted to one another?'

'That's what nature had in mind for the continuation of

our species,' I said, wondering when her ass would be grass. I was beginning to become aroused and looked forward now to her continuing to forget her slave manners. 'But we are not all attracted to one another, because some of us are men and women, not males and females. Men and women have learned or have been taught to become that way, unfortunately, as products of their environment from birth to puberty. But they can learn to go back to who they really are, males and females.'

'Would it be hard, do you think?' Nicki asked curiously.

I smiled, stirring in my trousers. 'I did it,' I said. 'You're doing it. We're happy. And if we can do it, anybody can. The point is, do they know that they have a choice? They can go back to being who they really are, as they were born, as happy and contented feeling males and females, and move away from being what they've learned to be, as unhappy, often lonely thinking men and women.'

'How would they learn?' Nicki asked.

'The same way you have, and do, and will again, now,' I said firmly with a frown. 'Stand up.'

'Oh,' Nicki gasped, startled at his command, but immediately knowing the reason why, and on top of that she did not question it. She cursed herself silently and stood up, blushing and with a racing pulse, but she did not question it.

'Do you know why I am going to punish you now?'

With shaking fingers and a wide-eyed gaze Nicki nodded, but did not look at him. Her nipples stiffened. The natural tingling arousal in her lower belly was obvious to her now because he was going to punish her again, and he was going to do it right then. Maybe it would happen now, her mind wondered as her lower belly tingled at the prospect.

'Pull your pants down,' I said seriously. 'But keep your

underwear on.'

'Oh,' Nicki gasped. The tingling in her loins matched the warming already on her bottom.

Your ass is grass now, girl, I grinned silently, watching my beautiful Greek virgin slave unfasten, drop, and then step out of her shorts, but keep on her dainty brief white underwear. And she did it willingly, because she knew it felt right. I assumed it did, anyway. It did for me.

I glanced at my watch, and then riveted my gaze on the dark nest of pubic hair hidden between her legs inside her panties. I had the rest of the morning and half the afternoon to have fun, and still leave enough time for her to clean the house and depart before Lauren and Marcena arrived home from their shopping trip.

Slowly I stood up and walked around behind her. She had two dimples, just above the top of her buttocks. I stirred.

'You are my beautiful Greek virgin slave, Nicki,' I said to her, gazing at the attractive hidden crease between her two firm peach cheeks. 'At least for the moment, and because of that you're also a natural submissive female, or you can learn to be. Do you want to?'

'Yes, Master,' Nicki said, knowing he meant her virginity. Her heart raced as fast as her pulse, wondering what he was going to do to her. He'd told her to keep her panties on so he wasn't going to do it to her. She could feel her buttocks becoming warm, and didn't know whether it was from the envisaged spanking or knowing he was standing behind her, looking down at them.

'If you truly understood what I've been talking about I wouldn't be punishing you now, would I?' I asked her. She didn't answer. Instead, she hung her head and looked away from me, then slowly shook it, just once. 'As a natural female, you'll be content from being submissive to me, if that's what you want from such a relationship.'

'I do,' Nicki reassured him honestly; feeling his gaze bore two holes in her body, one in each cheek of her bottom. Instantly she knew she'd forgotten again and decided it was too late. She was going to be punished for it anyway.

I let it go and believed her. 'You aren't weak in being submissive,' I told her. 'You're strong. Once you truly understand the submissive slave concept of a natural female your own ideas will become clear to you on how you want to act around me. It's not out of shame or embarrassment or fear that I want you to willingly serve my needs as your master, but out of pride and strength in your own femaleness.'

Nicki said nothing, feeling his gaze. He now stood in front of her, doing what he was doing, looking at her. She was proud, she thought then, of being his slave and of being a feeling female and not a thinking woman, which she believed her mother and twin sisters probably were.

She did not now feel complete in herself unless she was with him. And somehow she knew he would protect her body, teach her mind, and strengthen her natural female with his male strength and wisdom. She wanted to be everything to him and for him, as he was already everything to her. In her mind in the week just passed his memorable touch had awoken her several times, to find her hands on her breasts and between her legs while alone in her lonely bed. She had smiled softly then, believing how lucky she'd been in meeting him, in having him. Thoughts of him seemed to free her from the learned chains of her past thinking woman, and in that alone she felt very free, and without feeling guilty.

'You might think at first that my punishments are too severe,' I said, almost finished. 'But you should accept them gratefully, knowing that I always have your best interests at heart to make a better slave out of you for both our sakes.'

'I am grateful, Master, really,' Nicki said emphatically, believing her words to be true. She could feel his gaze between her legs, and the heat in her buttocks had now spread to her sex and lower belly.

'I know you are,' I agreed. 'But if and when I ever desire your body you'll happily give it to me. Then you can take pride and pleasure in knowing that you'll bring me much happiness. But the pleasure of giving your body is only one aspect of our relationship. The way we love, the way we trust each other, the things we share, and the respectful good manners we show each other always are all parts of this relationship. Do you agree?'

Nicki hung her head, feeling ashamed. She had forgotten her manners. She nodded instead of speaking, feeling as if she'd let him down already. Tears welled in her eyes. In her master's eyes she was beautiful, she knew that now and for that alone she could hold her head high and endure his punishments, whatever they were. She gazed down at her arms and legs, and then at the shadowy triangle of dark hair hidden within her panties. She was simmering and she knew it. He moved to stand once again behind her, and her buttocks felt the warmth of his gaze instantly.

'If I want you to be my slut,' I said to her, staring through her sheer underwear at the shadowy valley between her taut buttocks, 'then you will be my slut because I want you to be with every ounce of your natural female being. And if I want you to be my princess, then with every ounce of your natural female being will you strive to be the very best natural female princess you can be for me.'

Nicki blushed immediately when he used the word, slut.

She felt warm between her legs and knew she was getting wet. Everything he was telling her was true. She knew that. Her mind was his, to teach and to train, to explore and to know as only he could. She did not want to have any secrets from him, no mistrust between them. She knew already that she would probably never like his punishments, but she was realising that they were just his loving way of teaching her important lessons so she could be a better female for both of them.

'I want your female soul, Nicki,' I said, the emotion welling quickly as I spoke. 'I don't, and never will want the thinking woman of you in charge of your happiness, or around me, for that matter. When you kneel naked at my feet you'll never displease me, and the worst way you can displease me is to disappoint me. Do you understand?'

'Yes, Master,' Nicki said softly, on the verge of tears. His words were so meaningful to her, so beautiful, so completing. Kneeling naked at his feet was exactly what she wanted to do and where she wanted to be for the rest of her natural life as a female and his perfect slave. Nicki felt the warmth of her tears before she was even aware she was crying. He had called her sweetheart, a term of fond endearment. He had never done that before. Nobody had.

Her heart swelled to bursting point with loving affection for him in all ways. She wished he would just take her virginity then and there where she stood, and complete her deflowering properly. Then she would be physically bonded to him for life. She knew that truly. She had never wanted so badly to lose her Greek maidenhead in all her life.

I saw her tears and almost joined her with those of my own. I couldn't believe the emotional feelings she was bringing out in me; feelings I hadn't felt since I was a teenager discovering my first true puppy love. Except the feelings I had for her, I knew, were not those from a love of that kind. I gently stroked her glorious black hair as it flowed down over her shoulders like a dark cloak of mystery.

'Oh, Master,' Nicki sobbed softly, as his hand passed gently over her hair. She was beginning to realise that his role as her master was more difficult than hers was. And that she should be grateful that he even wanted to make her the very best female she could be. All she had to do was to stop acting like the thinking woman she had always been, then begin to act on each and every feeling that came to her instinctive or intuitive awareness. She just had to allow herself to be who she really was, a natural feeling female, and not what she had always been, an unnatural and mostly unhappy thinking woman.

'I'm a natural dominant male, Nicki,' I told her, knowing now it was true. 'I always have been. But like you and most people, who are generally unhappy and want something more out of life, I didn't always know it. For many years the thinking man of me suffered much loneliness and unhappiness because of it, but now my thoughts no longer lead my actions. Instead they support my natural male feelings, whatever they might happen to be in any given moment. And I'm proud of being a dominant male, Nicki, I really am. I deserve to be. It's my birthright, my right to natural long-term happiness, and I want you to feel that way too, but as a female.'

Nicki was still sobbing quietly. The emotion of the moment delivered by his powerful words was too much to bear.

'I – I am proud, Master,' she said hesitantly. 'I am.'

'I know you are, baby,' I told her, reigning in my own

surging emotions with my hand stroking gently down the centre of her back. 'And I want you to know that your willing female submission is a gift that I value as priceless. And when I take your precious Greek virginity – and I will take it, make no mistake about that – you'll give that preciousness willingly to me, and with all your natural female heart.'

'Oh,' Nicki almost cried, wanting him to pull down her panties and take it right there and then, to push it fully inside her, through her boundary no matter what the pain.

'And when I do take it,' I said. 'That wonderful gift from you will be the most prized possession I'll ever own, sweetheart, and only because it will have been me who took it. And it will have been you who gave it to me. Once I take it, Nicki, I'll always own that fact, and no one can ever take that away from me. Do you understand?'

Nicki finally felt herself crack and wept openly and unashamedly. She had never felt so much impassioned and heartfelt love for another human being; had never even imagined it could be so.

And while she sobbed he held her from behind, stroking her back, her shoulders, her ribs, the under-swell of each soft breast beneath her shirt. Then he stroked her buttocks and then deeply in between. His hand slid between her legs, lightly brushing the soft hair within her underwear, barely touching her.

Then finally and only because of her powerful bodily sensations her tears ceased, but they left behind their warmth of having been in other ways. His hand continued to pass slowly back and forth between her legs, feathering the sheer material canopy over her nest. He sanded her inner thighs and her damp crease with his light touch.

Her sex felt moist and hot and his gentle touch there was simply electric, each time his hand swept through her junction and burnished over the softness of her. She wanted him now, wanted him to take her and have her, to hang her virginity on his wall of pride. She wanted him to put it inside her, to break through what had always been waiting until she met the right man, the right male, and now she had. She realised fully at that moment just how fiercely she loved her master, and with a young virgin lust and fiery passion she had never thought she would ever be capable of. She was as happy and as joyous as any living human being had a right to be.

'Bend over and grasp your knees,' I told her firmly, standing behind her. Then I withdrew my leather belt from the loops of my trousers. 'Keep your eyes closed and face the front.'

Nicki gasped, startled out of her emotional thoughts and back to the reality of the moment. Her heart raced. Her punishment was about to begin. Slowly she bent forward and gripped her knees so firmly that her knuckles turned white.

'Get ready,' I warned her, my excitement rising with the warning.

Nicki's heart jumped and then beat so fast she thought it was going to explode at any moment. She wanted to beg him not to spank her, yet she did want him to. She was confused. She wanted him to penetrate her instead, to hurt her, to break her, to make her different in that way. And it was in the middle of that thought that her tender sensual world of the moment exploded in blinding debilitating pain as her bottom suddenly blazed in an agony she had never thought possible for one human being to feel.

And it was in the beginning of that agonising pain that she'd heard the loud slap that brought the blistering torment in her bottom with it. The incapacitating intensity of her anguish sent her mind and senses spinning crazily.

I quickly stepped forward and held her by the neck, then reefed her underwear down to her ankles.

'Step out of them,' I ordered her, watching her immediately do so. I grabbed them off the floor and lifted them to her face, then forced them inside her mouth as a gag.

'Leave them there,' I commanded firmly, feeling somehow that it was now time to break her thinking woman's spirit once and for all, for both our sakes. If she didn't listen she would now feel.

Nicki opened her mouth to cry out as he finished feeding something soft into her mouth. It effectively absorbed her cry of alarm and reduced it to only a muffled groan. It was her lacy white underwear. She could taste and smell her own musky arousal.

Her nostrils flared for air while she drew breath to scream her stinging pain away again, but it took all of her physical strength to keep her eyes shut and hold to the bent over position in which she stood with her hands gripping her knees. She felt herself buckling, losing her balance. With her white-knuckled fingers she squeezed the blazing pain into her legs with every ounce of concentration she could find. It ripped, torching through her mind. Tears stung her eyes mercilessly and her senses swam.

I drew back the leather belt and swung again, aiming as best I could for the centre of her buttocks. She jerked wildly when it slapped hard across her flesh, howling into the underwear wedged inside her mouth as two bright red welts seemed to magically appear across her creamy white buttocks. I was surprised at how calm I felt as I drew back for a third time and swung hard.

Nicki could not believe he was punishing her so harshly.

Her mind and body wracked with a pain she had never imagined possible. She bucked again and swayed, dipping at the knees, the tears swimming from her eyes while her body burned in hell.

I held her firmly again as I swung. She shrieked and writhed, then buckled at the knees and fell to the carpet on all fours, her buttocks trembling and twisting from side to side, but I followed her down and swung again. Her muffled whimper disappeared into the gag as she threw herself down onto the carpet, her buttocks clenching and unclenching, her hands stretched out in front of her as if she were trying to drag herself away from the pain and the belt by her fingertips. Her body was on fire, her mind ablaze.

Again I drew back and swung hard down across her lower buttocks, and again she screamed into the gag. Her ass was streaked with several raised welts that looked glorious to me as I hesitated when drawing back. It was time to stop. It felt right to stop. I threaded the belt back into my trousers while she sobbed wearily into the gag.

Nicki suddenly felt herself collapse, first mentally then emotionally and then physically. She cried openly and unashamedly, waiting for the next one, but strangely there was no more pain. She floated somewhere in the sky where it was cool and warm, her body turning numb to her sensory awareness of anything at all.

She waited, knowing what the blazing pain would feel like when it finally arrived, ready for it now, and strangely accepting its ultimate arrival with a submissive serenity. She was in a cool warm place somewhere, an unfamiliar place she had never been before where her mind now rested, waiting… waiting. But the pain never came. Slowly, gradually then she began to quieten her sobs of anguish.

She felt herself floating downward, back to the pain,

back to the reality of lying on the floor; naked from the waist down with her backside torching her body to death while it was still alive.

I knelt beside her in her agony and gazed at her scarlet-welted buttocks, wondering if I'd gone too far, but feeling I'd stopped at just the right time. Her woman's spirit had been broken, I was sure of it. Angry red stripes decorated her buttocks, looking sensual and attractive in their redness and in their unusual and unnatural markings.

Reaching to her mouth I removed her panties, hearing her gasp deeply and immediately. Then I leaned down and began to kiss that redness and her pain and hurt away, each welt and each risen inch of crimson flesh.

'Ohhh...' Nicki gasped, breathing deeply of the air. 'Ohhh...' she gasped again, startled as she felt his lips on her burning bottom.

'Open your legs,' I said firmly, then watched as she slowly parted them a little.

'More,' I told her more forcefully. She spread them a little more.

'More,' I insisted.

Nicki moved her feet wide apart, the pain in her bottom momentarily dulling from the awareness of the warmth of his kisses. He began to kiss deeply between her cheeks, his tongue gently, soothingly whispering away the hurt. Then he slid his lips and mouth further downward between her legs.

'Ohhh...' she groaned deeply, feeling emotionally drained and excited at the same time. Lifting her hips a little she was then rewarded instantly with the sensation of his tongue pushing inside her, inside the natural tightness of her virginity. Her loins tingled instantly and she raised her hips a little higher, to be rewarded yet again with the incredibly arousing sensation of the flat of his tongue dragging slowly from her stem to her stern.

'Ohhh…' she moaned again from her depths. Her own voice sounded to her as belonging to a wanton slut in its honesty of expression, but she didn't care, even of her thoughts about herself. All she wanted to do was feel; to feel his touch, his kisses, his exploring tongue as it slid upwards and buried itself in the very centre of her buttocks.

'Ohhh…' she cried honestly. He was her master, had punished her and now he was caring for her, loving her in a way she needed to be loved and cared for right then.

Her juices were strong and textured, slick and highly palatable, and I drank deeply of them with my tongue fluted inside her flooding well. It would soon be time…

Then I energetically continued to attend to the red brands on her bottom, and tasting all of her Greek virgin delights that lay betwixt and between, until finally she began to twist violently in my grip. Then she stiffened and groaned deeply for several long seconds, before collapsing fully relaxed into the soft carpet, with a long and contented sigh.

My slave, I thought tenderly as I rose and wiped her juices from my chin. My little Greek virgin slave was slowly changing into a natural feeling female, and through it all I knew that I, too, was changing for good. There was no going back now. I simply didn't want to. There was simply nothing and no one to go back to or for.

That night, a few hours after Nicki had left with a sore bottom, I stood looking at my cold-hearted affection-depriving wife as she came through the front door of the house. A flood of anger and resentment, as well as a surge of primeval adrenaline flowed into my loins from the wasted years with her. She hesitated momentarily when she saw me, then leaned back seductively against the door, while gazing into my eyes. I wasn't smiling.

My eyes danced as always, I could feel them, but now they felt dead to her. Then I thought of her body and how it would look if I surprised her and stripped her naked where she stood. I knew she loved the feeling of power and control her body had over me, and she loved using it as a currency, even more so to get what she wanted at various times. I'd seen her naked many times, but never against the front door of the house.

Then I changed my thoughts as she came off the door and walked silently right past me, her eyes clearly telling me of her woman's true feelings. I watched her pass by me without so much as a word and gritted my teeth. Not a matter of if, I decided, but when.

Chapter Ten

Two days later, just before lunchtime, my thoughts were interrupted with the sound of a knock on the front door. Rising from my small worktable I walked to it and opened it, to see Nicki standing there with a puzzled look on her face. In the morning sunshine I thought she was even lovelier than I had when I first met her. She wore a loose blue cotton summer dress. I showed her inside and into the room where I'd been working.

'Hi,' I said, wondering why she had come unannounced.

'Hi, Master,' Nicki said softly, glancing quickly at him as she settled. Then she dropped her gaze once more to stare at the tabletop. She still hadn't really figured out why she was there. It was just a feeling, something she had to do. Then she remembered and her backside warmed.

'May I sit, Master?'

'Yes,' I said. 'Something wrong?'

Nicki looked up and directly into his eyes, feeling the response forming instantly in her mouth. 'My bottom still hurts, Master, but… but it was worth it,' she said softly. 'I really mean that.'

I smiled at her tenderly, recalling her welted cheeks. 'Why do you seem a little ill at ease?' I enquired.

Nicki remained looking at him. How could she tell him when she didn't really know that one herself? She did know, at least a part of her did, but which part? And what exactly did that part wish by being there? She decided to wing it and see what happened anyway.

'It's… well, Master, it's just that I…' she stammered, not finishing her sentence.

I watched her give a nervous giggle. Then she took a deep breath, letting it out with a long slow sigh. I knew what her problem was, or rather, what it was not. It was the same one I had.

'The main reason I'm here, Master,' Nicki said. 'I mean, what totally freaks me is that suddenly it's okay with me if… if you…' she giggled nervously again. 'What have you done to me?'

'I've made an honest female out of you,' I said.

'Don't get me wrong, Master,' Nicki said. 'I think it's great. I just can't understand it. That's all. I feel like I always have a terrific time with you in some way I never expect. And when you, when you spank me I just can't remember the pain, only what you… you know?'

I knew what she meant, where she was going and what she wouldn't or couldn't say. She was leaving it up to me to interpret, if I could and I had.

'Yes, baby,' I smiled tenderly at her wide, uncertain eyes. 'I know.'

Nicki sighed at his use of the term of endearment. She felt a wave of extreme emotion race headlong across the ridges of her mind and body, but then she felt herself almost collapse internally and panicked. Now? Would it happen now? Would he do it to her now? Inside she was both frightened and excited. Then her thoughts began to fade. It was a very pleasant feeling of not caring, of now being unconcerned about her precious Greek virginity, or anything for that matter. It was wonderful to have a master who was responsible for everything.

'You don't want to be a Greek virgin any longer, do you?' I asked her, knowing it was time and why she had come.

'I – um – well, I – no, Master,' Nicki finally answered shyly and embarrassed, not game to look at him. That was why she had come; she realised that now. Then she began a thought that she never got to finish because he suddenly kissed her hard on the mouth.

'Ohhh,' she gasped breathlessly when he released her from his passionate and brutally stirring embrace.

'Have you come for me to fuck your wonderful Greek virginity away forever?' I asked, wondering if she'd find the courage to accept the vernacular and lift her head to look at me. She blushed hotly and her shoulders slumped and her head bowed even more. 'That's fine,' I told her. It was time, but I wanted to play. 'Tell me you want me to fuck away your Greek virginity.'

'Master,' she begged him, knowing it was a futile exercise. 'I want you to... fuck away m-my Greek virginity,' she sighed, defeated and hot and bothered.

'But you want me to suck your Greek pussy first,' I led her teasingly. 'Say it.'

Nicki's dress began to stick to her back, and the dampness between her legs just kept increasing. 'I want you t-to suck my Greek pussy first, Master,' she said, noticing the deepening of her own voice.

'Then you want me to penetrate you, straight through your virgin Greek wall.'

'Master?' she pleaded, feeling the perspiration form on her forehead.

'Say it.'

'Oh, um, I want you to... to penetrate me, Master, straight through my virgin Greek wall,' Nicki finished, very hot and bothered.

'And you want me to fuck you hard and fast.'

'Oh...' Nicki sighed, blushing terribly, 'I want you t-t-to fuck me, Master, hard and fast.'

I had chosen the right track to take. I reached over and lightly touched her breasts.

'Oh,' Nicki gasped. It was starting. Oh, it was finally happening.

I leaned over and cupped her face in my hands, then turned it gently to one side. Then softly I explored her ear with my tongue.

'Ohhh…' Nicki gasped as his hot breath and tongue filled her ear. She felt her head begin to spin, as if she were plummeting down a deep dark well where everything was calm, and it seemed the wrong place to even try to have a thought of any kind whatsoever. Again she felt the slight shift of her head. She then felt him lean close and gently tongue her other ear. She was becoming breathless and he'd barely touched her yet.

Her heart hammered her ribs mercilessly, the touch of his tonguing in her ear like a soft but forceful sledgehammer that tumbled her spinning mind and senses even more quickly down the bottomless well. She leaned into his grip, into his tongue, melting. Yes, yes, she thought joyously as her mind spun over and over.

She gasped as I ceased kissing her ears and held her at arm's length. Her eyes blinked several times, and then they opened fully and looked downward. Her eyes were milky and dreamy, and she looked beautiful. She looked radiant.

'Sit down,' I told her.

Nicki glanced up at him, then gazed down again, turned slowly and sat down. Then she looked up at him with an almost overwhelming expression of expectancy on her face and in her eyes.

'Will it… will it hurt, Master?' Nicki asked quietly, with just a hint of concern in her voice.

I gazed down at my lovely Greek virgin. 'Yes,' I replied.

'Of course it will, but you'll be too busy feeling wonderful to even notice.'

'Oh,' Nicki gasped softly, her mind quickly calculating the simple logic in that. It made sense.

'And I think you're eager to begin experiencing that special pain,' I suggested.

Nicki felt herself nod, not looking up.

'Stand up and remove all your clothing.'

At the first sound of his words Nicki was shocked, but the feeling never lasted long. This was the special something that had been waiting to happen to her since birth. Her heart began to race. Her blood pounded in her temples, and she held his gaze.

Slowly she rose to her feet, never taking her eyes from his. Her hands began to reach for her clothes. She removed them shyly, slowly, until she stood completely naked before him. She knew she was blushing from head to toe. Her hands moved quickly to cover her modesty, but her gaze remained locked inside his own.

'Do you want me to suck your virgin pussy now?' I asked her.

Nicki dropped her gaze from his, feeling and seeing her nakedness in front of him, somewhere deep in her mind as he would be seeing it. But when her eyes lifted once more to hold his, she knew it was time.

'Master, will you... will you suck my virgin pussy now?

Her pulse raced, her heart thumped, and her temples began to pound. She was a virgin. Another part of her kept reminding her of that fact – a virgin. She shouldn't be doing this. But she knew it was the wrong part of her mind that protested. It was the unhappy part, the thinking woman part.

I was beside myself with love and lust, deciding it was time for some cold steel between the third and fourth rib, time to really test her degree of willingness. 'Will you get undressed now, Master, and suck my Greek secrets?' I tasked her, thriving on the sensuality of the moment.

'Oh, Master,' Nicki breathed, feeling utterly hot and bothered. 'Master, will you take your clothes off now and, and suck my Greek secrets?'

I stared into her eyes, and then lightly slapped her dark patch of pubic hair.

'Oh!' Nicki gasped, her mind numb with a fusion of shock, raw sensuality and lust long dreamed about. Then he smacked her again, there, between the legs.

I watched her eyes close and her mouth peel open as I slapped her pretty muff. She inhaled deeply as I continued.

'You liked that, didn't you?' I tested.

'Yes,' Nicki answered immediately, knowing that what was going to happen was naughty, but necessary. The husband of her mother's friend? Sucking her? Smacking her? Taking her precious virginity? She felt herself moisten at the very thought of it all as she questioned herself. Then she simply didn't care.

I got undressed and smiled back at her. Her eyes never left my groin. 'Turn around now and bend over,' I ordered her, feeling my erection flex strongly.

'Try to touch your toes and spread your legs wide.'

At the sight of her following my instructions to the letter I suddenly became momentarily crazed with lust, as I stared at the incredibly sensual sight before my wide-eyed hungry male gaze. I drank in her utter Greek nakedness like a man who had just come out of a sensual desert and was dying of thirst. I just stood there with my mind struggling to retain some semblance of control over me, as well as the unbelievable situation I had created.

I settled onto my knees behind her, on the carpeted floor. Her complete and absolute mysterious nakedness lay trembling only inches from my face. I glanced down at my standing part. It was doing a fine job of doing just that, standing. I reached up with my hands and gripped her hips firmly.

'Oh…' I heard her gasp as I did so. Her bare flesh felt hot to my touch. My gaze centred on the lushness of black and curly pubic hair covering her junction, right before my eyes. I could easily see the ripe and full pink folds and secret places of her natural female.

My standing muscle flexed strongly, demanding it was time to begin, time to give her exactly what she had come for, exactly what she had been waiting for, exactly what I had waited for, the loss of her precious Greek virginity, one way or another.

Nicki could feel his closeness, the warm hush of his breath between her legs, on her buttocks and through the dark pubic hairs adorning her private loins. It thrilled her and excited her. It aroused her. The blood pounded in her temples as she gazed back at her master through her widely spaced legs.

'Oh, Master,' she gasped, as she saw the rigid muscle standing powerfully upright from between his thighs. It would soon be inside her. That would be deeply inside her. It seemed as if it were a long lance with a large smooth helmet. The sight of it captured her virginal gaze and attention entirely.

She felt her sex moisten even more, knowing full well that the husband of her mother's friend was about to do something that could never be undone, touch and take from her with his body, where no man had ever gone before. His hands felt powerful on her. She felt totally and completely controlled and submissive for the first time in her life, knowing what he was about to do to her.

With trembling hands and fingers I tightened my grip

on her naked hips, my fingers showing no consideration as they dug deeply into her soft flesh, drawing her mysterious Greek centre back slightly. My heart pounded as my mouth opened, and my eyes slowly closed.

As my face moved towards the heat of her virgin mouth I inhaled the fragrance of her heady sensual musk. My tongue coiled and readied to plunge and strike, like a snake in waiting. The last incredibly sensual and stirring sight my vision gave back to me was that of her curly black hair, and shiny glistening beads of sexual female fragrance.

The deep cleft of her sweet bottom lay decorated and centred with the darker-skinned, tiny necklace. It beckoned me strongly, so I licked the entire valley between her buttocks.

'Ohhh, *Master*…' she gasped, and then with a guttural groan myself, my open mouth forcefully attached and glued itself to her glistening, trembling centre. My invading tongue unleashed its thrusting ferocity immediately, spearing deeply and in rapid succession to relentlessly announce its firm and lengthy arrival inside the waves of her sweet-tasting molten lava.

'Oh, *Master*,' Nicki gasped again, exhaling deeply. Coloured stars swam before her eyes as the blood doubled its rush to her fevered brain and spinning senses. At the first touch of his mouth on her heated sex she buckled at the knees with the incredibly forceful and sexual onslaught on such an intimate scale. Falling forward she sank to the carpet on her hands and knees. But she felt him fall with her, sucking and tonguing more strongly as he followed her body down in its sudden plunge.

I kept her hips and buttocks held high and reached between her shoulder blades with one hand, pushing her upper torso flat and deep into the carpet. Then I forced my face and mouth even more invasively into her quivering Mediterranean apex, my tongue not once relenting in its savage invasion of her hot virgin channel.

'Oh, God!' Nicki gasped, laying her forehead upon her forearms and groaning at each rapid penetration of his living tongue. Her mind swooned and swam; drowning in a sea of never before experienced or even imagined sensuality. She felt powerfully free as a real woman, a female, for the first time in her life, and groaned deeply from the lowest pit of her loins.

The sound of her moaning found its way to my ears, causing me to instinctively plunge my tongue even more rapidly and deeply inside her clenching burrow of tortured femaleness. I buried my nose deep in the warm valley between her buttocks, feeling the tightness there. Doubling my efforts with my tongue's attack, my fingers clamped into the firm flesh of her thighs, holding me fast against her, her juicy centre impaled securely around the piston reach of my tongue.

My jaw began to ache from my tongue's forced extension each time I strove to stroke her even more deeply, straining to pierce through her hymen. I wanted to reach in earnest for her cervix, to touch it, to lick it, to announce my expected and timely arrival at such an intimate and private depth inside her female's virgin body.

Nicki felt her hips and buttocks suddenly jerk uncontrollably. They twisted and trembled, bucking from side to side with each brutal onslaught, until finally her tortured mind and physical senses could take no more. She climaxed violently in a blinding fury of unleashed passion and raw lust. Sensing it before she felt it, her orgasm rushed headlong to meet her. It came at her mind, her body and her senses at breakneck speed, and with a vengeance. She had no idea of how powerful the orgasmic tsunami of a virgin's sensuality would be. Then suddenly she lost it completely. At her mind and body's peak, her unconscious feeling mind took over her thinking mind for just a little while as she took time out.

Her body was wracked with the most incredibly intensive physical pleasure she had ever known. She felt herself rising from the floor, yet she knew her body remained exactly where it had been, climaxing over and over, until finally she shuddered and then collapsed sideways, falling heavily into the soft carpeted floor like a child's broken rag doll. Then slowly, gradually, she knew no more.

I slumped sideways with her, and then lay beside her buttocks, biting and gently raking with my teeth the trembling flesh. Suckling her I swallowed her virginal sap and felt her aftershocks, the physical reverberations of such violent orgasms to my very physical assault and invasion of her private female anatomy. I swallowed her body's warm outpourings, my mind and senses long affected and spinning crazily from the ingested intoxicating effects of her heady blend of liquid Mediterranean elixir.

Eventually she lay still in my oral grip, as lifeless as a limp doll. Only then did I release the contact of my mouth on her living Grecian centre. Then, retracting my tongue to the confines of its own lair, I sat slowly up and looked down at her seemingly lifeless form.

Then I smiled, knowing I had succeeded in draining her sensual and sexual life essence from both her mind and body, but only for the moment. And I had drained it right down and outward through her very sensual virgin core.

Leaning over her naked form I saw instantly that she'd fainted, and was now sleeping restfully in her present state of mental and physical exhaustion. I slowly stood and sat back down in my chair, my eyes never leaving her beautiful shape for a single second.

I smiled again, happy that things had gone the way they had. I decided to let her sleep a little while. Then I would wake her and take her. Glancing down at my groin, I knew I hadn't yet satisfied us both of our needs of the moment. Then I smiled again, but only for the moment.

After about fifteen minutes I quietly but firmly roused her, but before she could collect her waking thoughts I rolled her over onto her front and lifted her up to her knees.

Nicki moaned, uncertain and alarmed and not really sure where she was.

Wasting no time I took her fiercely and suddenly between the buttocks, deciding to leave her precious Greek virginity as the last treat for us both. I slid in easily on a coating of her own virgin oil, sensualising and sexualising her beautiful young bottom far beyond its natural endurance once again, until my beautiful Greek virgin slave blazed and fused with the second arrival of a series of fiery and violent multiple orgasms.

Nicki was in a world of raw lust, discomfort, and a haze of feral passion. She bucked and twisted on her hands and knees. When they arrived, her intense and seemingly endless orgasms raged and flamed throughout her mind and tortured body. The discomfort between her buttocks was intense, but the pleasure was even more so.

Then, once again, she collapsed and fainted, not knowing in real terms that she had taken him fully and willingly through the tight starfish of her bottom. She had begged for more in her native Greek tongue, for him to thrust even deeper, even harder and even faster. As the conscious awareness of her pleasure and pain faded from her present surroundings to a grey mist, she knew she was happier than she had ever been before in her entire life.

Again I let her drift where she had fallen, and again I had withdrawn from her. I showered, and then returned to sit and gaze down upon her naked sleeping form. She looked so peaceful, but then I figured that females always did when they allowed themselves to be just who they really were – females, and not women. I felt stirred beyond belief as I sat drinking in her Grecian beauty.

Nicki felt him roll her over onto her back. Then, like a wild animal falling upon its prey, he fell upon her liquid virgin warmth and openness in a rage of blinding passion, penetrating her wet, hot and slick centre with a fervour she had never imagined possible. He seemed like a wild animal in the way he was handling her, while she just lay beneath his intensity and welcomed his hard and lengthy arrival within her central core, after spreading her thighs wide.

Lifting her legs she locked them around the small of his back, trapping him there, as if to never release him from the heated and slippery confines of her clenching virgin channel, while he poised ready at her tight entrance. The pain of her seal being broken, her virgin woman dying to give birth truly to her natural female was a momentary flash in the sexual and sensual supernova of her rapture and sexual pleasure.

He speared her, arrowed and lanced her good. She knew her precious Greek hymen had been split beyond repair and redemption beneath the relentless onslaught of his cock. Her buttocks slapped the carpeted floor repeatedly, her ankles riding his lower back, offering her virginity to his rapid advances and retreats. Strongly, powerfully he rode her soft Greek saddle, spurring her mind and senses to greater and greater sensual and sexual heights, until she again exploded in blinding multiple orgasms of fire and brimstone.

'Oohhhnnnnnnnn!' she wailed, as it left her breathless and drained in its violent and intense aftershocks. Clinging tightly with her arms and legs she wrapped around him, before once again sensing her limbs and body collapse limp and lifeless onto the carpet. Physically and mentally shattered, she then fainted into a deep and exhausted sleep, her long and closely guarded virginity no longer a fact, but the living fiction of her female's permanent memory and wildest sexual fantasy.

When I roused her again I had her shower and dress. Then I bade her a warm and affectionate goodbye, knowing she loved me dearly, and that she knew I loved her just as fiercely. Feeling like a teenager, I then again went to the shower, turned it on full force and very hot, and showered again.

I remained under the steaming jets for over thirty minutes and emerged feeling like a new man, a new male. I dressed simply, made myself a strong coffee and downed a dozen cold oysters before settling down to work at my typewriter. Looking ahead, I knew who the next Greek virgin would be… one of her sisters. And when the time came, I knew the situation would take care of itself. Nature needed no planning or organising for it to happen.

I smiled. Nature already had her plan ready somewhere for their natural domination and submission – two more Greek virgins. I didn't know that plan yet, but I would, I was sure. Lifting my coffee cup, I smiled broadly. Then I drank slowly and very, very appreciatively. My beautiful Greek virgin was no more, but she was mine, forever. And so, too, would be her sisters. I had a mission now, for happiness in abundance for the rest of my natural male life.

Chapter Eleven

'Athena just has no confidence in herself whatsoever lately, Master,' Nicki said, over dinner on the following Friday, when the subject of the individual observed personalities of her sisters came up as a topic of conversation. 'Appolonia isn't much better, but mum encourages them wherever she can.'

I smiled. Another long week had gone by. Lauren had gone to stay over at Marcena's house. They were going out for the evening for a few drinks, and she'd not wanted to drive home with alcohol in her blood. I had taken advantage of the opportunity to spend time with my beautiful slave, and invited her over for the night. Her sisters had stayed home.

Nicki looked beautiful in a white dress. We had finished eating and were sitting comfortably beside one another in the lounge, talking, or rather, she was. We were both relaxed. It was great to be with her again. It had been such a boring week. Ignoring Lauren had become more difficult without it ending up in an argument. My time remaining with her was limited. I was becoming more certain of it with each passing day. I nodded.

'I just figured they were both quiet girls,' I replied, finishing the last of my wine. 'They are twins, after all. If one were quiet you would expect the other to be.'

'Yes, I know, Master,' Nicki agreed, knowing he was right. 'I was just giving you what I know about them.' She smiled, sipping her wine. After dinner and the clearing of the table they had settled into the lounge with fresh glasses of wine. She felt wonderful and was glad he had invited her over, but she was scared to death of being caught. She was sitting in her favourite chair. Her legs were curled up beside her.

'They'll come out of their shell,' I said. 'Just like you did. They just have to meet the right male, that's all.'

'Yes, Master,' Nicki said, knowing he was probably right. If her sisters were lucky they would meet someone like her master. She looked intently at him. For a few moments she wished she could show him just how much she cared for him, but was afraid of scaring him off. Then she puzzled about that thought. It wasn't like her to seek attention obviously, but since losing her virginity she had noticed she had been feeling very feminine, a lot more than she usually did. She was changing and she knew it.

I looked up and smiled, then leaned over to kiss her lips. The kiss lasted several seconds, wherein her tongue had strangely given the not so subtle invitation, not often received in that manner, that I should heed the call of the wild and follow her up on that invitation. It was working, I concluded. Her female was merging with her woman. She had an itch that needed scratching. Then I ended the kiss and relaxed back into my chair with a sigh, watching her do the same. Then she gracefully got up. I remained quiet, wondering where she was going.

Nicki smiled sweetly, and then slowly sank to her knees before his chair. She rested her hand deliberately on his groin, and squeezed him softly. What was being squeezed was immediately not soft. His strong male eyes began to dance. She loved the sensual feeling of her master's body rising under her control, especially when it had her hand wrapped around it.

'Do you mind, Master?' she asked, smiling up at him, and squeezing more firmly.

'Maybe,' I replied.

'Maybe?' Nicki echoed, not unaware of the dancing glint in his eyes or the warmth between her thighs. She had never seen that look before. It was almost telling her that she had no choice but to continue what she was doing, and submit to his demand if he made one, whatever that might be. For a brief moment she wondered why she had never seen that look in his eyes before.

Our eyes locked and loaded. It was male dominance, pure and simple – and female submission too. I knew it, knowing I'd won. Her hands left me and slowly undid and pulled down my trousers. Her eyes riveted instantly on my erection as my underwear came away. Then her misty gaze swept slowly back to my face. I pushed the recliner fully back and closed my eyes, clasping my hands behind my head to wait… and I was not kept waiting long.

'Good *girl*,' I groaned. 'In fully, please.'

'Mmmmm,' was the only reply I heard from my beautiful Greek slave, who now had my missile stuffed into her warm, wet mouth. My eyes pinched shut tightly when I felt her lips compress. Her other hand cupped my balls and gently began to twist and tug in time with her mouthing ministrations of my standing length.

'That's *very* good…' I sighed, knowing I was once again in good hands.

'Mum can't even get them to be really confident,' Nicki told him later. She was making them both a cup of coffee now that she'd finished pleasing her master in the way she knew he absolutely loved. 'I have more confidence than the two of them put together. Well, now I do, anyway. I get so worried about them sometimes. And lately their college grades have begun to slip, as well.'

I let out my breath slowly. She brought the coffee and joined me at the kitchen table. The smile came easily to my voice with my genuine response. 'I'll have a chat with them, if you like,' I told her. 'Probably won't help much, but you never know.'

Nicki settled onto her chair and rested on her elbows.

'Really?' she asked. 'You would do that?'

'Maybe they just need a different point of reference,' I said. 'Who knows? A male's point of view on things, maybe?'

'Probably won't help them much, even if you did,' Nicki said, and then sipped her coffee. 'They can be a bit obstinate at times, especially Appolonia. You should see her with mum when she gets her mind set on something.'

I smiled. 'Well, I could have a general chat first, sort of get an unobtrusive overview, if you really want me to.'

'That would be wonderful, Master,' Nicki replied gratefully. She felt with the way they just lounged around lately, staying in their rooms all weekend or moping about the house, that her sisters would turn into wallflowers. It puzzled her that they had actually gone to the dance. Then she wondered why she felt as if she couldn't stop looking at him as he drank his coffee. She also wondered why she was getting wet, and she knew she was. Then she smiled; it was just being with him.

I smiled, grateful for a window of opportunity, no matter how small. 'Don't worry, we'll get to know each other, somehow.'

I finished my coffee and placed the cup on the table. It seemed that most mothers were their own daughter's problems, I had read somewhere. I watched her finish her coffee, my mind returning to the feeling of those innocently skilful lips around my penis, and I stirred.

Then my thoughts shifted their point of focus. Not

knowing how much Nicki had told the twins about me, I was sure it was something, no matter how small or insignificant. I hoped that whatever it had been was enough to arouse their natural curiosity about me.

Then I stirred again beneath the table, thinking about her discipline training to come, as well as the last two remaining twin Greek virgins, that were yet to feel my dominant presence. I decided then without a doubt; I deserved all three Greek virgins.

Chapter Twelve

'And that's the whole story, Mr Davis,' said Athena, feeling that she had no self-confidence whatsoever. She had even gone to the extent of training for and achieving a first-degree black belt, but even that had not helped. She dabbed at her eyes with a tissue and sniffed a couple of times.

Her chin hung low to her chest as she sat, ashamed and depressed in the big chair in his lounge. She couldn't seem to sort out her problems, with her sisters or with people at school, as well as the teachers. Her grades had been slipping lately. Now it seemed to her that all was lost unless she could somehow get a handle on her confidence problem. Then she again burst into silent tears of personal frustration and shame, dabbing her eyes with several already wet tissues.

I gazed sympathetically at the doleful sight of the attractive Greek girl sitting opposite me in the big lounge chair. I was well aware how cold and cruel college and teachers could be, and in Athena's case it seemed they had been.

I sighed and recalled my last time with Nicki on Saturday, before she left. Nicki had never suspected a thing until I was deep inside her, and then it was too late. She had been doing the dishes at the sink after we'd finished breakfast, and once penetrated from behind had willingly gone along for the ride, although her ears had been straining for the sound of Lauren's car in the driveway.

I smiled softly for Athena and her problems, having allowed her the time to tell her story and get it all off her chest for the first time in who knows when.

Athena sniffed a few more times and nodded, hating the idea that she needed someone else to help solve her problems. She had never needed anyone before. It went totally against her beliefs and martial arts training to have to need someone now – and the husband of her mother's friend, at that.

'Thank you very much, Mr Davis,' Athena offered, grateful at least for someone to finally talk to about it all.

I nodded in silent acceptance, compassionately appreciating the young woman's situation. I liked her already and knew that the attractive Greek virgin who sat sniffing across from me just might be ready to lose it. At least, I hoped so. I decided then to use her own natural Greek pride and her training in the martial arts to help her as well as to help myself, to her, for as long as I wanted to in the future.

'It's okay,' I said with a warm smile in my voice, seeing her look up at me with teary eyes the instant I did. 'But you must be prepared to help me help you in whatever way I think is best for you. I've managed to help Nicki, as you know, and you've tried to fix your problem consciously, but you've failed. Sorry to put it as blunt as that, but you wish me to fix your problem in order that you can retain your college grades and increase your natural level of self-confidence all round, so I have to look at it clinically. Do you see that?'

Athena burst into frustrated tears once more, taking several minutes before calming down again. She knew she had failed. She did not need the husband of her mother's best friend to tell her that. After trying so hard to come to grips with her seemingly complete loss of confidence, nothing seemed to be working, in spite of her martial arts self-discipline training. It just hadn't worked.

Even though she had not made her mind up about Mr Davis yet, she accepted that someone like him might be able to help save her grades and her personal dignity. He had helped Nicki so there was at least a chance he could help her. She had nothing to lose, and everything to gain.

She also realised that with his help she might just be able to get everything in her life back together again. Not that she had anything else in her life besides her college. She just didn't have the time to mix with friends, aside from Appolonia and Nicki. She was either studying or training, or she was sleeping, and that was her life, such as it was. Yes, she decided, she would do whatever Mr Davis asked her to do in order to help save her college grades and her self-respect.

'Yes,' Athena answered. She felt very humbled by her problem. She had failed to be able to successfully fix it. 'What you say is true, Mr Davis.'

I decided not to offer her my first name to address me with. That would keep the authority in one corner... mine. I watched her burst into fresh tears once more, and felt sorry for her even more so. I allowed her another few minutes before deciding to end her wallowing in self-pity. Then I spoke, my voice containing a little more firmness about it, in tone and in volume.

'Athena, be quiet,' I said quietly but firmly. 'Please, listen now.'

Athena felt the change in tone rather than the meaning of the words he said. She sat bolt upright, holding back a sniff. She was surprised by the inflection of his tone. He sounded like her favourite martial arts instructor. Mr Davis had sounded just like him in authority with the words he had just spoken to her.

She looked at me with different eyes than she had when

she first arrived. Nicki had called and told me that Athena had come home from college in tears, and then thrown a temper tantrum, saying she was never returning. Nicki suggested to Athena that she come. I'd been lucky; it was one of the nights that Lauren attended a charity meeting. Athena had told her mother she was having a study night with a friend, to help her with some maths problems.

Athena had almost not knocked on the front door at first, but finally she did, losing her thoughts altogether when he opened the door and she'd seen his face, even though he was the husband of her mother's friend.

Something was going on in her lower belly because she felt warm in a not unpleasant sort of way. In fact, she felt warm in a very strange way. Not that his gaze suggested anything other than polite good manners. He had always treated her sister with respect, Nicki told her. Yet, she puzzled. There was just something about his eyes that made her feel, well, sort of intimidated, yet warm in places she knew she should not be feeling warm in.

As I sat silently gazing at another lovely Greek virgin I felt myself stir as I always did when I planned to dominate Nicki for my own agenda. Athena was a beauty by any culture's standards, but by my own standards she was a real sensual vixen, a winner, solid of frame, with no shortage of flesh in all the right places and with all the right shapes to go with it.

Her long black hair, like Nicki's, would cascaded down her back when allowed to hang free from being tied up in a bun, as it was right then. I imaged briefly how she would look with a collar around her neck and handcuffs on her wrists, and I stirred again, wondering what her neat Greek ass would look like with my red handprints adorning it.

I just sat there, saying nothing, and gazing at her politely with a hint of a smile on my face. The controlling aspect of it all had me as hard as a rock while I waited for the right moment.

Athena could feel herself becoming warmer between the thighs with every passing moment he continued to gaze into her eyes, but strangely, she did not feel uncomfortable with his silence or his staring politely at her. Nicki had told her he was comfortable to be with, although she added that she didn't know why, only that he was. She began to feel relaxed in the deep chair. Each breath seemed to become a little longer in exhaling before inhaling again. It was a very strange but not uncomfortable experience indeed, she concluded.

'Now, Athena,' I said, 'Nicki had a confidence problem that she told me about when cleaning the house one day. Did she tell you about that?'

'Yes, Mr Davis,' Athena said quietly, her emotions under control again.

'Good,' I said. 'Her problem really based itself on her assertiveness, or rather the lack of it. And she didn't understand the differences in her day to day personality.'

'Oh,' Athena said, interested. Nicki didn't tell her that.

'Yes. There are certain differences in a young woman's make-up that unfortunately they don't teach you at college. It's a pity, too. If they did you wouldn't be sitting here now, feeling miserable.

'I wish they had,' Athena agreed, wondering what the differences were.

'They teach you many important things at college,' I told her, gazing into her deep Greek eyes. 'Including how a woman should act, how a woman should talk and think and dress and behave around boys and all people. But they don't teach you about the other important side of your personality, that deals with your moment by moment feelings.'

Athena sat curious and interested. He was right, she agreed. They didn't teach her anything about her feelings, nothing at all.

'Everything you think and learn they can teach you,' I continued. 'But all those natural feelings you feel, those that are unique especially to you, they don't teach because they can't. They could advise you about them, but they don't because they can't teach them.

'Only you know your own feelings, and only you can teach yourself how to manage and satisfy them in the natural way that nature intended, because you were born first with your feelings as a complete female, before you learned how to think or were taught anything at college. Don't you agree?'

Athena sat spellbound. Everything he was saying made perfect sense. No wonder Nicki had been helped. Her personality was terrific these days. She felt her head nod.

'How I was able to help Nicki,' I said, 'was to explain the difference between the woman in her personality and the natural female she had been born. Once she got the basic understanding and had a little practice, it came quite naturally to her in only a couple of talks. But Nicki had promised me that she would do anything to fix her problem.'

I paused and took a few quiet breaths while I watched her. Then I continued.

'Some aspects, not all of them, but some, have to be learned the hard way simply because you've learned to think your way into the messes you get yourself into, instead of feeling your way around them or out of them as the case may be at the time. In other words, if you've learned anything that is not in your own best interests

139

you can *unlearn* them. Does that make sense?'

Athena nodded, totally agreeing with him. She'd never thought of things that way before.

'With Nicki, she was able to unlearn all of the things that were not in her own best interests that did not make her feel happy, and that had always made her feel guilty about herself.'

Athena nodded, knowing exactly what he meant. She was amazed he knew so much about women.

'Unfortunately,' I said. 'You have learned as a thinking woman to override your natural feelings. It should be the other way round. You should act on your natural feelings for your own personal happiness whenever and wherever they arise, then support them with your creative thinking to enjoy them even more so. Does that make sense, too?'

'Yes,' Athena answered quietly. Everything he was saying made sense, she concluded, believing already that he would be able to help her.

'You can look at it this way,' I said to her, setting the trap for control. 'Your thinking learned woman does not like your natural feeling female to be in control of your personal happiness, because she's been taught or she's learned that that's the way it's supposed to be. Television, schools, parents; everyone tells you how to do, to be, to think, to act and to behave, irrespective of whether you feel it's right for you.

'Your poor female just doesn't get listened to when it comes to her own natural feelings, and special needs that nature provided you with to be happy upon this earth. Seems a bit unfair, don't you think?'

Athena felt herself nodding while he was speaking. She was enthralled with everything he was saying, simply because it made so much sense. No wonder he was able to help Nicki. He knew so much about women. She wished then that he had been one of her teachers. His wife must feel very lucky to have him.

'In a way,' I said, 'you could almost liken the learning thinking woman in you as a real bitch, never allowing you to act on your natural feelings about anything that feels right for you, always overriding your feelings with learned thoughts or behaviours.

'They think that because they work for someone else or other people they must work for you too, but they don't. That's the sad reality. Other people's thoughts and ideas will never work for you in real happiness terms, which is necessary for your moment-by-moment natural happiness.

'But they aren't your thoughts. They're someone else's. I think your personal happiness is so important. If that's okay, then everything else in your life will be okay, too. But if your personal happiness as a natural female is not okay then nothing will be okay for you, even when things appear to be going well. Does that make sense, too?'

Athena was still nodding. She was being blown away with how much he knew about her without actually knowing her.

'Of course it does,' I agreed with her. 'However, you have to be prepared to have the courage to accept whatever it takes to get the job done. That will put your natural feeling female back in charge of your personal life and happiness, and relegate your cold-hearted thinking woman to her rightful second place. If you're not prepared to do whatever it takes to get the job done, then you can look forward to being the way you are now for the rest of your life, if that's all the happiness you really want from it.'

Athena's eyes stung with the tears of her sadness. They trickled down her cheeks as she nodded in agreement with him.

'It all depends on what sort of happiness you want from and for your life, Athena,' I told her, settling back into my chair. 'The short-term lonely happiness of your learned thinking woman, or the long-term natural happiness of your natural feeling female.'

She was taking it all in. I could see that just from the look on her face.

'It's up to you, just as it was up to Nicki. She chose the long-term natural happiness of her feeling female and hasn't looked back, but you would know better than I would about that. You live with her, I don't. So in the end it's up to you, but if you want my help, as Nicki did, then I'm not interested in helping your learned thinking woman achieve short-term happiness at the expense of your natural feeling female. Do you understand that point of view?'

'Yes,' Athena heard herself say quickly. She knew what she wanted and it wasn't short-term happiness and the loneliness that went with it. She wanted long-term natural happiness. She wanted her feeling female to be in charge. Her learned thinking woman had only made a complete mess of her life's happiness to date, as well as her confidence.

'So,' I finished, hopeful and confident. 'You can think about it and let me know. Talk to Nicki some more about it, if you like. But if you decide to support the natural happiness of your feeling female and ask me to help you, I'll be very disappointed if you go back to supporting your cold-hearted woman at the first hurdle.'

She stared at me, wide-eyed, and I continued laying down the rules.

'You'll have to unlearn many unnatural aspects, and find the courage to act on many natural feelings of personal happiness that your thinking woman has denied you in

142

the past. Does that sound fair to you?'

Athena nodded, her tears gone, her determination replacing them as he spoke. She didn't need to talk any more with Nicki. Everything she'd told her about him had been true. If anyone could help her, he could, if she had the courage to unlearn things that did not make her happy and learn new things that allowed her to act on her natural feelings. No, she did not need to talk to Nicki any further. She'd made up her mind already.

'I don't have to speak with Nicki,' Athena said confidently. 'I deserve to be happy and I'm not. I haven't done anything wrong to anyone or anything. But I'm never happy, no matter how hard I try.' Tears were welling again in her eyes, but she was not stopping now. 'Whatever I have to do, I'll do. I won't go back. There's nothing to go back to. Please help me like you helped my sister.'

My heart went out to her in her anguish. I reached over and grasped her hand lightly, then squeezed it comfortingly.

'Of course I will,' I told her. 'But no going back, okay? It would be very embarrassing to you, if you had to admit to your sister that you didn't think your personal happiness was worth a little pain of learning along the way, and I know that won't be the case, will it?'

Athena couldn't answer him, but she slowly shook her head in agreement while the tears flowed freely into her hands, that she brought up to cover her face.

The natural male in me rose from my chair and stepped to hers, holding down my hand for her to take when she opened her eyes.

'Come here, you special little female,' I said warmly. 'I think you deserve a hug of support for your courage from another human being, don't you?'

Athena blinked through tear-filled eyes and saw his hand outstretched. She took it, allowing him to help her stand.

She felt emotionally beaten and drained, and when he encircled her with his arms she melted into his chest, feeling safe and secure and cared about as a human being for the first time in her life. Her anguished sobs disappeared into his chest with her tears, while he held her close for several minutes. Then he held her at arm's length and smiled tenderly.

'Everything is going to be fine, Athena,' I said to her tear-streaked face and puffy but pretty eyes. 'Everything is going to be just fine.'

The feeling of genuine sympathy and concern in his eyes and on his face was too much. Athena hung her head and began to sob pitifully again, and did not resist when she felt his hands on her shoulders gently pulling her back to his safe, caring embrace.

This time, without choosing to, her arms went around his waist. He tightened his grasp around her shoulders and back and she sighed, feeling genuinely cared for. She also noticed another feeling, one that originated deep between her thighs and in her lower tummy, and instantly felt ashamed.

She felt herself blushing. Then she noticed his smell. It was a strong smell. It was a man's smell. She wondered, too, if he'd held Nicki like that, and then decided he must have if he'd been able to help her. Then she wondered if Nicki had felt as she was feeling now, like she did at night in her bed sometimes, when her fingers feathered her own virgin nest.

Deliberately I kept my hips away from hers, lest she feel the hardness and rampant strength of that which had rapidly grown between my legs since taking her into my arms for comfort.

After several more minutes of holding her gently, but firmly, I once again held her at arm's length and smiled into her tear-stained face and watery eyes. On Friday evening Lauren and Marcena were going for drinks again, and again Lauren had told me she would be staying over at Marcena's house. Nicki had also told me she had college assignments to do. That left me free with the house all to myself.

'No more tears,' I said warmly. 'If you can make it Friday at six-thirty we can begin. If you change your mind just ring me or tell Nicki to tell me, so I don't expect you. There'll be no hard feelings and I'll only wish you well. Okay?'

Athena's mind had already been made. She nodded, but there would be no going back to the miserable unhappiness of her past if she had anything to do with it. 'I'll be here,' she heard herself say, then felt better already.

I smiled, and then led her to the door.

'Our little secret,' I said, opening the door. 'I think your problem is your thinking woman. And Nicki is Nicki and you are you. What works for Nicki may not work for you, and vice versa. Our little secret.'

Athena smiled and nodded, knowing exactly what he meant. A secret it would be, just between the two of them, and Nicki. But even with Nicki, as he'd said, Nicki was Nicki and she was different. She was her own person.

'See you Friday, happy girl,' I said.

'Absolutely,' Athena emphasised. Then she spun on her heels and walked away, feeling a confident spring in her step that hadn't been there for a long while, if it ever had.

I closed the door, grinning. Winners are grinners, I concluded. There's no challenge like no challenge, and this time I wouldn't need any hypnosis. I had my own natural male confidence, and if necessary, I had Nicki.

Chapter Thirteen

'Any second thoughts?' I asked Athena, once she had settled into the lounge chair opposite me, on Friday night at six forty-five. I'd had two days to prepare my thoughts and strategies. During that time I had come across the stories of Gor, the mythical sister planet of Earth where all the women were made slaves by males and by nature. The dominant theme of the Gor stories flew straight home to my heart and mind. The concept suited me perfectly. I wasn't sure just how I would go about using that concept, but I knew I thought along those lines already.

'Not really,' Athena said. She was nervous, but determined not to let it show. Her mind had been on nothing else since she'd seen him last.

'Not one question?' I asked. Her face was serious, as if she were going for a job interview.

'Curious would be a better word, I guess,' Athena answered, with a nervous flicker of a smile. She had taken notice of Nicki's moods over the past two days, and reassured herself that her sister's personality had definitely changed for the better.

'Curiosity is good,' I smiled. 'As long as it's tempered with the correct amount of natural discipline for doing whatever it takes to get the job done, when it comes to your personal happiness.'

Athena nodded, but said nothing. She had already decided how important her personal happiness was going to be to her from then on. She didn't want to go back to the way she was if there was a chance she could change. There was nothing worth going back for. She was always miserable.

'Athena,' I said.

'I'm sure,' she said immediately, politely cutting him off. She had wasted enough time in her life already and wanted to get on with whatever help he could give her.

'Speaking of Nicki,' I added, 'did you get a chance to speak further with her for advice of any kind?'

'Yes,' Athena nodded. 'I didn't tell her about anything we spoke about,' she told him. 'You said to keep it a secret, but she did ask me if it all went okay. And she was happy that I had decided to ask you for help and that you said you would. I don't think she'll pry, though. It's not her style. Besides, she's changed, I think. Keeps to herself a bit, but she's better than she used to be.'

'Once you know something, Athena,' I said, 'you can't un-know it. Nicki knows now who she really is, and she couldn't un-know that fact even if she wanted to. There's too much personal happiness at stake… hers.'

Athena nodded, agreeing with him. She knew that Nicki always seemed happy these days, quiet and a little withdrawn, but always happy and always with a little smile on her face as if she knew a secret that nobody else did.

'No going back, then?' I pressed, happy with her responses so far.

'No,' Athena said, shaking her head. 'Nothing to go back to.'

I chuckled to relieve a little of her tension. She laughed nervously with me, but only for a few seconds. Then her face became serious again.

'Athena, the best place to begin is at the beginning. I'll take it now that we have begun and will proceed accordingly. Okay? And expect you to honour the commitment you said you had towards your own happiness in the future, about doing whatever it takes to get the job done.'

Athena nodded, but said nothing. She did notice, however, that her heart rate had picked up a bit. She felt like she was at the beginning of something really important.

'Good,' I said, feeling a surge between my legs. It wasn't sensuality. It was the feeling of dominance, of control, of a natural power bestowed upon me by Mother Nature. 'Then let's begin with teaching you what you are right now, a learned thinking woman, and introducing you to who you are, a natural feeling female. I'll never say or do anything without a reason. I'll also never say or do anything without there being a lesson in it for you and your happiness, which you will always see ultimately if you're willing to keep in mind the bigger picture of your personal life and long-term happiness.'

Athena nodded, feeling her inner tension begin to mount. She was excited and nervous both. She swallowed; her mouth was dry.

'Who are you?' I asked.

Athena felt instantly dumb. Her thoughts ran chaotic around her mind for several seconds, but she couldn't string two of them together to make a sentence. Then she did.

'Athena?' She answered nervously. She mouth was so dry. She tried swallowing again, but could hardly find any moisture.

I enjoyed the tempering of her female's spirit already, before plunging it into the furnace like a Japanese Samurai sword. 'No, that's your name,' I told her. 'Who are you?'

Athena felt as if she were in front of her college principal being asked sticky questions to which she had no answer. 'I'm a… I'm a… woman,' she finally got out.

'No, that's *what* you are,' I told her patiently. 'Who are

you?'

Athena's gaze rapidly darted left and right, and then back at his face. Then she struggled with, 'I'm... I'm my mother's daughter.'

'No, that's your bloodline. Who are you?'

Athena began to blush from embarrassment. She felt really dumb and didn't like the feeling. Obviously he knew the answer he wanted her to say, but she couldn't for the life of her figure out what it was. She felt hot and nervous and just a little bit intimidated. His tone, although understanding, was beginning to sound a little firm as if she should know. She looked quickly left and right, then sighed, defeated, and shrugged her shoulders. She felt embarrassed to the extreme, knowing she was blushing from forehead to knees. She was also becoming just a little angry and wondered if humiliation was a part of the deal.

'Do you think the patch of dark hair between your legs was given to you by nature just to keep you warm in winter?' I said seriously.

'What?' Athena's mouth dropped open. She was stunned. Her mind questioned her indignantly. How dare he talk to her like that? Did he talk to Nicki like that? Did Nicki like being talked to like that? How was talking indecently going to help her overcome her lack of confidence?

'Well?' I pressed, plunging her into the fiery forge for some tempering. The pain of her embarrassment and growing anger would toughen her female's spirit to break out of her woman's shell, and would be worth the sacrifice in the long run.

Athena finally managed to get her mouth to close. She glared at him. 'Why did you speak like that?' she snapped angrily.

149

'You know where it is,' I said coolly, feigning sudden indifference. 'Close the door on the way out, and good luck.' Then I looked away and picked up a book that lay beside my chair on the small table. I opened it and pretended to begin to read, ignoring her completely.

Athena's mouth had once more dropped open without her knowing it, and without her seemingly being able to close it. She just sat and stared at him, and again her mind barraged her with questions. Did he just dismiss her? He'd told her to leave and close the door on her way out? What was the matter with him? How was all this helping her? Then she managed to close her mouth again and swallow. Her mouth was dry. She felt hot and embarrassed and intimidated.

'Go?' she croaked.

I glanced casually at her. She looked fit to burst. Her face was a bright crimson. I figured her breasts would be, too. Her eyes were two glaring orbs of anger, humiliation and embarrassment that stared at me without blinking. I smiled politely.

'Look, Athena,' I said patiently, 'it would seem that we both have better things we could be doing with our evening. Obviously your definition and my definition of whatever it takes to get the job done must come from different dictionaries. You didn't ask for my help to teach you the English language, so no hard feelings. You can leave now.' I gazed back down to my book and once again pretended to indifference as to whether she stayed or went.

'I...' Athena began, and then stopped. Her pulse pounded in her ears. She could feel her heart racing, knowing she had been right. He was dismissing her like a schoolgirl. Embarrassed and humiliated in the extreme, her temper was rising because of it. She could feel it, and again her thoughts assaulted her thinking mind with questions for which she could find no answers. Definitions and English language, what was he talking about? And why was he being so rude to her? Nicki didn't tell her about that side of him. Wait until she got home.

'I—' she tried again to speak and suddenly found she could, but stopped, simply because she couldn't think of anything to say.

I looked back at her in her confusion and anger, and then decided she'd suffered enough and hoped I hadn't gone too far. I put the book back down on the table, still open as if I intended to go back to it at any moment.

'Listen, Athena,' I said bluntly, 'I told you I never say or do anything without a good reason. And I also told you that such reasons would always involve a lesson, in some way that would help towards overcoming your problem. I didn't ask you to come, remember?'

'I—'

'It's obvious to both of us that you're not ready to learn who you really are for your long-term happiness, so you can stay as what you are and sort out your problems on your own. Now, be a good girl and do that. Sort them out on your own, and close the door on your way out. Okay?'

For the third time Athena knew her mouth was open, and she couldn't remember the last time she'd blinked. Her eyes were tearful in her anger and embarrassment, but she wasn't crying. She wouldn't cry in front of him, no matter what.

Once again she tried to speak, but nothing came out. Her mouth was dry. He just sat there, staring at her, waiting for her to get up out of the chair and leave, just because she didn't understand he had only been trying to help her. Her anger and embarrassment grew. She felt hot all over.

He was dismissing her like a schoolgirl who had done something wrong just because she wouldn't do whatever it took to get the job done; the job of her personal long-term happiness.

I sat and held her gaze, wondering whether she'd get up and go, or remain sitting and stay. One of us would have to change their attitude, I mused, and it wouldn't be me. Of that there was no doubt whatsoever. Then suddenly I thought I noticed a slight softening of her look – a little less anger.

Whatever it took to get the job done, the thought ran through Athena's mind. Reasons for everything he said and did that all had to do with her long-term happiness. Stay as she was and sort out her own problems, because she wouldn't do whatever it took to get the job done.

And then another thought occurred; a different thought entered the foray of her chaotic and confused mind. Her woman wouldn't let her do whatever it took to get the job done, her thinking woman, the one that had caused her so much unhappiness already.

Then it suddenly seemed to her that someone had turned on a light inside her mind. She had agreed to do whatever it took and now she wasn't, but she had meant it, was determined to. Now she wasn't, but it wasn't her. It was her woman, her thinking woman. Then everything became clear. She knew what he was talking about.

'Mr Davis—' she began excitedly, but he cut her off with a raised hand. He looked back down to the table and picked up the book. She knew what he'd been talking about. She knew now. She understood.

'Mr Davis—' she began again, but he pushed his hand towards her, palm open, again indicating that she should be quiet. Then he pointed to the door and flicked his fingers abruptly. It was another dismissal.

She burned with embarrassment and shame. He wouldn't even look at her. Tears welled in her eyes and overflowed down her cheeks, but she was not crying. That was just what her tears were doing. Frustration raged inside her mind and body. Her fists clenched tightly in her lap.

He glanced at her. Quickly she drew breath to speak, but again he beat her to the punch with a flick of his fingers. She hated that. She was losing her temper. She could feel it. He wouldn't let her speak, just wanted her gone. She understood now, but he wouldn't let her speak and wouldn't let her stay.

'Out,' I said menacingly, intending to unsettle her a little more. I sensed her breaking point was near.

'No,' Athena said stubbornly. 'No, no, no.'

'I beg your pardon?' I said angrily, feeling myself being drawn into my own created scenario.

'I know now,' she blurted. 'I know. I understand. I do. It was my fault – no, not mine, my woman's fault. It was her fault. Don't make me go. Please, don't make me go.'

It had been a close one. I thought I'd lost her for a moment.

'Then who owns the patch of Greek hair between your thighs?' I asked, matching her tension level to keep her up there and out of control.

Athena was stunned again, but only momentarily. 'I do,' she answered. 'I do.'

'You do, or your thinking woman does?'

'I do,' Athena insisted. 'I do.'

'Why doesn't *she* own it?' I questioned.

'Because it's mine,' she said quietly. 'It's mine… not hers.'

'She thinks it's hers,' I stated. 'She's always thought that. She thinks everything you've ever felt has been hers, because you've let her. Your weak female has let her.'

153

The tears of Athena's state of mind overflowed her body once more as she answered. They streamed down her face, but she wasn't crying. In her mind she wasn't crying. 'I haven't,' she denied. 'I didn't know about her. I do now. I'm not weak, I'm strong. I just didn't know. Please, I didn't know she did all those things.'

I sat there and said nothing. My male heart reached out to her female in her anguish and distress. The pain of rebirth can be painful, I thought, at any age. The tears meandered down her cheeks, but she wasn't sobbing. I wondered then if she even knew she was crying. For the first time then I felt her strength, the natural strength of her female.

'Then show her,' I coaxed, and she flinched at the words. 'Show her who is the stronger.'

Athena felt as if her blood boiled in her veins. She felt angry, but strangely, not angry with him now. 'I'm stronger than she is,' she said. 'I am. I am.'

'Then show her how strong you are,' I encouraged, getting into the sincerity of everything I was saying. 'Show her you're not ashamed of what's between your thighs. Show her that.'

Athena's tears rolled down her flushed cheeks. 'I will,' she breathed, losing control and knowing it, but not caring. 'I will. I can.' Her fists balled and clenched tightly.

'Then show it. Undo your jeans. Be strong and have the courage to take down your jeans, right now, and show her that you know why it's there, between your thighs; that you know it's there to allow you to feel good as a natural female. That it's there so you can enjoy being who you really are, a natural female who can feel good about herself without feeling guilty or ashamed.'

Athena hesitated, not sure what to do. She was, but she wasn't.

'Show her how strong you are then, Athena, if you've got the courage. Or have a good cry and go home. Pull your jeans down and show it. To her. To me. To whomever you feel like showing it to. Show it now, or have a cry and go home to your sisters.'

Athena sobbed as her hands crept to the button on her jeans. Her blazing, watery eyes never left him as she unzipped them, and pushed them down to her knees, lifting her hips slightly to ease their passage. Then, after a slight hesitation, her eyes never leaving his, she rocked her hips slightly again and slid her white knickers to her knees as well.

'There,' she whispered, glaring at him through tears of frustration, anger and sadness, 'I do what I like. I do what I like.'

It was a moment when whatever I was going to say next simply would not do.

She lay there in the chair, glowering at me as if in defiance of the devil himself. Like a moth drawn to a brilliant flame I was out of my chair, kneeling and grasping her ankles, easing them apart as far as the restrictive denim would allow.

I slid my grip to her calves and lifted them, while pressing between her thighs. Her virgin thicket lay exposed to me, the pink lips of her peeping through the dark canopy.

'Oh,' Athena gasped; shocked, startled and confused. 'No, what are you…?' But her question went no further than to drown in a sigh of extreme pleasure when she felt his warm mouth latch firmly over her sex and begin to lick and suck.

I barely heard her groaning or gasping, but I knew she was. The taste of her was intoxicating as I hungrily and passionately fed on her slick crease. Her core pulsed against my tongue each time I licked or suckled it deeply. I was rapidly becoming lost in a world of Greek virgins. Holding her calves high kept her knees back against her breasts. She couldn't move.

I slid my mouth down the slippery gorge of her cleft and tasted her on my tongue, before arriving there in fullness and depth. Oh, I groaned loudly, fluting my tongue and sucking her juice into my mouth. Then I struck it deep and I struck it hard, as far inside her tight virgin channel as I could.

'Ohhh, nooo, ohhh...' Athena heard herself groan with sensations and feelings she had never felt before; could never have imagined before. His mouth was between her legs, licking her, sucking her, chewing firmly on her lips and teasing her spot. Her struggles were rapidly fading and turned to groans, while her hips began to grind without her conscious will to make them do so. She rolled her head from side to side and tried to sit up or move in any way, but he was holding her legs up. She couldn't move.

I drank as she flowed. Her lacquer was thick and creamy from the source of her Greek virgin Nile. Almost out of control myself I dragged the flat of my tongue, rimming her nether necklace as I pushed her calves further back, which lifted her buttocks a little more. And then I dragged her upward, my tongue split her crease, opening her seeping slit to collect her slick pollen on the next trip down, which I did, and then swallowed. I held firmly to her calves while her unexpected orgasm raged through her body.

'Ooohhhnnnnnnn!' Athena groaned from her wildest fantasy. She was losing her mind. Her thighs shuddered. Her breasts quivered and her tight pussy flamed with wave after wave of sexual fire and brimstone, which pleasured her tortured mind.

Her eyes pinched tightly shut as she stiffened and tensed, sobbing her bliss in the lounge of her mother's friend's husband. She could hardly move, and didn't really know she was or even wanted to. Her knees were held up and apart while he feasted on her virginity. She felt as if she were his dinner.

I was relentless in my aggressive mouthing of her succulent virgin flesh. Knowing it had never felt a man's mouth before drove me on. She was pure, her sex weeping its joy, her channel spilling and overflowing its banks, only to find my mouth waiting to suck her overflow over my tongue and into my deeper male belly. My tongue whipped rapidly from side to side as she suddenly came again with a virgin vengeance, only more strongly so.

'Ooohhhnnnnnnn…' Athena cried out uncontrollably. He was eating her while she again climaxed so fiercely. Oh, he was eating her pussy.

I held her tightly, knowing what was happening with her young virgin body, but not caring. The suddenness and intensity of the cunnilingus had spiralled her into multiple orgasms. I was giving her female feelings she wouldn't forget in a hurry. Maybe next time she'd know what I was talking about when I touched on the difference between that part of her and her thinking woman. I held her tight, in her virgin moment of female self-awareness.

Athena sighed wearily, and my fingers dug into her shapely calves as her female introduced herself to her woman, in no uncertain terms. Her clitoris strummed gloriously between my lips as she wearily came one more time, with a pure female whimper, until finally she drew a deep breath and collapsed even more deeply into the chair.

Slowly I moved my face away from between her thighs. My chin glistened with the slippery joy of her female's forced liberation. Slowly I lowered her feet to the floor, leaning back a little and seeing once more her dark pubic triangle, like an attractive shroud of Greek mystery.

And as I did she sighed deeply. Her eyes were closed and relaxed, which was the way her face and body looked as her legs fell loosely apart. I gazed fondly down at her, resting in her settling virgin afterglow.

Her lips parted slightly. I smiled with heartfelt tenderness and left her to bask in her own natural female glory, while I rose and went to the bathroom, returning with a warm hand towel. Then gently I lifted her ankles again, just high enough to be able to softly wash and dry between her thighs.

I lowered her legs and wiped my face, returned the towel to the bathroom then soaked it in the basin. Then I returned to my basking beauty. Reaching down, I grasped her by the wrists and pulled gently, encouraging her to rise to her feet. With a groan and then a soft sigh she followed my lead, and within moments I had her standing listlessly.

Her eyes remained closed as, holding her steady with one arm, I pulled up her underwear, then after a little bit of a struggle I got her jeans back up over her hips and around her waist. I did up the button and then zipped her up; one complete, almost untouched Greek virgin package once again. Then I lowered her limp body back down into the chair. She sank into it with a long sigh and I let her hands lay gently in her lap.

Going to the kitchen I made us both a cool drink, then returned and placed mine on the small table. I opened the limp fingers of her right hand and wrapped them around the glass, then slowly let go and sat back down with a contented and victorious sigh, along with an inner smile of satisfaction. I was on my way, and so was she. It would now only be the dance of time as it had been with her sister, and as it was yet to be with her twin.

As I studied her calm face her eyes gently opened, blinked a few times, then closed again. Then they opened and remained so. Her gaze moved slowly left and right, as someone might look when first becoming conscious after a general anaesthetic. Then they settled on me.

Truth time, I thought.

Briefly her gaze travelled down to her lap, where her jeans were fastened, but then her dark eyes came back to my face. The awareness of everything that had happened showed immediately in the eyes behind the gaze, but she said nothing, just looked at me.

I smiled, but said nothing. Then she seemed to notice the glass of iced water in her right hand. She looked at it, then back at me, then back at the glass again, and lifted it slowly to her lips and drank deeply, her gaze once more locked and loaded onto mine. The moment of truth would soon be here. My heart picked up the pace, but I forced myself to remain calm, and prayed.

'Welcome to the world of your natural feeling female,' I said. 'How does it feel to feel good about yourself without feeling guilty or ashamed?' I fell in love with Athena in the next second, with her answer. It didn't come from her eyes, because they gently closed. And it didn't come from her body language, because her body seemed to deflate even more deeply into the chair upon which she reclined.

Her answer came from the shape of her lips as she sighed sweetly, and gently smiled. That had been her answer, a Greek female virgin's gentle smile.

159

Chapter Fourteen

Lauren had again left early to go shopping with Marcena, and that was fine with me. An easy truce had settled over us in the week, not of hostility, but of acceptance that neither of us liked the other any more. I had risen reasonably early, given that it was a Saturday morning.

The first waking thought I'd had was of Athena. A warm feeling of fondness accompanied it. The first image to enter my thoughts was of her dark Greek virgin shrine, glorious when she lifted her hips a little and pushed her jeans and knickers down to her knees. And my erection accompanied that image, more virulent than my usual morning glory. I had arranged to meet her again the following Wednesday, when she had a day off.

I wondered, as I sat typing for a magazine, how I would eventually get Nicki and Athena, as well as Appolonia when she eventually got with the program, to agree to share me. I was really happy for the first time since I could remember, and I intended to remain that way. I knew, however, that I would not be satisfied with just two of the sisters. I wanted all three all to myself, and if possible for the rest of my life. And I was impatient.

As far as my marriage went, I now realised fully that it was not a matter of if, but when we would separate. I didn't really like the idea of a messy divorce, and I didn't think she did either. Half of everything we had would suit me fine, and that included the house. I didn't want to live there any more. I wanted a fresh start somewhere, maybe up in the mountains with the clean air and singing birds, and lots of privacy where I could be alone with my three Greek slaves. There were no doubts in my mind that I cared deeply for both Nicki and Athena. I also had no doubts that I would care just as deeply for Appolonia, as soon as I got her into my stable.

I had already been thinking about her, and how I could bring it about. The main thing was, as I saw it, that I was enjoying life as a male for the first time in my life, and simply didn't want it to end. I hadn't turned into a control freak, but the natural dominance of being a male along with the natural submission of females, to me just felt right in every aspect.

How many years I had remaining I didn't know, but I did know I was going to live them as a male, in every sense. I smiled then and went back to my typing, wanting to finish it before Nicki arrived to do the cleaning. I had decided not to take her to the beach; there was still work for the magazine I had to finish before I could call the weekend my own, and besides, I had a few surprises for Nicki...

She arrived promptly at ten. I let her in and was genuinely glad to see her. She must have been glad to see me too, because once I'd shut the door she wrapped her arms around my waist and hugged me strongly.

'Mmmmm,' I whispered, leaning forward to kiss her forehead. 'What a wonderful way to greet your master.'

'Mmmm,' Nicki sighed in return, letting go of him to gaze into his dancing eyes. She loved the way they did that, and credited her presence as being the cause. It made her feel good about herself.

'I've missed you, baby,' I said. She leaned into me once more, her arms encircling my waist again.

Nicki released him, feeling as if she belonged to him. It

was a wonderful feeling, of utterly belonging to someone, of being owned. She followed him into the lounge, where he sat down in his chair.

'Athena seems a little different, Master,' Nicki said quietly as she sat at his feet. Thank you for helping her.' Her arms rested over his knee, her fingers interlocked and supporting the weight of her arms.

I smiled down at her and rested my hand over hers on my knee. 'In what way does she seem different?'

'Happier, I think,' Nicki replied. She was enjoying the warmth his hand had over hers. 'It's as if she's doing some deep thinking, maybe? She's been quiet this morning. I tried to talk to her about it or answer any questions she might have, but she didn't seem to want to.'

'That's okay,' I said, squeezing her hands. 'She'll be fine. I'm glad I was here to be able to help, and proud of you too, for asking on her behalf. I've got some more work to do with her yet, but she's on her way. I don't think she'll have a problem with her self-confidence for much longer.'

'I don't think so either, Master,' she said, believing the words. Appolonia should see him too, she thought. Then the stuck-up bitch might come down to earth a bit and not treat her like a little girl. She was only a little older. That was all, not a generation.

She loved both her elder sisters dearly, but when it came to favourites Athena always treated her like a friend, whereas Appolonia made her feel like a child in the way she spoke down to her. Athena would lend her clothes, but Appolonia wouldn't let her get near hers. She didn't know how Appolonia's secret boyfriend put up with her. She was always bossing him around.

'She wants to change,' I told her quietly, admiring the memory of Athena's determination, and the fact that she'd been crying without realising it. 'That's the main thing.'

Nicki sighed, wishing both sisters could feel like she did, could have a master like she did and could feel as happy as she did. Athena and Appolonia never smiled much, unless they were trying to get something from her or their mother, or someone.

She smiled up at him, wishing that both her sisters could smile with the same heartfelt happiness she'd been smiling since meeting her master and losing her virginity, but she knew she couldn't ask him to help Appolonia, too. He'd think her entire family was a bunch of emotional cripples. It was enough he was helping Athena. Maybe Athena could bring Appolonia down a peg or two, once her master had helped her get her self-confidence back.

'No housework today?' I asked, frowning slightly.

Nicki's eyes widened. She'd forgotten. She had been so happy just sitting at his feet and talking it had never entered her head.

'Oh,' she said, startled and fearing for the temperature in her bottom. Then she jumped up to her feet. 'I—'

'It's okay,' I said. 'But you better hop to it now.'

'Yes, Master,' Nicki said quickly, about to turn and head for the closet where the vacuum cleaner lived.

'And Nicki,' I added, 'you can leave your top here with me.'

Nicki gasped, then smiled. She loved his surprises, never knowing from which quarter they would come. Grasping the hem of her T-shirt with both hands she quickly whipped it up and over her head, revealing to his appreciative gaze her full young breasts, naked and exposed. She felt the embarrassment begin as a warm flush, but accepted the feeling now as cherished. Shyly lowering her gaze from his, she then turned, heading for the closet.

I was hardly able to wait to begin my life over again, but with different people in it this time. Then I sat back in my chair and clasped my hands behind my head, enjoying the highly erotic sight of my bare-breasted Greek slave as she leaned forward, pushing and pulling the vacuum cleaner back and forth while she cleaned the lounge. Those wonderful breasts and glorious nipples jiggled and jostled as she worked diligently on her allotted task.

My thoughts then turned to her sisters as I watched Nicki cleaning the house, and when I couldn't see her I could easily hear the various noises she was making, which told me that her efforts in doing the job were still earnest and sincere. I had no idea of the personality of Appolonia, other than the vague references to her selfishness that Nicki had dropped from time to time. I knew I would have to find out more about her, in order to create a natural strategy that would have the potential to get her with the same program as her sisters.

A while later Nicki reappeared. Fine beads of perspiration glistened on her forehead and in the valley between her breasts. She looked gorgeous. Her dark brown nipples looked erect and pliant. She flopped down in her chair, looking completely exhausted. It brought back memories as I sat eyeing her breasts, with her knowing I was doing it.

'Remember the very first time you flopped into that chair, exhausted?' I asked.

Nicki was blushing at him staring unashamedly at her breasts, but she was not ashamed or embarrassed. Instead, she felt proud that he wanted to.

'Yes, Master.' The memories of him using her own strong Greek mind to make her undress in front of him immediately came flooding back. She felt herself blush some more and was amazed; even after all she'd been through with him. It made her feel hotter than she already was. Then she had a sudden thought, and added, 'Appolonia has a stronger mind than Athena's or mine, and she's got a lot to learn about being nice, I can tell you. Even mum can't get her to do things she doesn't want to do. You should try that mind trick on her.' Then she laughed.

I laughed with her, not being able to believe my luck that she had brought up the very subject I had been thinking about. Without knowing it, Nicki had given me the opening I needed.

'Is that right?' I said. 'Surely she can't be that different from Athena? After all, they're twins.'

'Different?' Nicki scoffed. 'Ha! Chalk and cheese, Master. That's how different they are.'

'Really?' I said. 'I always thought twins were identical in character and nature, as well as their basic looks.'

'Maybe in some twins,' Nicki replied emphatically, shaking her head. 'But not with my sisters. They don't like the same foods or wear the same clothes, and they don't think the same way, either. And Appolonia is selfish, whereas Athena is always doing things for us. They're both strong-minded, though, like I am, but Appolonia's the strongest. She's the eldest, but only by an hour or so. The way she goes on sometimes you'd think she was our mother. I feel sorry for her boyfriend; she treats him like she was his mother, too.'

'That's interesting.' I had the opportunity I'd been waiting for. Now I was optimistic. At least we were on the right topic.

Nicki was thinking hard about how she could get him to try and make Appolonia a better and happier sister, but so far she was too embarrassed to tackle it directly with him as she'd done about Athena.

'What sort of hobbies does Appolonia have?' I asked, carefully probing. I didn't want her getting the wrong idea and think I was only out to steal the cherries of her sisters.

'Hobbies? Appolonia's only hobby is reading books, and herself. Athena and I have to wait our turn for the bathroom every day because she takes so long getting herself ready. She takes forever. Athena has her martial arts, and I have… well, I have… you now, Master.' She felt herself blushing again.

'Yes, sweetheart, you do. And I have you, too.'

Nicki's heart surged as her master's eyes began to dance for her in that special way.

'Have you finished the cleaning?' I asked, needing to think and plan.

'No, Master, sorry, I was just having a little rest. I'll do it now.' She jumped up and raced back to work, feeling her breasts swaying firmly as she hurried. She felt hot again, and knew it wasn't from the climate inside the house.

'Good girl,' I called after her, enjoying the sight of the cut-off shorts encasing her neat bottom, and I remembered the first time my hand had caressed her gorgeous Greek ass. My groin stirred seriously, but lazily. It was going to be that sort of morning.

Chapter Fifteen

'I can't believe what… that I… what happened,' Athena confessed shyly and hesitantly. She sat nervous and embarrassed in the chair opposite him, on Wednesday morning at ten o'clock. Her thoughts had been on nothing else all week. Sleep had been hard to find, and although tired, she had relived the entire event in her mind a dozen times or more each day since. She thought she felt good about it, but she just couldn't believe it had happened.

'It did,' I said. Although seeking to ease her mental anguish I was impatient and determined to make the day a special day for us both. 'And you can't take it back. But you can pretend it didn't happen if you feel you've gained nothing from the experience, as far as your personal confidence and happiness is concerned.'

'No,' Athena said quickly, 'it's not that. It's just that… it's just that… oh, I don't know. I seem to be a little confused, that's all. I wasn't expecting—'

'Self-discovery comes in many ways,' I said, gently cutting her off in mid-sentence. 'Personal happiness and confidence comes the same way. You can always expect the expected, but the nicest surprises and the most profound growing experiences usually arrive with the unexpected.'

Athena bowed her head, too embarrassed to look at him. 'You can say that again,' she quietly said.

I decided to cut to the chase. 'Athena,' I said, looking squarely at her face to catch her gaze when she looked up. She did in the next second, and I did. 'Who are you?'

Athena blushed instantly, knowing the answer he wanted. She had thought about the difference a hundred times already. 'A female,' she said softly.

'Good girl.' I smiled. 'That's right, a female. And what nature of female are you?'

'A… a feeling female,' Athena answered quietly.

'Yes, a feeling female. And what has been responsible for your lack of self-confidence and unhappiness as you see it to be?' I wanted to see if she'd given any thought to the basic concept.

'The woman in me.'

'And what nature of woman in you would that be?'

'My thinking woman.'

'And do you believe that?

'Yes.' She was sure now. She understood the difference between the woman in her and the female in her. She just wished she had known about it a long time ago. The whole idea seemed to be so simple yet it made so much sense. It was just difficult to get used to the idea of acting on her feelings as they arose in her and not her thoughts.

'And who is responsible for your long-term happiness and natural self-confidence?' I asked.

'I am,' Athena said softly, holding his strong gaze.

'And who are you?' I asked.

'A female.'

'What nature of female?'

'A feeling female.'

'Who should act on your feelings at all times and lead your moment by moment decisions each day?'

'I should,' Athena said quickly.

'And who are you?'

'A feeling female.'

'And should you be influenced by the learned values and beliefs of your thinking woman when it comes to your personal happiness and self-confidence?' I asked, working my way slowly around a circle with no end and no beginning.

'No.'

'Why not?'

Athena thought for a moment.

'Do you really have to think about your answer?' I asked her firmly. 'Feel it, and then say it exactly as you feel it. That's the beginning of practicing to be the female you've never been, but always should have been.'

'Because my woman doesn't know how to feel,' Athena said quickly. 'She's only learned how to think.'

'Good girl.' I smiled.

Athena smiled back at him, feeling relieved. She also felt better than she had when she'd first arrived.

'And do you really believe that? I mean, does it really make sense to you in a way that you feel you can incorporate that belief into your life and times?'

'Yes,' Athena answered, knowing she did. 'I do.'

'Who has the most natural strength and courage?' I asked.

'I do.'

'And who are you?'

'A feeling female.'

'A natural feeling female,' I corrected her gently.

'Yes, a natural feeling female.'

'Why are you a natural feeling female?' I asked.

Athena began to think, and then stopped herself when she saw him frown slightly. 'Because I was born first,' she said.

'Good girl.' I smiled at her.

Athena felt as if she had just gone to the top of the class. His smile caused her to feel warm all over. She blushed as the memories came flooding back. She lowered her gaze from his eyes.

'What will you do at any time in the future,' I went on, wanting to ease her embarrassment quickly, while she was on a roll, 'if you feel like doing something that feels natural and right that would make you happy, but your thinking woman says no because of her own learned beliefs and values?'

'I'm in charge of my happiness,' Athena said confidently. 'It's my life and I'm in charge.'

'And who are you?'

'A natural feeling female,' Athena said, feeling surer than ever that she was on the way to living a better life.

'What if you feel like doing something you'd like to do to make you happy and feel good about yourself without feeling guilty, but you've never done it before and your thinking woman says no?'

'I'd do it,' Athena said confidently.

'Even though you might be nervous or it might embarrass you, or even humiliate you?'

Athena blushed again, but soldiered on. 'Yes,' she said quietly, looking down at the carpet. She felt warm all over, and it wasn't from the temperature of the lounge in which she sat.

'And in knowing then that who you are is really who you are and not what you are, can you recognise as a natural feeling female that your gender biology is real?'

Athena blushed again and felt warmer than she had. 'Yes,' she answered him.

'Then you can recognise also,' I said, 'that as a male my presence around you, and yours around me, will affect your body and your emotions?'

Athena just nodded; too self-conscious of her blushing to be courageous enough to trust herself speak.

'Do you remember how angry you became when you

thought about all the misery and unhappiness your thinking woman has caused you so far in your life? Compared to the natural happiness you could have had if you'd been strong enough to take charge of it, as is your natural right as a feeling female?'

'Yes,' Athena nodded, feeling that anger and determination flood instantly back into her mind and body.

'Are you sure?' I pressed, noticing her fists clenching.

'Yes,' Athena said confidently.

'And you believe you now have the confidence and courage to take personal charge of your feelings as they come up in your awareness, moment by moment?' I probed, heading her towards the capture pen. 'And then act on them if it feels right for you to do so, no matter what your thinking woman tries to tell you to do?'

'Yes,' Athena said firmly, the tension in her fists.

'So, that patch of hair between your legs is not there for your woman's benefit, or to just keep her warm in winter?' I baited.

Athena blushed, but she answered quickly and positively. 'No.'

'Is that a fact?' I asked dryly.

'Yes.'

'Or a fallacy?'

'No,' Athena said forcefully. 'A fact.'

'And does believing that fact make you feel courageous and confident as if all of your natural self-confidence is beginning to come back to you?'

'Yes,' Athena said confidently.

'Do you feel strong enough and confident enough yet to ignore or to override your thinking woman's protests and do whatever you feel like, whatever feels right for you to do, in belief without question and faith without doubt?'

'Yes.'

'How would I know?'

'I do,' Athena said forcefully.

'How would you know?' I asked.

'I do.'

'Whose patch of hair is it between your legs?'

'Mine.'

'Really?'

'Yes.'

'Are you sure?'

'Yes.'

'Whose breasts are they?'

'Mine,' Athena said firmly, knowing she was blushing.

'Whose lips are they?'

'Mine.'

'Whose bottom are you sitting on?'

'Mine,' Athena said firmly, and then blushed some more.

'Really?'

'Yes.'

'Really,' I said. It was not a question, but a non-believing one word statement.

'Yes,' Athena said determinedly.

'So, you would do anything you felt like doing with any of those areas that are yours,' I led her. 'And have the strength and courage to overcome your woman's beliefs and your own embarrassment in doing them if you felt like it?'

'Yes,' Athena said without thinking, and when she did think a split second later she blushed again. She felt hot and bothered and warm in all the wrong places, but felt confident, and that felt good.

'Even to the point where you'd agree to punish your thinking woman if she ever attempted to deprive you of your rightful happiness?'

172

'Yes,' Athena snapped.

'And do you think you've developed the natural honesty to admit the absolute truth of those natural feelings whenever they arise, and then have the strength to act upon them?'

'Yes,' Athena said firmly.

'Really?'

'Yes.'

'Is that so?'

'Yes.'

'To act without thinking, just because it feels right, or is what you feel like doing?'

'Yes.'

'Really?'

'Yes.'

'I don't believe you.'

'It's true.'

'Do you remember how I treated you the other night?' I explored, giving her the feel of a little cold steel between the third and fourth rib.

Athena felt herself blush afresh. 'Yes,' she said, but with little conviction.

'Did it make you feel good?'

'Yes,' Athena said without thinking, then blushed some more as the erotic images came flooding back.

'Did it feel right?'

'Yes.'

'Your thinking woman didn't think so, did she?' I tested.

'No.'

'But she was wrong, wasn't she?'

'Yes.'

'She deserved to be punished, didn't she?' I led her.

'Yes.'

'Are you sure?'

173

'Yes.'

'Really?'

'Yes.'

'And you can remember the feeling of my mouth and tongue between your legs, can't you?'

Athena felt as if her face was beetroot red. 'Yes,' she said quietly, but held his gaze.

'And if you felt like it, or it felt right, you'd do it again, because that's your natural female right. Is that true?' I challenged.

Athena nearly swooned with embarrassment. 'I... um... I—'

'Are you still a weak female?' I prodded. 'Trodden under by the stronger will of your thinking woman?'

'No!' Athena flamed instantly, knowing she was not weak, but strong.

'Then if you felt like it or it felt right for you would you override the protests of your thinking woman, and accept my mouth and tongue between your legs again?'

'Oh,' Athena gasped, hot and truly bothered. 'I... I...'

I sighed in an exaggerated manner. 'You're weak as a female, Athena,' I goaded her. 'Maybe you should go home and consider who is really in charge of your life and times. It seems to me you're still happy for it to be your thinking woman.'

'No,' Athena snapped, embarrassed still. 'I'm not. I'm just not used to... I'm just—'

'You're still a weak female,' I said. 'And that's okay too, if that's the way you want to spend the rest of your life. But why waste my time and yours with the lie that you feel you deserve to be happier than you've been?'

'I'm not weak,' Athena said. 'I'm not a weak female. I'm just not used to... to... to being spoken to like that, that's all.' She felt flustered and embarrassed, but she

174

also felt angry. She hated being called weak, because she did not think she was.

'Athena,' I said patiently, and sounding like it, 'you can't even bolster up the courage as a female to tell the truth about a simple honest question. Instead, you let your thinking woman take over and answer for you like a little girl who doesn't know and can't recognise the natural feelings of her own human nature, and who is too afraid or embarrassed to admit them even to herself.'

'I'm not weak!' Athena snapped angrily.

'Then give your natural feeling female the freedom and courage to tell the truth about how she felt about having my mouth and tongue between your legs.'

'I did.'

'No, you didn't, and you know you didn't,' I goaded her further. 'Your female liked it, because it felt good and natural. It made her feel good about herself without feeling guilty. But your woman didn't because it didn't agree with her learned beliefs about what she thinks should feel good for you. Does that about sum it up correctly?'

'No,' Athena denied.

'Then what is the truth? As a female do you have the guts to believe without question, in faith without doubt that you did like my mouth and tongue between your legs?'

'I... I...'

'Okay,' I sighed. 'Have a nice day. Come and see me again when you find your female's natural strength of character.'

'Oh no, I mean yes,' Athena blustered. 'I did like it!'

'And did it feel good?' I asked quickly.

'Yes.'

'And did it feel right?'

'Yes.'

'And did it matter what your thinking woman thought?'

'No.'

'And will it ever matter what she thinks when it comes to your personal happiness?'

'No,' Athena said emotionally. 'It won't.'

'Then if you wanted to feel those feelings again, now that you've admitted you liked them because they felt right, would you willingly choose to feel them again if you felt like it?'

'I… yes.'

'No matter what thoughts of protest or embarrassment your thinking woman might try to impose upon your right to happiness as a natural female?'

'Yes.'

'No matter what?'

'I said, yes.'

'Even if it meant punishing your woman for getting in your way?'

'Yes.'

'Really?'

'Yes.'

'Really,' I said, sounding unconvinced.

'Yes,' Athena insisted, 'I would.'

'You would?'

'Yes, I would.'

'You would what?' I led her carefully, keeping my face as serious as I could, knowing her pain and my patience were all for the greater cause of us both.

'I would choose to do that,' Athena blurted without thinking. 'I would punish her.'

'And do what else?'

'That.'

'You can't even say what you know you want to say and feel,' I baited her. 'And you tell me you're strong? As I said, Athena, you—'

'I would have your mouth and tongue there!' Athena spat angrily, livid at his constant reference to her as being a weak person.

'You would?'

'Yes.'

'Didn't hurt that much to tell the truth, did it?' I smiled.

'No…' Athena said quietly.

'The question is, do you have the strength and confidence to act on your moment by moment feelings now?'

'Yes, I do,' Athena said firmly.

'Would your feeling female like my mouth and tongue between your legs right now?' I asked, giving her the entire apple at once, to see if she'd choke. I held my breath while she stared angrily at me. I gave her five seconds.

'Don't think!' I snapped, watching her flinch, startled. 'Feel!'

'Yes!' Athena yelled instinctively.

'Yes?' I pressed, questioning her sincerity.

'Yes!'

'Really?'

'Yes.'

'Really,' I said flatly, and then looked away as if I didn't believe a word she'd said.

'Yes,' she went on hesitantly, 'I do.'

'You do what? Have some courage if your happiness is that important to you, or go home.'

Athena was angry and fit to burst. He wasn't going to dismiss her again. She knew what she wanted and she wasn't weak. She wasn't weak.

'I want your… your mouth, and… and tongue… between… my legs,' she finally said, saying it as she felt it, her confidence and anger ebbing. She'd begun to feel weak and hesitant, just as he said she was. 'I want your mouth and tongue between my legs,' she repeated quickly, but this time confidently, as she wanted to feel, as she wanted to sound, as a feeling female, not as a thinking woman.

'When?' I snapped; locking the gate and snapping her collar closed.

Athena shook her head, her emotions in a spin.

'When?' I said more firmly.

'I—'

'When?' I raised my voice at her, and the tears of frustration and anger overflowed the rims of her eyes and ran freely down her cheeks. She stared hatefully at me for calling her names that weren't true. Her fingers clutched the armrests of the chair.

'Go home,' I said dismissively. 'Now, go home.' Then I looked away from her blazing eyes and picked up the book from the small table beside my chair.

'No,' Athena said, 'I won't go home. I won't. I'm not weak. I'm not.'

'No?' I said quietly, indifferently, looking at the open pages of the book.

'Now,' Athena said calmly, feeling hurt by the way he was treating her, as if she didn't matter, as if she was a non-person all of a sudden. 'I want your mouth and tongue between my legs, now. Right now. There, are you satisfied?'

'Are you satisfied?' I countered. 'As an honest female for a change?'

'Yes.'

Inside I smiled and padlocked the gate, but outside I turned slowly, placing the book back down on the table. When my eyes met hers I did not smile. She gripped both arms of the chair, her knuckles white, her lower lip trembling very slightly. She breathed quickly through her slightly open mouth, her eyes two saucers of determination and indignation. She was in the yard, the gate locked. She was mine. It was only the dance of time now.

'Right now?' I asked her, quietly.

'Yes, right now,' she insisted.

I held her gaze steadily, the moment of truth having arrived for both of us.

'Then get up and take your jeans and panties off, but leave your top on,' I said quietly but firmly. 'Now.'

Athena felt her fingers tighten on the armrests of the chair. His eyes told her he wasn't kidding. She wasn't weak, she thought. Her heart raced. She felt hot all over. Her legs felt as heavy as lead. But he was the husband of her mother's friend, she reasoned.

'Now,' I repeated. 'Or get out.'

Athena rose elegantly. Her hands moved to the waistband button of her jeans, while her eyes stared at him. She had to keep her resolve. Her pulse increased and she could hear her heartbeat inside her head. The button popped undone, and her fingers tugged down the zipper. She stepped out of her flat-heeled shoes and moved them to one side with her feet. Then she pulled her jeans down over her hips and thighs, her gaze never leaving his for an instant.

He wasn't smiling and he wasn't angry. His face was impassive. His eyes held hers as if they were locked together in mortal combat. She let her jeans fall down over her knees and held them loosely while she stepped out of them. Then she dropped them in a pile on top of her shoes. Her knees felt like jelly, and they actually trembled. Her fingers also trembled as she reached for the waistband of her white panties, and hesitating briefly, she then slid them down over her smooth hips and thighs too. Then her face burned with the utter embarrassment of him seeing her intimate body exposed like that.

She lifted her knees one at a time and stepped out of them too, letting them slide from her fingers onto her jeans as she straightened up and held his gaze. She fought for all the strength she could muster to not grab her clothes and bolt out of the house. Her hands instinctively came together to cover her Greek modesty, while her skin glowed from unease as she held his gaze evenly.

'By your sides,' I said firmly, watching her shyly move her hands away from the dark curls that covered her junction. My stomach knotted in unison with the instant strengthening of the human muscle between my legs. Then I deliberately lowered my gaze from her eyes and stared directly at what I knew to be virgin Greek territory at the apex of her shapely thighs. If my cock had a voice I knew what it would have demanded right then, and in no uncertain terms.

Athena's skin simmered with the humiliation of standing there, naked from the waist down. Her hands hung by her sides, with him staring at her lower belly. Her heart hammered mercilessly against her ribs, showing her no mercy at all. Each breath was a tremulous pant as it flowed hesitatingly between nervously parted lips. But she felt something else, too. She wanted to be looked at in that way, and in that place. To herself she admitted that fact, and found it to be liberating despite the humiliation and embarrassment she felt so strongly.

'Turn around,' I instructed her firmly.

'What?'

'Turn,' I said forcefully, 'now.'

Athena obeyed slowly, her heart racing.

'Bend forward and hold the armrests. Your woman needs punishing to show her that you are really the boss.

Doesn't she?'

Athena did not believe what she was hearing. Her heart hammered in her ears.

'Who's the boss?' I prompted. 'You or her?'

'I—' she began, but he cut her off.

'Athena,' I said firmly, 'if you don't know who the boss is by now you never will. If you haven't the courage as a natural female to punish her and put her in her place when she gets out of line, you can get dressed and leave now. It's your life and happiness, not mine. Make a decision for once in your life, and don't be weak.'

'I'm not weak,' Athena said emotionally.

'Then make a decision for yourself. She either deserves to be punished and put in her place, or she doesn't. Which is it?'

'She—'

'Yes or no,' I snapped.

'I—'

'Get out,' I hissed. 'Get dressed and get out.'

'No,' Athena pleaded.

'Yes or no,' I repeated.

'But I—'

'Get dressed and get out!'

'Yes!' Athena screamed, tears streaming from her eyes.

'Yes, what?'

'Yes, she does!'

'She does what?'

'Deserve to be punished!' Athena babbled, crying and not aware of it.

'Really?'

'Yes!'

'Someone has to master her, don't they?' I began to lead her into her role.

'Yes.'

'You haven't been her master, have you?'

'No,' Athena said, knowing it was true.

'She needs a master, doesn't she?'

Athena nodded.

'What does she need?'

'A master.'

'Really?'

'Yes!'

'You've let her make your life miserable,' I pressed, 'haven't you?'

'Yes,' Athena said quietly, knowing it was true.

'And you need a master too, don't you?'

'I—'

'Don't you?'

'Yes,' Athena acknowledged, her shoulders sagging.

'Say it,' I coaxed.

'I—'

'Say it.'

'I need a master,' she said wearily.

'Am I your master, Athena?'

'Yes,' she said instinctively.

'Say it.' I waited quietly, patiently.

'You're my…' she eventually whispered, 'you're my master…'

'Pardon?'

'You're my master,' she repeated.

'And are you happy about that?'

'Yes, Master.'

'Will you always be?

Athena nodded, drained.

'Then bend forward and hold the armrests, now.'

Athena gasped, but felt herself immediately obeying and holding the chair. Her mind raced, her pulse throbbed, and a tear dripped onto the cushion. She felt defeated and drained.

I smiled fondly at her creamy white buttocks, which trembled as I gazed at them in their Greek purity. If only she knew how much I loved her, of the wonderful future I had planned for all of us, I thought, knowing she was about to come all the way home to who she really was. Her thinking woman would soon cower from her natural feeling female in fear, for the rest of her life.

Stepping to her left side I rested my left hand on her lower back, and without warning brought my right palm down hard on her right buttock. She squealed and leaned further over the chair. Then I swept my hand down again on her left cheek. Again she wailed and jerked further over the chair. Two red marks began to crimson their way into the centre of each glorious cheek.

Alternating then, I spanked her cheeks one after the other until I had counted fifteen for each side. My hand throbbed, and she'd pressed her face down into the cushion upon which she previously sat. Her vulnerable bottom was raised invitingly. Each cheek was now a lovely blotchy red, trembling as she sobbed into the cushion, but I was determined to break her thinking woman's spirit at the very beginning of our relationship. I gazed at her ass, my groin as hard as granite. There was something so incredibly erotic about the sight of a freshly spanked bottom, but I knew, somehow, that her woman had not yet reached her limit.

Athena could not believe what had happened, what was happening. Each whack on her backside stung maddeningly. She had never been spanked by anyone, not even her mother. Her bottom flamed and her teeth had clamped down on the cushion with each jolting spank. She'd thought they would never end. She was crying, but determined to see it through. Then suddenly her bottom again exploded into a nightmare of blistering pain.

Ten more smacks on each cheek I delivered with precision, then began to smack the backs of her upper thighs down to her knees. She almost buckled a couple of times. I could hear her wailing into the cushion, but it was muffled. Again I returned to her bright red bottom and began laying into it, intent on breaking her spirit. As yet she had not called for me to stop, only babbled her pain into the lounge chair.

Athena was losing her mind with it all. Again and again her buttocks erupted in pain. Her legs threatened to fold at any moment and her frame jarred with the force and sting of each strike. Her bottom blazed.

I stopped, my hand throbbing, my heart racing. Her backside was entirely devoid of un-spanked flesh, and was now an attractively deep crimson all over. Gently then I began to caress her beaten skin. She flinched, and then relaxed.

Athena sobbed, but she was aware. She was aware of his hand as it caressed her flaming buttocks. His fingers glided gently between her legs, brushing lightly, feathering her black nest. She groaned from the relief of the silent hand, and began to accept the pleasurable sensations that were beginning to pool in her lower belly. She was wet, and she knew it. It felt like a soft tickle as it slowly seeped from her Greek virgin source over her upper thighs. She couldn't believe it. Her body was numb from the pain and the pleasure, and she didn't know how she had managed to stay on her feet…

I swung hard. The belt from my trousers whipped mercilessly through the short distance to her scarlet behind and landed with a reassuringly resounding *thwack*. She rocked into the cushion and buckled at the knees, wailing, but I followed her down and swung a second time. Again she wailed, and pressed her face deeper into the cushion. The redness of her buttocks was now a more lustrous hue than that caused by my hand. I swung again and again, striping her ass from top to bottom and directly over her wet sex lips, while she howled into the cushion.

Athena couldn't take it. The pain was tremendous. She had never imagined hurting so much from anything. And then it seemed to fade. It was still there, but she realised it was somehow bringing forth the deep pleasure she was beginning to experience.

Her nipples began to burn. She groaned deeply each time the belt strapped across her backside, but her groans were losing their anguish. She could somehow sense that, and could feel her orgasm approaching, and knew it would be intense in its origin.

I couldn't believe it, but I was happy. Again and again I swung the belt, and now she was straining back into its arc. Again and again she pushed her bottom towards the belt's fiery arrival, her knees bracing against each onslaught delivered. Her wailing had turned to deep groaning acknowledgements of each strike.

Then I stopped.

It was time.

I don't know how or why I came to that conclusion, but I knew it was.

Dropping the belt to the floor I began to gently caress her stunningly red buttocks and thighs again. After only a few moments her sobbing ceased altogether and she sighed. I continued stroking for several more minutes, and her bottom continued to gently push back into the gentle pressure of my hand. I glanced down at my groin. My trousers had tented well and truly. I smiled. Not for much longer, I thought, remembering Nicki. Not for much longer.

I reached for her shoulders and gently pulled her back upright. It was time. She stood facing the chair, her head bowed, the occasional sniff or sob the only thing I heard from her. My gaze found her delicious bottom once again. It was so red – a deep, dark and beautiful red. My cock pulsed impatiently.

I turned her around. Her face was red and flushed, her eyes puffy, but her gaze, her gaze met mine with an acceptance that almost brought tears to my eyes. Then I eased her back down into the large chair, watching her hiss and grimace sweetly as her punished bottom sank into the cushion.

She sighed, wondering what was happening, but not really caring if her unspoken questions were even heard, let alone answered. Everything was just floating around her and she felt so wonderful and free… so free.

Yes, I thought proudly, not just a little relieved; it worked every time.

'Athena?' I began, as I stared down at her.

'Yes?' Athena heard herself respond. Her gaze drifted to her groin and saw the lushness of her own dark triangle. Her whole world was the feeling sensations that were swamping her embarrassed mind.

I watched as she breathed through her moist, slightly parted lips. She sank down further into the chair. I decided to try and split her personality away from herself for complete inhibition, without any personally attached guilt.

Athena felt strange, as if another part of her floated somewhere above as she sat half-naked in the big chair, no longer attached to the world or any of its problems. She wasn't even really aware of her own body, just who she really was, floating free above the world, looking down from heaven itself as she sat there in front of him.

'Athena, is it your woman that holds all the

186

embarrassment?'

'Yes,' she answered, wondering why she was talking about herself. Then she lost the thread of the thought.

'And your woman will do exactly as she is told by you, as a female,' I continued, using the third party dissociate technique I'd read about. 'That's how she'll stay balanced and under control in your life. And you want to keep her balanced and controlled for the sake of your personal confidence and happiness, isn't that true?'

Athena knew he was right. It made sense. 'Yes,' she answered, her voice trailing off and sounding distant. She felt wonderfully detached, light and floating, just waiting for the next word to come along.

'Are you prepared to ensure she keeps her balance, so that you'll feel no shame or guilt when she tries to deny you your rightful happiness and natural self-confidence?'

'Yes,' Athena answered, feeling herself floating down slowly from wherever she had been. She knew she couldn't allow her woman to be in charge of her life's happiness any longer. That would be just too sad for her. She didn't like to be sad or lonely. Yes, she concluded rationally, she would do whatever it took to get the job done. She closed her eyes and breathed deeply.

'That's fine,' I said, with a smile in my tone and a lump in my trousers. 'You can open your legs wide now and remain relaxed, then help get your life back to perfect and natural balance, without guilt, inhibition or shame, and responding fully in whatever way and manner feels right to you as a natural feeling female. Do you understand fully?'

'Yes,' Athena replied softly, allowing her eyes to slowly open. Everything seemed a little hazy. She moved her feet one at a time and let her thighs loll to each side. For just a moment as she gazed into his eyes she wondered if she was asleep, having a dream that she was awake, or she was awake and having a dream that she was asleep. Then her gaze dropped from his face to her parted knees. She blushed immediately and felt hot and very, very bothered.

I slowly let out the breath I'd been holding, and watched the half-naked Greek girl stare at her own dark sex. She seemed to be deep in thought. With my heart racing and my pulse pounding in my temples I slowly removed all my clothing. Her eyes watched me and widened, like a frightened filly about to be saddled for the first time.

'Lift your feet and put them on the armrests,' I commanded her firmly. Then I knelt down before her. Slowly, each foot at a time, she obeyed me, and my gaze zeroed into the depths of her virgin forest like a laser weapon. My cock speared and aimed in anticipation of following the laser guidance of my eyes, but I overcame the powerful urge – with considerable difficulty. She reclined in the chair just staring at me, her eyes two sparkling spheres of astonishment and apprehension.

Athena was numb with the flood of sensations that surged through her mind and body, upon seeing him undress and then gazing at the erect muscle between his legs. She could hardly breathe. She knew what she must look like with her feet on the armrests of the chair, but her focus of attention between his legs had been such that she simply obeyed without question or thought when told to place them there. She was astonished at the shape and form of him, never having seen an aroused male up close and personal in that way.

He knelt between her legs. She was shaking with confused excitement, just gazing at him as if in shock while her eyes searched his face and his groin. His eyes danced.

I placed my hands on her knees and widened them a

little more, waiting for her reaction – any reaction. I silently congratulated myself; there was none. I could smell her natural body perfume and breathed it deeply into my lungs, my body hardening, thickening, and lengthening between my legs as I did so. What I was now doing seemed dreamlike, as if I was in a dream, as she seemed to be. I watched myself place my hands gently on her inner thighs, my fingertips near her glossy pubic bush.

'Oh…' Athena gasped at the feeling of the warmth in his hands. Her heart raced. Her breath rasped.

'Oh…' She heard herself murmur, anticipating, excited and afraid, wanting yet not wanting. She closed her eyes to escape the tension of the moment. This couldn't be happening.

I rested my hands as she muttered something unintelligible and turned her head to one side. She opened her eyes a little, then closed them again, rolling her head back to a central position on the back of the chair. I edged my fingers closer to her dark forest. The natural beckoning pinkness of her Greek female lured me, but I took it slowly this time.

Athena felt a little disorientated, wondering why she was shaking. Somewhere in the back of her mind and awareness she was trying to make sense of what was happening, but it was difficult to put everything together. What was she doing? Oh yes, she was keeping her life in balance.

'Oh…' She gasped deeply when his hands moved again. Then she gave up questioning or wondering and felt herself sink even more deeply into the comfortable chair.

The more I gazed at my delicious Greek virgin the harder I became between the legs, and the more I stirred to life in the deepest part of my mind and awareness. It was all about control. I knew full well that part of the strength of

189

my lust and passion was because of the gloriously beautiful sight before my eyes, but the other part was purely because of the total and absolute control I knew I'd had over the entire situation from start to finish.

Then, without any further thinking, I drank in the full sensual sight of her wonderful female form. Nothing of her remained hidden from me.

Again I smelled her body perfume and inhaled it deeply into my lungs, knowing the inevitable would happen, but only when the time was right. She was young and healthy, and like Nicki, was not from my world, yet not like Nicki, which made her very different and very exciting.

She lay back into the chair, her flat stomach tensing and relaxing while I watched her. Her beautiful face lolled to one side. My fingers were millimetres from her lustrous nest. I gazed at the Greek virgin heart of her as if I'd never seen a female so revealed. The throbbing in my head and my own rigidity intensified like never before, as my hands moved closer together between her legs, resting there comfortably.

Athena rested on the edge of the most incredibly tense and agitated state of mind she had ever experienced. Aware she was partly naked, and that her legs had been moved wide apart, she felt the her that had been somewhere else and looking down was slowly coming back to merge with her happening reality.

I spread her succulent sex lips, gazed at her and drunk with craving. I decided to possess her virginity quickly, so I reached beneath her, lifting and pulling at the same time, until her buttocks nestled tight between my thighs. Then I lifted her knees back and pressed her thighs against her breasts.

Athena grunted softly and her eyes opened and widened. He had dragged her body to his and he now loomed over her. Her knees were pinned back on her breasts as she gazed up at him with wide, glistening eyes. The part of her that had been slowly coming back to merge with her happening reality now did so quickly as the situation began to clarify in her mind, a jigsaw of some kind finally piecing itself together, clicking into place.

She gasped at the sudden realisation of it all. No, he couldn't. He was her mother's friend's husband. He couldn't. But he was. He was there, right there. His body was there between her legs, long and stiff and demanding. She was staring between her knees, pinned by his tight grip to her breasts, right at it, and it looked rigid and too big. Then he grunted and moved and she couldn't see it any more.

'Ohhh...' she cried out, struggling desperately with the sensation of it being placed at her river's mouth. No, he couldn't. He was her mother's friend's husband. He couldn't. But then he did, pushing himself inside her a little way. Her virginity, her thinking mind screamed at her; he was taking possession of her virginity.

'Oh, nooo...' she cried, unsure of what was about to happen, but another part of her, a different part of her, widened her knees a little more as he prodded with his hips and sank a little deeper inside her narrow virgin breach.

'Athena,' I said to her, staring down at her. 'Athena, I'm going to fuck you now. I'm going to take your virginity. Your woman doesn't want that, does she?'

Athena felt her head roll from side to side, but she could feel him there, right there, just inside her and pushing against her tightness. It was hurting. It was hurting...

'But your female does because it's time for that to happen. Doesn't she?'

Athena stared up at him, wide-eyed, her moist and

pouting lips slightly open as she breathed, not believing what was happening. But somewhere inside her a part of her did. And it was that part of her that nodded, just once. He saw it, and let the natural weight of his hips press down, causing her to grimace and bite her lip. Then his fingers tightened behind her knees, making her grimace again as they clamped into the tendons there. She held her breath and his fingers tightened again, as if getting ready for something. He couldn't. He couldn't. But her mother's friend's husband was pushing, pushing, his jaw tensed and his eyes fixed, luring her, enticing her and seducing her. They danced, strong, dominant and piercing.

'Ohhh...' Athena gasped, her breasts squashed against her knees as she arched her back and filled her lungs. Pushing, he was pushing into her... inside her. She stared up at him but no words came from her open mouth, only rapid pants. His fingers tightened again behind her knees.

It was going to happen. He was stabbing with his groin, struggling to possess her, but it was going to happen. He was straining, pushing harder and deeper, using the natural weight of his hips. It was happening. It was going to happen; just as she'd dreamed many times it would happen. And then it did. With sweat beading his brow he pressed down on her knees, squashing her beneath his weight, and suddenly thrust with an animalistic grunt, sinking deep inside her.

'Ooohhhh!' she shrieked. He entered her quickly and deeply with his first incisive thrust, penetrating her tight virginal channel and pushing through to where no man had ever gone before.

I pierced her defence with the force of my first thrust, and with deliberate intent I broke her virgin seal, tearing it like rice paper. She sobbed, her eyes screwed tight and her fingers fiercely clutching the cushion on either side of her head.

'Ooohhhh,' Athena cried beneath him, in pain and pleasure both. Then she shuddered and held onto him tightly, but another part of her told her to relax, that it was time and that everything was exactly as it should be, as it was going to be and as it was meant to be.

I couldn't help but groan with undiluted pleasure. Athena's virgin channel was tight – tighter even than Nicki's. I began to fuck her as she lay beneath me, then suddenly felt myself tighten, knowing it was all about time. Repeatedly I buried my erection deep inside her but managed to hold back each time; never believing it could be so incredibly marvellous; so tight, so sensual, so satisfying, and so final. I began to fuck her faster and faster, deeper and deeper, savouring the feel of her, reaching for the stars in my own mind while she lay, inert and inexperienced beneath my heaving body.

Her breathing began to deepen and turn to ragged pants. She was lost and she knew it, but she didn't care. Her gasps became moans of pleasure.

I was immersed in her tight liquid channel. My groin slapped against her tight Greek slit. I shifted my grip and held her ass in the palms of my hands, almost fully off the chair. My moment was rapidly approaching. But I didn't want it to; I wanted to enjoy this innocent beauty for a while longer yet, so I pulled back and gritted my teeth.

Athena cried out with the sheer depth of that which was impaling her like a rapturous battering ram. It was only a matter of time, she sensed, until her pleasure would explode into the skies. Her eyes opened. She saw nothing but him and bliss, receiving him, guiding him, helping him, and urging him faster and deeper. Her nails raked his tensed arms as he rutted against her.

'Oh, *Jesus*...' I groaned deeply, and my dam burst, emptying its boiling seed deep within her writhing Greek centre, anointing her there, that virginal part of her that had yielded and received me so wondrously.

'Oh, *yes*,' I cried out again with a deep groan, while my body emptied for several long seconds. Then I let go completely in a seizure of relief and fell upon her bodily, gripping her, holding her, my thrusting now involuntary and in the hands of the gods. Her knees slumped to the sides; her legs sprawled on either side of me.

Athena sighed, sensing something happening deep inside her physical sensory awareness. It was happening. Oh yes, it was happening. She cried, quickly thrusting herself to the brink and hovering there, tipping with each and every thrust, yet somehow not falling over the precipice of pleasure as if she were somehow being held there, not being allowed to fall just yet.

'Oh, please...' she whispered, and then her senses swam and her mind spun as she felt him move again, and again, inside her, languidly now after his intense crisis, but moving nonetheless. He was still erect and able to reach deep, filling her gloriously, fucking her again... and then it happened.

'Ooohhhnnnnnnn,' she cried as her mind suddenly burst, erupting in a special song of extreme rapture and bliss, in unison with her body. Sensations of an utterly glorious nature exploded.

'Ohhhhhhhhh,' she cried from her soul. Her body and mind swam into a deep dark river that felt warm and safe. Then suddenly it was very quiet. Her awareness returned gradually. His resting weight was not unpleasant. His smell was wonderful. She sighed deeply, happy and content, careful not to move lest she disturb his peace. And then she sighed deeply and closed her eyes.

I felt her breathing deepen and her body go limp beneath me, except for the gentle rising and falling of her breasts. Raising myself on my elbows, gazing down at her in admiration, I was in awe for the wonderful Greek virgin she had once been for me. Then I smiled.

Slowly I withdrew from between her tight sheath and stood again, gazing down at her resting naked beauty. Collecting my thoughts, I spoke to her.

'We're finished,' I said firmly. 'You've done well and should be proud of helping yourself keep your life in balance. I'm sure your thinking woman knows her rightful place now.

'From this moment onward, as a natural female you'll feel more comfortable around me and want to be near me more often. You'll daydream about what it would be like if we were always together, and you'll be happy to share what you have with those you love. Go to the bathroom and clean yourself, then return and get dressed and sit. You've done very well.'

Athena had opened her eyes when he first spoke. 'Yes,' she said slowly, without thinking. She had heard and then felt the command, clearly from deep within herself. She sat upright, knowing what had happened, that she had lost her virginity, that he had taken it and she had let him, had wanted and needed him to. She had done her part and had no regrets. It was time to go. All would be well again now. She was happy. She had done well. He had said so.

I watched her sit up slowly, wearily, then rise and walk through to the bathroom. The toilet flushed and within minutes she was back. She dressed quickly, her eyes focussed as she put on the last of her clothing. Then she sat opposite me again and looked down at the carpet.

'I will call you and you will come,' I instructed her firmly. 'Unless I want you sooner.'

'Yes,' came the instant reply, and Athena knew she would. Her pussy and her backside throbbed.

'Or you will call me as a feeling female when you feel the need.'

'Yes,' Athena heard herself say, knowing she didn't want to leave. She felt drained.

I watched her blink several times and then slowly she raised her head. Her gaze focused directly upon my face. I smiled at her and spoke again. 'It was time,' I said firmly, the moment of truth having arrived, 'for you to grow as a natural female and put your thinking woman into second place.'

'Yes,' Athena answered without thinking. She looked back at him. 'I know that now.' And she did. She had lost her virginity, given it to him, allowed him to take it from her, painfully and wonderfully, but she had no regrets. And he had punished her woman for bringing her so much unhappiness because she had allowed it to happen. She would never again be the woman she used to be. She no longer wanted to be. She would be female from now on. For him, she would always be a natural female.

'Who am I?' I asked, hopeful.

'My Master,' came the words to Athena's lips, as she lowered her gaze to the carpet and wondered why she felt good about saying them. Then she thought of Nicki and that velvet collar, and she smiled.

'Good,' I said, relieved. I rose from my chair, watching her rise with me. Then I led her to the door and ushered her out without another word, but inside my male mind was speaking volumes of the future I would have with her.

Athena smiled quietly and confidently to herself as she walked from the front door of his house. She wondered if he was going to give her a collar too.

Chapter Sixteen

The following morning Appolonia, angry and there on a mission, sat across from Mr Davis. She half-smiled, politely, calmly, but inside her heart pounded. He had agreed to see her from her earlier phone call and now she was there, looking at him. Athena had told her he was helping with her problems.

She was nervous, but determined to get to the reason why her twin sister had come home with a red bottom. Athena had tried to hide it, but Appolonia walked into the bathroom to get some of her things, saw her twin sister's poor rear, and was shocked speechless.

Appolonia knew nothing of Mr Davis other than from a visit or two, and that he was the husband of her mother's friend. But there was something, she noticed, as she sat there, waiting for him to answer her question; a feeling, and a sensing she just did not understand. But she made the thought go away, needing to concentrate. She needed to keep her mind on things.

Appolonia was the eldest sister, only by an hour, but she was the eldest and she felt responsible, but she was also frustrated as well, with many things. She wanted a known relationship with her boyfriend; her mother didn't know she had one. She didn't love him, but it was better than having no one. He had recently touched her intimately for the first time, but she stopped him before they went too far.

'Nothing that she didn't want, didn't agree to, and had needed for a long time,' I finally answered her, having allowed a little time for some mild intimidation. I could see that Appolonia was nervous, and I could also see that she was probably more determined in nature than either Athena or Nicki. I decided not to do what she would be expecting me to do – defend myself. I couldn't believe my luck at unknowingly having created the opportunity to begin work on her welcoming to the fold.

'What?' Appolonia gasped, becoming angrier; he didn't even show remorse for his actions. 'She agreed?' She held his penetrating stare, wanting him to see she was suspicious of him. But she felt intimidated, and didn't like it one bit.

'Yes,' I said casually, 'she did.' I was just staring impassively at her, allowing her to lead the conversation wherever she wanted it to go.

Appolonia began to feel strange. She found she could not look at him for lengthy periods, even though she wanted to stare him down, just to let him know she wasn't to be taken lightly. His eyes bothered her, but she didn't know why. They were strong and captured her completely each time she gazed into them. She did not know whether to feel suspicious of him looking at her that way, or just wait and see what happened next.

'I don't believe you,' she said. Her own voice sounded strangely different to her ears, not as confident as she'd wanted it to sound. She wanted to stay angry, but her mind seemed to be floating at times, as if trying to get away from his gaze. She did not like the feeling of the loss of control she was beginning to associate with looking at him. It was as if his gaze was somehow drawing away her will to stay angry.

She put her awareness into alert mode, fighting to do it. She tried to prepare herself to retain control of the conversation. He was not going to get away with hurting her sister like that. She just couldn't believe how casual he was sounding about the whole thing.

'I don't care what you believe,' I told her quietly, but sincerely, and I didn't. I knew the trouble she could cause, but somehow I didn't think she would.

'You don't care?' It angered her that he was so indifferent in his attitude and answers.

'Are you jealous?' I asked suddenly, wondering where that question came from.

'Jealous?' Appolonia gasped, shocked by his question as well as the flush that immediately bathed her mind and body. It drove her thoughts further away from her anger. A part of her felt far away, her sense of control of the situation drifting with it.

'Yes, jealous, but too embarrassed to admit it, even to yourself,' I provoked.

'Too embarrassed to…?' Appolonia could not believe what he was saying. She felt extremely flustered, and then blushed.

I saw my last beautiful Greek virgin blushing, and knew I had her measure. Women always blush when they realise they've lost complete control of their mind or body, or someone has discovered a truth about them; a sexual side effect of feeling controlled or helpless. Women are women and females are natural females. I smiled to myself, mentally preparing for the next phase of her eventual submission.

'Even now your woman's mind is thinking thoughts of a sexual nature,' I stated confidently, but casually, as if talking about the weather.

'I beg your pardon?' Appolonia was shocked to the core at the way he was speaking to her and what he was saying. Her mouth was dry, and for some reason, bizarrely, she suddenly imagined his hand caressing her thigh, feeding the fire in the pit of her stomach. She imagined his hand moving, spanking her like he'd done to her sister, feeling his arm holding her in a captive embrace, his voice even more persuasive than his deep gaze. She was agitated, her heart pounding. She wanted to stop imagining such things, to be angry for what he'd done to Athena, but she couldn't.

'Jealousy of your sister's natural female happiness isn't a crime,' I said.

'What?' Appolonia gasped incredulously. 'I'm not jealous of Athena.' She felt hotter than ever, light-headed, the air-conditioning cooling the anxious sheen of her thought's effects on her forehead. Her hand moved to rest on her knee. She squeezed it and drew breath instantly when her thighs pinched together, and a chill passed over her body as the slow fire between her legs began to seethe in earnest.

I left my incensed Greek virgin alone to her thoughts, knowing she was deepening her anger as well as her own trap with every thought she was having. Then I spoke.

'Everything I said and did was for her own good, just as she wanted me to,' I stated. 'She came to me for help with a confidence problem.'

Appolonia listened to his voice through her angry mind and sensual thoughts. He was right, she admitted; Athena had been having trouble in that area lately, and couldn't seem to do anything about it on her own. 'That doesn't give you the right to punish her,' she argued, finally giving him some curry of her real thoughts. She was intimidated by the authoritative tone in his voice, but recognising it was there angered her even more. She wasn't quite sure what to do, so she didn't look at him directly for a few seconds. She had been trying to stare him down, but it was a futile gesture. There was something about his eyes.

They were compelling. And then suddenly, for no reason she could fathom, she imagined leaning forward and kissing him. Her traitorous heart picked up its beat the instant the image came to mind. What was wrong with her?

'I didn't punish her,' I said patiently, as if explaining myself to a child.

Appolonia hated being patronised. 'Don't talk to me like that,' she snapped, imagining herself kneeling between his parted thighs and undressing him. She shook her head a little to clear the disturbing images, and mentally pulled off his shoes, then reached up and unbuckled his belt, undid his trousers, then lowered them down his legs and off.

Her trembling hands found his underpants, stretched obscenely at the front, and they too were removed and discarded. She then undid the buttons of her dress, letting it fall to the floor. Her lacy underwear disappeared next, until in her mind's eye and imagination she was naked and completely without shame or guilt about what she was doing, as she leaned forward and took him deeply into her mouth and throat.

'I'll talk to you any way I like,' I told her firmly. 'Besides, you like me talking to you like that. It makes you feel good. That's why you want to be happy like your sister is now.'

The sound of his voice snapped her out of her unwanted daydreaming, but she'd only heard the last part of his sentence.

'What?' she said, angry with herself now. 'Are you kidding? Are you crazy, or what?'

'You want to experience what your sister experienced, and you're jealous and angry because you don't quite know how to go about doing that,' I said calmly, as if we were merely passing the morning with polite conversation. 'It's not a crime to want to be spanked.'

'What?' Appolonia was incredulous. What kind of a man was he? Her buttocks clenched tightly as her knees pressed firmly together. She was livid at him and at herself, but in her head she heard his deep grunt of pleasure as she took him orally, and she was happy.

Then she shook her head again and quickly collected her thoughts as well as her anger, not understanding her imagination's behaviour. 'I don't know what your game is, Mr Davis,' she said, trying to remain calm. 'And I don't know why you're speaking to me like this. But if you think you're going to get away with spanking my sister, you've got another think coming.'

I said nothing, but I could see she was imagining plenty, getting increasingly agitated by her lurid thoughts and my indifference to her.

'Oh, how dare you try to intimidate me?' she suddenly blurted, finding any silence between us impossible to deal with. 'How dare you spank my sister, and how dare you tell me I'm jealous of her being spanked? How dare you?'

'Because I can.' I smiled easily, and paused. 'And because you need me to spank you so you can be happy too, like Athena,' I eventually concluded.

Appolonia shook her head in bewilderment. 'No, I don't,' she insisted, rising indignantly to her feet. It was too much. He was too much. 'I don't need you to make me happy,' she told him. 'I don't need you for anything. I don't need *anybody* for anything!'

'So who else is going to love you?' I said, as amazed at the words as she was.

'What?' Appolonia exploded angrily. 'How dare you speak to me like that?'

She stood glowering at me. I was about to tread a

dangerous path, I could feel it coming, but I couldn't stop.

'Who, Appolonia?' I provoked, pushing her to the limit. 'Who is going to love you?'

Her eyes blazed and her breasts rose and fell as she breathed rapid and shallow breaths, then she drew back her hand and swung down with real venom at his head. He instinctively ducked a little to the side, but managed to parry the blow and at the same time rather fortuitously grab the hand that was intent on assailing him. In an instant she was toppling off balance as he tugged, and with a squeal she tumbled on top of him.

She squealed again at the force of her fall. Immediately she tried to get up, but found she could barely move. Quickly he'd pinned her arms by her sides as she sprawled on top of him, breathing in his male smell as she gasped and struggled. Then he moved beneath her and the chair reclined, so that she found herself lying fully on top of him, an unmistakable lump pressing solidly into her lower tummy. She was mortified.

I couldn't have planned it better myself and I smiled a self-congratulatory smile, while holding her arms pinned to her sides. I could have planned it worse, but I couldn't have planned it better. She struggled admirably, but I remained in total control. My third beautiful Greek virgin had just fallen right into my lap, literally. Quickly shifting my hold on her upper arms to her wrists, I moved both hands behind her back and up a little, pressing them against her lower back, in the graceful dip just above her delightful bottom. I then gripped her crossed wrists in one hand and grabbed a handful of her lustrous black hair with the other, and pulled firmly, lifting her face from my shoulder. She tried to free her wrists but my strength was too much. I simply gripped them even more tightly in my fist, making her groan and wince.

Appolonia tried wriggling free and kicking her legs, but he adroitly wrapped his own thighs around hers, preventing her from doing anything much more than lie there on top of him, in his embrace, breathing heavily from the intense but brief activity. The undeniable lump ground against her lower belly each time she tried to move, persuading her to yield and remain still.

'Let me up,' she said quietly. 'Please, let me up. Let go of me.' But he didn't. Instead he pulled her head up even more, gazing appreciatively at the smooth skin of her throat.

The script now discarded because of her unanticipated reactions, I began acting from instinct alone. Her throat looked so smooth and delicious I couldn't resist, so I raised my face and kissed her there. She was warm to my lips, and I could feel her racing pulse as I sucked deeply on her fragrant flesh. She tried to say something and struggled anew, but it was a weary attempt to break free of my clutches. I sucked her throat, gently drawing my lips up under her chin, then kissing repeatedly just below her ear as my grip in her silky hair held her just as I wanted her. Again I heard a pitiful gasp and again she renewed her struggles, but I easily held her, my legs around hers and one hand pinning her crossed wrists together in the small of her back.

I worked my lips back to her chin, slowly following her sculptured jaw-line with feathery kisses and soft murmurs of reassurance. Her lips were full and moist and pouting, and slightly parted from her exertions. I had a date with my destiny, and my last Greek virgin was it. So moving decisively, I acted with deliberate intent.

Appolonia was confused and tired... and she was aroused. The persistent lump, impossible to ignore, moved against her if she moved. He was kissing her throat and ears, and he was quietly talking to her, comforting and encouraging...

Appolonia whimpered as the fingers entwined in her hair tightened and his lips swooped to smother hers, his tongue trying to force its way inside her mouth. She sealed her lips tightly shut, but immediately felt his fingers tighten even more in her hair. The pull on her roots was excruciating and made her squeal, and the instant she did his tongue breached her valiant defence and invaded her mouth, duelling with hers.

I reached hungrily into her, feeding on her futile struggles, kissing her deeply and possessively. She would not miss her own date with destiny, and she would not miss her date with me.

Appolonia gasped into his throat, inhaling his male scent and rapidly becoming breathless. Tears stung her eyes as his insistent tongue explored and defeated her.

Her mouth tasted sweet and fresh, as was her breath. As I kissed her soft lips I could sense a weakening in her, and congratulated myself as her tongue responded tentatively to mine, confirming what my instincts were telling me, and then I felt her tummy pressing down, just a little, on the acute swelling trapped inside my trousers. It was a supreme moment in my life.

Appolonia began to feel faint, not even realising the slight movement of her hips or the import of the message it transmitted. And then the kiss ended and he released her hair. She rested her forehead on his shoulder, and he gently stroked the soft down at her temple as she lay quietly, waiting for whatever was to come.

The chair straightened up again and with apparent ease he manoeuvred her listless form, so that she found herself facedown across his lap with her wrists pinned behind

205

her back once more. Her flushed cheek rested on the arm of his capacious chair, her toes touched the carpet on the other side of his legs, and still that lump pressed perniciously into her tummy while she breathed slowly through slightly parted lips, her eyes closed. She felt drained and defeated, yet stimulated and aroused.

I held her firmly, gazing down at the tautness of her dress, pulled over her mouth-watering bottom. Then I smiled and just sat there for several minutes, slowly regaining my breath. Any last struggles had long since passed, and it was worth it, I thought. She was worth it. They were worth it, all three of them, and we were worth it. I smiled again, lifted my hand, paused, savouring the moment, then swung it hard down to impact on the soft firmness of her glorious Greek virgin rump. There was no challenge like no challenge.

'Ow!' I heard her shriek.

'This is what you want,' I said decisively, repeatedly sweeping my open palm down across her delicious buttocks, quivering within the dress beneath each fresh impact, 'don't you.'

'No,' Appolonia cried. 'Please stop. Let me up!' But he ignored her and continued to spank her with a remorseless rhythm. The tears of utter humiliation spilled from her eyes, but she wasn't crying. Again and again his hand landed heavily on her bottom, and again and again she shrieked as it did, each smack seeming harder than the last.

Upon reaching twenty I stopped and rested my hand on her thigh, caressing it idly. She tensed, expecting another volley that never arrived. I heard her sigh. She wasn't crying, but I knew I had only just begun.

Appolonia's backside burned excruciatingly. Her heart raced and her pulse thrummed in her temples. She was relieved it was over and breathed deeply, fighting to suppress the tears of humiliation at being placed over his knee and smacked like a naughty child. Her mind and body flooded with new and strange sensations, and she wondered if Athena had experienced the same confusing feelings.

Then she cried out as her bottom exploded again beneath the impact of his cruel palm. 'This is what you want, but didn't have the courage to ask for, isn't it?' I demanded forcefully, repeatedly and steadily sweeping my hand down to scald the delicious Greek buttocks that lay hidden – for the moment – within the relative safety of her dress. In normal circumstances the hem reached halfway down her slender thighs, but in her sprawled position across my lap it had ridden higher and stretched tightly across her thighs, just a few inches beneath the smooth cheeks of her bottom. I changed the direction of my next few smacks then, and reddened her bare thighs above her knees, upward to the tight hem of the dress.

'Nooo!' Appolonia shrieked as he smacked the back of her thighs. She was nearing her limit and she knew it. She sobbed deeply between spanks. Her bottom blazed and the back of her legs stung. Then he was smacking her bottom again, several more times, and then he stopped. She groaned, her heart racing, not believing what was happening to her.

Her arms ached, still pinned behind her back, and the lump was still there, pressing up into her tummy, and she shook her head on the armrest in weary denial as she felt his fingers working the hem of her dress higher up her thighs. 'No,' she mumbled weakly, but he kept on tugging and easing on both sides until she felt him get it up over her sore buttocks to her lower back. She burned with shame, the humiliation of it all almost too much.

Devouring the wonderful site before me, laid out on my lap, I slowly raised my right hand, my left still holding her wrists, and smacked over the sexy white cotton panties that encased her lovely Greek bottom. She shrieked, struggling again, but I held her exactly where I wanted her. Again and again I smacked her backside, every luscious inch. She cursed me, making me smile through gritted teeth, but by the time I'd counted twenty and stopped to rest my palm on her punished cheeks, she was sobbing passively.

My erection strengthened beneath her feminine weight as I pulled her white cotton panties tightly between the glowing cheeks of her bottom, like a thong, and she sighed instinctively as I gently caressed her punished flesh. She gasped between sobs, not sure whether to expect more pain or just relax and enjoy its absence. She sighed and sniffed, and eventually calmed and laid still across my lap, accepting the healing touch of my hand as it soothed her scorched flesh. Then I stopped moving my hand altogether and just let it rest lightly and possessively across the centre of her superb bottom.

Appolonia sighed deeply and shuddered on his lap. No tears now, no pain, and no soothing hand – just nothing. She felt drained, physically and emotionally, but she also felt good, somehow, as if a great load had been lifted from her shoulders. She pondered that feeling as she lay there across his lap, no longer noticing the lump pressed into her tummy, accepting its living presence as if it had always been there. She lifted her head for a moment, and then settled her damp cheek down again on the armrest of the chair.

'That's what you wanted,' I said quietly, after a while, after a peaceful silence. 'Wasn't it?'

Appolonia didn't answer right away, but eventually said,

'No.' There was no anger or resentment in the word, just a statement of fact.

'That's what you needed,' I said. 'Wasn't it?'

'No,' Appolonia eventually replied, for the moment enjoying an unusual freedom from everything and everyone.

'You feel better now, don't you?'

'No,' she lied, not caring.

'Be honest enough, as a natural female, to tell the truth for once,' I said, but Appolonia simply lay there, the occasional sniff the only thing breaking the comfortable silence that settled between us.

'But you do feel better for having just been spanked, don't you?' I pressed quietly.

Appolonia thought about that for a few minutes. She did feel better. She felt free, for some reason, but she wasn't sure what she felt free of, or from. Her mind felt light. She knew she hadn't cried like that since a child, and even then she couldn't remember crying in the same heartfelt way. 'Yes,' she finally said, knowing it to be true. The spanking had caused her to break and cry her heart out, so she figured it was the spanking that had caused her to feel better.

I smiled and affectionately squeezed her buttocks as a reward for her honesty.

'Oh,' Appolonia gasped softly. And then she gave in and relaxed fully, despite the presence of the lump pressing up into her stomach.

'Ooh,' she sighed, barely a whisper, then feeling absolutely drained of energy she closed her eyes, resting in the deep peace and warmth of her buttocks as her thoughts began to wander.

I sat watching Appolonia's angelic expression for a while, and so engrossed in her pure beauty I completely lost track of time. I'd been thinking about Nicki and Athena, and the life with Lauren I no longer wanted. I thought Appolonia must have dozed off beneath the soothing of my stroking hand over her reddened bottom, and wondered if I would have to content myself with only two beautiful Greek virgins after all.

Appolonia sighed. She'd surprised herself by drifting off for a few seconds, and had imagined images that disturbed her now as they ran fresh in her resurfacing mind. She had to leave. It wasn't safe for her to remain there, to remain on his lap with his hand caressing her bare bottom. And it wasn't necessarily him; she didn't completely trust herself.

I was beginning to have second thoughts about my grand plan, as alluring as it was to me. It was simply the ethics of it all, given Appolonia's negative response to her spanking. It should have been different, I figured. I felt a little disheartened, but I had never known such wondrous and natural happiness as a dominant male. With a feeling of acceptance almost akin to defeat, I released her wrists from behind her back and gently moved her arms down beside her, and then lifted her shoulders until she sat sideways, squeezed beside me on my chair.

Slowly then, without a word, she stood up. I steadied her by holding her hip with one hand, staring at the deep white V of the white cotton panties I'd turned into a thong at the back. With an ease of movement she adjusted her underwear, and her dress whispered enticingly as it fell smoothly back into place around her mid-thighs, and then she surprised me by turning and walking proudly to the kitchen, surprising me again a few moments later when she returned carrying two cold drinks.

She handed me one, before sitting opposite in the large chair. I glanced at her grip on the glass, noticing the toned sinews in her tanned arm, flexing as she lifted the refreshing drink to her lips to sip.

I looked at her face. It seemed relaxed and calm, but her eyes were wide. She was staring at me without blinking. I waited and raised my eyebrows. She didn't respond or move in any way, so I rose and stepped closer to her. Her eyes widened, but she didn't move, didn't speak, just sat staring up at me in a strange way. I laid a hand on her shoulder, but she didn't respond to my touch in any way. I squeezed her shoulder.

'What's wrong?' I asked, but again she did not respond. 'Waiting for an apology?' Then I reached down and took the iced drink from her fingers, and placed it on the small table. I placed my own glass there as well.

Appolonia was uncertain, and gazed up at him, wondering what was going on and what was wrong with her. She had not been expecting him to let her up, let alone leave. Perhaps he didn't want her, and with that thought she was shocked to be immediately swamped with feelings of rejection that hurt her deeply. She wanted to leave, but she didn't want to leave. She didn't know what she wanted or needed right then, and felt confused by such intense, conflicting emotions.

Her mind clouded as if a fog had settled over her. Her thoughts stopped. She heard nothing, saw nothing, felt nothing, and feared nothing. Then, just as suddenly, the fog cleared. She felt as though she'd awoken from a deep and refreshing sleep. She felt different somehow, then instantly came to life beneath his grip on her shoulder. She looked up at him. She looked around the room, then back at him.

'Share a thought,' I said, getting nowhere with my own. I looked down at my hand and slowly withdrew it from her shoulder, then took a step backwards, wondering just what the hell was going on. I was puzzled by her reaction and behaviour. It had been a stupid plan, I realised, cursing my greed. To seduce one beautiful sister had been beyond my wildest dreams; two was incredible. I should have stuck there, not pushed my luck.

'I have to be somewhere, and I'm late already,' Appolonia said flatly.

'Stay where you are,' I ordered on nothing but an impulse, my heart hammering in my chest. I was commanding her. She had been about to rise from the chair but she froze, and then settled back down, her fingers clutching the armrests tightly, I noticed. Her clear eyes stared up at me, mouth slightly open, but she said nothing, did nothing. I just stood there, not knowing exactly what was going on with her, but not willing to touch her again.

I waited and watched the gorgeous Greek virgin for many minutes, in silence. She could have got up and left at any time, but she didn't. She just sat and looked up at me with wide, clear eyes. My work with her sisters had seen me develop immense patience, but after more than five minutes she still had not moved, or uttered a single word.

Appolonia had never felt so strange in all her life. Drawing a deep breath she desperately tried to figure out what was going on with her, and in the still silence she then noticed the look in his eyes.

She wanted to go, but she wanted to stay. She wanted him to make her stay, and in realising that fact she made up her mind to leave. So gathering herself she rose and looked at him squarely. She could not believe the day's events, or her reaction to them. Her bottom throbbed warmly, comfortingly.

'Don't ever do anything like that again, Mr Davis,' Appolonia said quietly but firmly. 'I think maybe you want to make a move on me, and maybe on Athena or Nicki too. But don't, okay? You're much older than us, and you're my mother's friend's husband.'

I gazed at her clear face, marvelling at her youthful beauty. Despite the harsh words, her eyes were warm and questioning. Then, without thinking of any possible consequences, I moved even closer. My fingers slowly lifted to her shoulder and rested there again, our eyes locked. I watched her closely. As my fingers touched her shoulder her expression seemed to relax and soften.

Appolonia sighed, feeling the heavy cloud of emotional confusion settle back upon her. She didn't want to go and she didn't want to stay, but he was letting her go. He had spanked her and hurt her, and then he had soothed her. But now he was letting her go. She couldn't think, couldn't concentrate, but remained gazing at him, waiting for him to answer some unasked question. She felt very tense, in a strange world she'd never visited before.

I waited, but she didn't move or say anything. Her gaze never left my face. It was the strangest situation I think I had ever been in. I stared at her eyes. The glazed look was back; as if she were somewhere else or deep inside her own thoughts. I reached up with my other hand and lightly touched her cheek, my eyes never leaving her face. Then suddenly I sensed that strange look leaving, as if it was another part of her mind somewhere. I withdrew my touch and waited.

Appolonia wondered why she felt so good. She had felt tired and sore when first getting up from his lap, but now it was time to go, so she moved away from him towards the front door.

'Stop,' I said, and watched as Appolonia stopped, her back to me, her arms loose by her sides. She did not turn to face me, so I moved closer and stood behind her, savouring the shapely curves of her bottom, savouring the fresh scent of her flesh and her hair.

I moved around to her front, her eyes looking directly ahead, at the buttons on my shirt, her breathing slow and completely relaxed, and I leaned closer and kissed her slightly parted lips.

'Oh,' Appolonia sighed into his mouth. It was a gentle kiss, a tender kiss. Her breathing and pulse immediately increased, and confused, she stepped back away from him and gazed into his eyes. But he moved smoothly and leaned close again, this time allowing his tongue to gently force its way inside her mouth. He touched her tongue with his, which induced an immediate and instinctive gasp as she remained absolutely still, unsure of what was happening or what to do.

The kiss ended, and she felt a little breathless. He was studying her face intently, and she just couldn't decipher her conflicting emotions of rejection and attraction for him, to him, and by him.

After a few more minutes of silence between us I took a step to the side. Appolonia's gaze didn't move, but now focussed towards the front door, the view again unobstructed by me or the buttons on my shirt. Then I waited.

After a minute or two she walked to the door, without giving me another glance, opened it, then closed it behind her and was gone.

For a long while I stared at the finality of the closed door, then slumped down in my chair, having to adjust my position to ease the stiffness in my trousers that was now an irritating distraction, feeling sad at the thought of only possessing two beautiful Greek virgins.

Chapter Seventeen

On Monday morning Lauren again left before I awoke. She had taken to sleeping in one of the other rooms, and that was fine with me. Nevertheless, I felt optimistic and positive. I had the feeling that something was building. I wasn't sure what, but I sensed it. I had been typing for only about fifteen minutes, when the doorbell rang.

My heart picked up the pace a little as I walked to the door. It was Appolonia, as I sensed it would be, wearing jeans and a pretty pink short-sleeved shirt. As usual she wore no make-up – like her sisters, she didn't need it – and her long black hair shone healthily, caressing her shoulders like a shining dark waterfall.

I gazed at the girl, speechless; such was her radiant beauty at nine o'clock on a Monday morning. I smiled, really happy to see her, and an uncertain, fleeting smile was returned. Then she lowered her eyes as I invited her in and closed the door, her arm brushing mine as she passed. She stood awkwardly for a moment, looking down at her neat feet, and then silently accepted my unspoken invitation to sit in the same chair she had on her last visit.

'Would you like something to drink?' I asked.

'No, thank you,' she answered politely, without looking up at him. She had hardly slept at all since previously leaving the house. And what sleep she'd had was troubled, giving her little quality rest with which to face each subsequent day. She looked at her hands, resting together in her lap, wondering if she was making a big mistake, wondering what she was doing there. Her courage was failing her rapidly, and she knew it. Another few minutes would be all she could take before running from the house, humiliated in the worst possible way, never to return. Feeling silly for just sitting there, gazing dumbly down at her lap, she at last took a deep breath and raised her face, looking up into his dancing male eyes, which caused her little remaining resolve to dissolve even more rapidly. She wished she'd never come, and couldn't remember why she had.

'How is Athena?' I asked.

'She's fine,' Appolonia replied quietly.

'How is Nicki?'

'She's always fine.'

'And how are you…?'

Appolonia hesitated. She lowered her gaze and stared at her lap, wishing she hadn't come. 'I'm fine,' she eventually whispered.

I knew. One look into her eyes, and I knew. In fact, my heart knew before my head did. I hadn't known it before, but I did then. And that which I thought I'd figured out regarding her previous behaviour, had been wrong. I marvelled at the myriad lessons I had yet to learn as a practicing male. Now all I had to do was figure out exactly how to satisfy her quest and reason for being there.

'Why are you here?' I asked frankly, testing her female's mettle for what lay ahead.

Appolonia lifted her gaze, feeling the tears instantly. She shouldn't have come. She knew that now. She felt hot and bothered and blushed again. The embarrassment and humiliation that swamped her was something she did not think she could endure, or want to endure. She thought she'd worked it all out, but she hadn't. She should have known better. 'I'm sorry…' she whispered, standing, 'I shouldn't have come—'

'You're weak,' I said, cutting her off, and she said no more, did no more, just stood before me, head bowed, staring down at her feet.

'Look at me,' I said. 'Look at me.'

Appolonia raised her face, her eyes wide, shimmering with unshed tears. She should never have come.

'Can't you find the courage to tell me what you've come here for, what you *want?*' I pressed. 'What you *really* want from me, as a female?'

Appolonia felt the sheer weight of his words upon her, and the shame was hard to endure. She would leave, and this time there would be no turning back. She shouldn't have come.

'Appolonia…' I urged her to have the courage to ask for what she wanted from me.

Appolonia froze and stared straight ahead through her tears. She wasn't weak; she was strong, she had courage. She just wasn't feeling very courageous at that moment, that's all. She had been when she'd left home, but she wasn't now. Now she just wanted to curl up and hide.

I placed both hands gently on her shoulders, and squeezed reassuringly. 'Isn't your happiness worth anything to you?' I asked, intentionally loading the question.

The tears began to meander freely down her cheeks, but Appolonia made no response. There was nothing to say, and she held his stare as his hands moved from her shoulders, and sank slowly, together, down to hover lightly against her tummy, his knuckles just brushing against her pink shirt and the waistband of her jeans.

'Oh,' she gasped, but his strong male gaze held her. Her pulse raced.

'I'll take what you want to give me,' I said resolutely, undoing the single button on her jeans with a finger and

217

thumb. 'What you need to give me.'

'Oh,' Appolonia gasped, 'don't.' She tried to back away, but the hands at her opened waistband held her easily in place in front of him.

'And you want me to take it, don't you.' It was intentionally a statement, not a question.

'Oh, um,' Appolonia mumbled, confused, but he held her and lowered the zipper of her jeans with a finger and thumb. Then she froze as he slipped his hands inside the opened jeans, his palms against her hips, and began to ease the tight blue denim down.

Appolonia shook her head a little, meandering tears glistening on her cheeks. 'You shouldn't be doing that,' she whispered, looking searchingly into my eyes. 'Really, you shouldn't…'

'But this is what you want,' I stated flatly, bending very slightly to ease her jeans over the delicious curves of her bottom and down to her thighs.

'Really, you shouldn't…' Appolonia murmured, with little conviction.

'But you want me to,' I told her.

The air felt cool on Appolonia's upper thighs. She glanced quickly down, and then back up to his dancing eyes. The triangle of her white panties was now visible between her thighs, just beneath the hem of her pink shirt, and her jeans were almost down to her knees, pinning her legs together, making her dependant upon him for her balance. Feeling insecure she held his upper arms for support.

'You do want me to, don't you,' I stated, my fingers brushing her thighs, barely enough for her to feel, but enough for there to be no mistaking their presence. 'It's what you came here for.'

'No, it isn't, please,' she said softly, shaking her head,

her wide eyes shimmering. And then she gasped sweetly and instinctively nibbled her lower lip as my fingers slipped between her trapped thighs, and my knuckles grazed her virginity through her white cotton panties. 'Does that feel nice?' I gently asked, and she made no reply, just held my stare, uncertain of what else to do.

It was time to press on.

'Turn around,' I whispered, and watched victoriously as, without a physical or verbal objection, she meekly and quietly complied, as though in a dream. 'Give me your hands,' I ordered, and as she put them behind her back I crossed them and locked her wrists together in my fist. Then I held her close, her inert fingers trapped between us, pressed against the stiffening muscle within my trousers, and I kissed her neat ear, inhaling deeply the healthy fragrance of her hair. 'Okay, Appolonia?' I asked sincerely, and slipped my free arm around her front, embracing her securely, my bicep brushing her breast, my palm on the smooth warmth of her toned tummy, just beneath the hem of her pink shirt, my fingertips just touching the waist of her panties.

Appolonia's eyes closed and her head rested back against his shoulder as she felt his hand move down, slowly, inch by inch, until his fingers burrowed between her thighs, the edge of his thumb rubbing her virgin lips through her dampening panties. Strange sensations ran up and down her spine and she felt light-headed as his fingers moved back and forth, becoming gradually more and more insistent. Squeezing her thighs tightly together she went limp in his overwhelming embrace, but he held her easily.

I smiled and gave myself a mental congratulatory slap on the back. My hand was trapped between her lovely thighs and against the wet warmth I found there, seeping through her panties. She was turned on, of that there was no mistake. My beautiful Greek virgin was turned on, and this is what she'd come back for. I was close, and there'd be no stopping me now, so I pressed my forefinger against the damp cotton and a little way between her virgin lips, enticingly at the entrance to her tight, unexplored channel – her priceless treasure and my greatest find.

Appolonia gasped deeply, feeling his moving presence at the entrance to her warmth.

'I'm touching you,' I whispered into the tiny shell of her ear, circling her tight virgin rim. 'Just like you want me to.'

'No,' Appolonia mumbled, but felt her body yielding to his deepening touch, 'I don't, please.' But in her heart she knew she lied, and the seepage of her juices increased, just for him.

'Yes,' I said into her ear, forcing the tension from her thighs as I embraced her, feeling her soft breast against my arm, and her inert fingers trapped against the swelling in my trousers. 'You do, and you did before. You wanted me to take your virginity before, but you weren't ready to give it then. But now you are.'

'No,' Appolonia cried, but with little conviction, and then she relaxed her thighs, only for a moment and only a little, but it was enough. His persistent finger seized the moment and wormed inside the tight Greek virgin channel between them, taking damp white cotton with it, until his palm cupped her mound.

Hell, but she felt good, and cupping her sex I squeezed her back against me even more tightly, trapping her inert fingers even more so against the intense swelling in my trousers. I let go of her wrists, managed to extract my hand from between us, and wrapped my arm around her breasts, enabling me to hold her even more securely in my embrace.

'Oh…' she gasped deeply, her head resting limp against my shoulder, her knees beginning to weaken and tremble. 'No, don't…' she whispered weakly, no longer able to deny the sensations running up and down her spine and gripping deep in her stomach.   'Yes,' I said, feeling her succumbing by the second. I moved my finger in and out of her beautiful clutching depths, feeling it pass evenly over her hard virgin pleasure-jewel.

Appolonia gasped and languidly rolled her head from side to side on his shoulder. He was there, right there. She panted and her knees dipped slightly, but he held her easily.

'I want your Greek virginity,' I whispered into her ear, 'and you want me to take it, to have it, to possess it.' I was close, so close to my goal, and at that moment my erection flexed and pulsed between us, against her inert fingers, very nearly embarrassing me, very nearly causing me to deviate from my path, but I didn't. I took a deep breath and eased my groin away from her a fraction, just for a moment, until I was in full control again.

Appolonia moaned, rolling her head slowly from side to side on his shoulder, her eyes closed.

'You don't?' I goaded relentlessly. 'You don't want me to take your virginity? Then I was wrong. I thought that's why you came here this morning. But obviously I was wrong…'

Appolonia groaned desperately as the finger slipped from within her tightness, and then the hand was gone from between her thighs. It wasn't going to happen. She'd blown it at the last moment. Tears squeezed from her closed eyes and trailed down her hot cheeks.

Then his intense embrace eased and he pushed her forward a little. She almost stumbled, the jeans still around her knees and effectively binding her legs, but she managed

221

to steady herself, her mind in a spin, wondering what was going to happen to her.

'Go home, Appolonia,' I said decisively, knowing I didn't want her to, knowing she didn't want to. Her next move was crucial and I held my breath, hating the knowledge that there was little more I could do to claim my beautiful Greek virgin, that it was completely up to her now. I stood behind her, savouring her beauty, basking in the sight of her delicious bottom, imagining my red handprints there and wondering if beneath her white panties there was still some fading evidence of the spanking I'd given her.

Appolonia couldn't think, couldn't move, couldn't breathe, and was barely aware that her jeans were still down around her knees. He didn't want her – that's all that mattered. Then, slowly, she turned in a hesitant shuffling motion until she stood facing him, her hands at her sides. Raising her face, her watery eyes found his.

'Please…' she whispered, and that single heartfelt plea was the sweetest, most beautiful word I had ever heard in my life. I'd taken a huge gamble. I'd handed the ultimate decision back to her; relinquished control of the situation, and now, looking at that beautiful girl standing before me, I knew I was about to be rewarded.

And for one immeasurable moment in time our gaze's locked, while her female finally and honestly introduced herself to my male, and my male finally and fully understood her own. And in that timeless, special moment of utter female submissiveness, I smiled. She did too, carefully, hopefully. And right then and right there, I fell in love with my third Greek virgin, and she fell in love with me.

'Appolonia,' I said, quietly but firmly, 'take off your jeans, panties and shoes, but leave your shirt and socks on.' I was back in control, and she recognised that control, and it compelled and it incited her.

I was excited as she lowered her eyes and her face momentarily. She stepped out of her flat-heeled shoes then reached down to her knees. After pushing her jeans down to her ankles she stepped out of them too, as well as her white cotton underwear. Then she straightened up as a half-naked Greek virgin and looked at me, tearful and shy. Her arms hung loose by her sides, and she made no attempt whatsoever to cover her modesty.

Then she looked at me again, nervously.

'Come here, girl,' I ordered her quietly, and she immediately stepped slowly to me. Her pretty pink shirt only added to the teasingly sensual vision of her. She came to me and stood quietly, looking nervous and embarrassed. I pointed to the large lounge chair upon which she had previously sat, and spoke gently.

'Stand there and face it, holding the armrests,' I said firmly, pointing the way.

'Oh,' she gasped softly and lowered her gaze, then turned and moved slowly to the chair. She bent over it, placing her hands on the rests as instructed. I said and did nothing, except watch my third Greek virgin in her final waiting time. She stood naked from the waist down, her legs spread only slightly, bent over and waiting for the inevitable. The vertical valley of her creamy Grecian buttocks smiled at me in my earnest endeavours for the benefit of all. My body stirred aggressively in the direction of the two peach cheeks before it.

'Appolonia,' I said firmly, and then moved to where she stood leaning forward, but she didn't look back over her shoulder in my direction. I felt myself flex even further as I stood directly behind her mouth-wateringly submissive form, studying the smooth complexion of her

223

bare bottom, and the toned curves of her legs.

'Spread your feet a little,' I said from immediately behind her, hearing a soft gasp accompany the slow widening of her stance, first the left foot, then the right, and watched spellbound as the shadowy valley between her buttocks tightened a little with her movement. My hungry gaze veered into her nether depths, and I hardened even more.

'Wider,' I said, quietly gazing at the subtly striated corrugations of her nether necklace. Then I leaned over her from behind, inhaling deeply of her body's natural virginal perfume. Hardening further, my trousers tenting significantly and with my heart beating furiously, I reached forward and grabbed a handful of her thick dark hair, and gradually pulled back.

'Oh!' Appolonia cried.

I moved my other hand up between her thighs and grazed her lightly from behind.

'Oh!' Appolonia cried again when her body heat suffused with the touch of his palm, her breath quavering. She felt controlled as he touched her while holding her head firmly by the hair. Controlled, and it thrilled her deeply.

I slid my hand against the soft flesh in the tight gap between her inner thighs. Her skin felt cool compared to the warmth of her sex. Then I slid my fingers upward again, a little higher between her legs.

'Oh!' Appolonia gasped, feeling light-headed. She tried to lower her head, but the feather-touch on her moist lips by his brushing fingers caused her to accept the pain of being held exactly as he wanted her.

'Oh!' she gasped, straining against the hold on her head, her treacherous body responding to his touch. Gently his fingers explored the unique curves of her swollen lips and their softness.

'Oh!' she gasped again, and accepted him controlling

her.

I sighed deeply. Pure virgin oil greased my fingers as they passed through and forward, moving slowly upward to the lair of her secret sphinx.

'Oh!' Appolonia heard herself gasp, as if the sound had come from the lips of another. Then she gasped again and groaned disconcertedly as he gripped her hair even more firmly in his fist.

My groin ached as my fingers worked their way between her chaste folds, back and forth and from left to right. And then, in circular motions, I began to massage her oiling median with my thumb.

'Oh…' Appolonia softly gasped again, aware of her hips beginning to sink a little and gently rotate. They urged downward onto his fingers and she strained once more, dipping her back a little in search of some relief from the hand gripping her tightly by the hair. But there was none.

In the palm of my hand began to pool the untainted droplets of pure liquid from her first real virgin arousal. Gradually the gentle gyrations of her hips were becoming more and more urgent, as was I. My fingers slid and circled her slippery crease while my thumb disked the tight entrance to her virgin's private retreat. Then slowly, I slipped my thumb up into her virgin's tense shelter.

'Ohhh…' Appolonia gasped, shuddering, as he slowly reached inside her. Her heart stopped then started again, but at a much faster rate. She began to pant rapidly between parted, moist lips. She strained again as the sexual sensations flamed outward from between her legs to her breasts, now accepting the pain of his grip on her hair as simply a matter of fact.

Her undefiled quiver was liquid warm and definitely active. My thumb lay buried partly inside her slick tube. My fingers began to massage the kernel of her happiness and her moans swiftly became more and more compelling.

'Ooohhhh…' Appolonia moaned softly, sinking and gyrating against his hand and fingers. She strained against the intense pleasure, wanting the pain that went with it. They came as a package in her feeling mind, pain and pleasure, deeper pleasure and deeper pain, again and again until finally her body stiffened, her eyes closed, and a long-celibate groan of pleasure, pain and anguish erupted slowly and sensually from her parted lips.

'Nnnnnnnnno…' she groaned expressively and deeply while he held her, writhing and trembling, by her hair. Pain and rapture of the most intense kind crashed over her like huge surf at the beach. Her hips rocked uncontrollably for several seconds while the pain in her scalp balanced her emotional scales, and all the while he continued moving his thumb inside her fibrillating quiver, his fingers danced maddeningly over her vulva.

Finally, and with a shuddering sigh, she calmed and became still once again, leaning forward, her hands on the armrests, legs spread, breasts thrusting and her throat arched smoothly as her head was held back, panting deeply but hesitantly. Then she felt him release his tight grip on her hair.

'Ohhh,' she sighed, her head wearily dropping forward.

I removed my hand then lifted my fingers to my lips, first smelling her virginal aromatic musk, then tasting her first real blend with the tip of my tongue, smiling appreciatively as if I was about to sample the finest of wines from a very selective and special vineyard. I placed my glistening fingers into my mouth as if they held a delicacy unknown, and sipped that fermented virginal liquor.

'Stand up now and face me,' I ordered. My groin strained for release, and although desperately wanting to feed the gorgeous virgin the destined length where she stood leaning over the lounge chair, I did nothing more. Instead, using every ounce of self-discipline, I stepped back, and then watched her as she slowly straightened up.

She gazed ahead for many quiet seconds, before finally turning to look at me. I smiled as if something special had just happened. Her gaze was deep and dreamy, then she returned my smile shyly, acutely embarrassed at having just been masturbated by the hand of her mother's friend's husband.

Then I stepped close and scooped her up into my arms to carry her upstairs, determined that she would have her formal, ultimate, and irreversible deflowering in comfort and style upon the freshly made sheets on the bed of her master. Her face pressed tightly to my chest as she clung around my neck, all the way up the stairs, my feelings for her blossoming a little more with each step. For once the bed I slept in, the marital bed, would bear the weight of a couple in love.

I closed my eyes and suppressed a hiss of delight when Appolonia's wet lips and sweet warm breath caressed my bare skin, nuzzling my stomach and just, gingerly, kissing down to the first growths of my pubic hair. I sat on the edge of the bed while she knelt between my open knees, her breasts wedged softly between my thighs, my hands resting lightly on the back of her slowly bobbing head, guiding her whilst giving her the encouragement to go with her instincts. I couldn't suppress a hiss of delight when her lips and nose bravely pressed a little lower into my pubic growth, and her hot cheek inadvertently but silkily caressed my pulsing erection, which speared up from my groin alongside her diligently moving face.

'Ohhmm…' Appolonia moaned to herself in the joy of being able to give him something in return. She had only needed to be shown the way. She had not needed to be shown how, even though he had tied her hands behind her back.

My nostrils flaring I inhaled deeply again, my chest rising and my stomach hollowing as I gazed down at the innocent beauty kneeling tightly between my thighs, her head bowed in my lap, lips and tongue working obediently but unseen. Her clear flesh was a healthy colour and unblemished perfection.

Then I gripped her shoulders and pulled her up, her breasts cushioning my erection for a few wonderful moments, tempting me to stay right there, but then higher still, pulling her upward, guiding her limp legs over my parted thighs, sitting her on my lap, the veined underside of my standing penis pulsing against her toned tummy. I held her around the waist and pressed my face to her cleavage, breathing the sweet, intoxicating freshness of her flesh. And as I hid there, rocking gently to and fro, I felt her heat against the root of my erection, snugly cocooned between us.

Opening my eyes I stared at her enigmatic beauty, her eyes closed, her lashes fluttering, her cheeks flushed, her lustrous dark hair tousled about her angelic face and shoulders.

Working blind I released the leather belt from around her wrists, and then rolled her onto her back. I moved over her. Her legs opened instinctively and her eyes glazed as she looked up at me with a heart stopping intensity.

'Oh…' Appolonia moaned, pressing firmly upward against his hardness when she felt him arrive at her welcoming gates, and instinctively began circling her hips.

'Oh, *fuck*,' I groaned. I couldn't stand it any longer,

her closeness, her scent, the feel of her submissively beneath me. It was time…

Appolonia gasped as he pressed, apprehensive and a little frightened. She tensed from head to toe, lying beneath his weight. Something was building in him, and in her. She could feel it in her virginal heart, telling her it was going to happen. She held her trembling breath, waiting to see what he would do next, not knowing herself.

She could feel the pulsing girth of his penis fitting the length of her wet cleft as he moved. She breathed hesitantly, waiting, her fingers digging into his biceps, and then she knew the waiting, that endless dance of time as a thinking woman, a virginal thinking woman, was finally over. And then she felt him lifting her slightly as he wedged two pillows beneath her bottom, raising her hips and positioning her virgin sex perfectly for him to fulfil his goal.

He covered her again, resting on his forearms, pinning her motionless with his weight and his stare, and then she whimpered and bit her lip as his hips moved and he breached her, slowly but surely. He penetrated her to the core with one long, slow, relentless thrust, impaling her with a stretching fulfilment that stole her breath away. She strained against his weight, feeling skewered beneath him, but it felt wonderful, the pain of her thinking woman's death no longer even a memory.

'Ohhhhhh…' she wailed, flinching as he rutted against her, the pace of his hips increasing feverishly, then suddenly he stiffened and thrust deeper than ever, exploding with a guttural male grunt.

'Oh!' she cried in wonderment, squeezing her thighs tightly with him fully trapped inside, milking the last drop of his fluid until finally he lay replete on top of her, his forehead resting heavily on the mattress.

I heard her whispering softly in my ear as she hugged me like a child, and we lay like that for several wonderful minutes. Then her hips began circling gently beneath me and gradually my strength returned. I moved one hand down and cupped her buttocks, and searched her deep warmth there, quickly finding the star-crossed tightness of her warm nether necklace waiting. As I lay my face on her shoulder and kissed her throat, I slipped a fingertip just inside her there.

'Ah!' Appolonia squealed, shocked and startled from her afterglow. She clenched her buttocks tightly around his invading finger, but quickly felt the discomfort and igniting passion both when that finger inexorably penetrated her bottom. Her breathing faltered as she tried to fathom the sensations, both mental and physical.

His arms held her, his finger intimately inside her, licentiously exploring her last virgin passage as her heart began to thump against her ribs. She gasped again as his finger began moving inside her bottom.

My strength returned, I hardened quickly inside her tight mooring, and felt the strength of her bottom each time she clamped my hand between her cheeks. My penis expanded inside her tight sheath, throbbing. She groaned and shuddered several times as I lay on top of her, grinding my groin down to savour the deepest penetration I could. I knew she wasn't pretending; she was pleasing me instinctively as a female in training, but doing that which now came naturally.

Appolonia felt wonderful, finally free and safe, allowing his pleasure to heighten her own natural passions. 'Oh, *yes…*' she whispered as she fucked him while he fucked her, intensifying her pleasure. She wanted to be possessed by him totally as a female, to be taken by his strength, gloriously free now of all restraints and inhibitions. She ground her hips against the two invaders of her body, huskily and feverishly encouraging the deep penetration of each.

I heard her cry out when my finger reached deep between her flexing buttocks and I fucked her vigorously. Her tight virgin sheath felt like a second skin over my throbbing cock. I thrust more forcefully inside her with rigid finger and erect cock, to match her rising urgency, and gradually she became exhausted and even more relaxed, allowing me even deeper explorations with each deep thrust. I was in heaven. My eyes closed and I gritted my teeth as I picked up the pace, rutting on top of her beautiful, weary body. I opened my eyes briefly and savoured the sight of her. Both of us were breathing hard and fast.

Appolonia groaned repeatedly and her body glistened, coated in a sheen of perspiration as she moved urgently beneath him and with him, in perfect time with his thrusts. Her climax approached headlong to meet her with a vengeance, beginning deep as a raging fire. 'Oh, yes!' she cried repeatedly, feeling controlled and possessed by his raw maleness.

I felt like a coiled spring, expecting my body and mind to snap and unwind at any moment. Incoherent sounds came from her gasping mouth. I balanced the deep thrusts of my bloated cock and my stiff finger, igniting and inciting my lust and dragging yet more tortured cries of delight from her lungs, released after so long being held captive by the loneliness and discipline of her culture.

Again and again she gave and received, lifting and turning and twisting, until at last, unable to hold back any longer, she imploded in mind and body both, joining with him at his peak. Crying real virgin tears she then carried him over the crest and into the deep abyss of two humans now fused together as one.

After several long minutes, while her panting and gasped utterings lessened in my ears, I breathed deeply and felt myself calming, then I sighed as we both drifted in our cooling afterglow until we slept.

When I later opened my eyes she was still nestled with me, still joined to me while she dozed peacefully. I felt her warmth and instantly stirred inside her.

'Ohhh,' Appolonia gasped softly from her dreamless sleep. Then she breathed quietly and sighed. For a moment she was not sure where she was, or if it had been a wild and wonderful dream. Then she rolled her head listlessly to the side and saw him watching her, and she smiled. Her lips pressed to his cheek and she gently kissed him. He responded by pressing down slightly, drawing a sweet gasp from her, and barely awake she wanted to tell him how she had visited the heavens in their lovemaking, but she didn't. Instead she allowed herself back to dreamless awareness and wished for her moment of virginal deflowering to never end.

Reluctantly I eased myself from her and sat up on the side of the bed, and gazed at her beauty in full resting nakedness. Without a word she then rose to her feet, and then padded, comfortable in her nakedness before me, through to the bathroom.

When she returned I was dressed and sitting once again on the edge of the freshly made bed. She sat down beside me, and took the hand I offered in her own. I smiled.

'Your female mind will not forget this day, and neither will I,' I said with complete honesty. 'I've lived most of my life unhappily, as a thinking man, but I chose not to any more. Now I live as a natural feeling male, and wish only to be in good company with natural females of like nature. I've taken what you wanted to be taken, what you needed to be taken. And for that special gift I will always love you dearly, and will always welcome you, if you wish to be with me.'

Appolonia nodded, and the tears of her heartfelt and natural happiness rolled down her cheeks as she listened. She never wanted to leave him. No matter what it took, she never wanted him to tell her to go.

'In a few moments you'll leave, but hopefully, only for the time being.' I paused again for a few seconds before continuing, feeling a little sad without really knowing why. 'Whether you're with me or away from me, I want you to remember what I took from you today, what you wanted me to take from you today, without guilt and without shame. In that same way did I take the gift of your precious Greek virginity,' I told her seriously, planning for a possible future that was not too far away.

'If you accept me as your male and your mate, know truly that I am a dominant male, and that I have my natural place in any relationship we might have together, just as your natural place as a submissive female awaits you if you choose to join me. I have a lot of love to give you as a male, and I have a lot that I wish to receive from you as a female.'

Again I paused, speaking from my heart for the first time in my life, and hoping she was piecing together in her conscious mind and awareness that which I was offering.

'Before we meet next I want you to consider what your life has been like and what you'd like it to be like, and who you'd like it to be with. Sharing your days and nights with people you love can be a wonderfully uplifting experience. A family of natural males and females can be a family to belong to, even more so… as a family within a family.'

'Yes,' Appolonia said unbidden, and nodded. He had won a place in her heart and mind. She was his, in any way he wanted to have her, to take her, to use her and to love her. She knew that and wanted to sit naked at his feet forever. And she took heart and consideration at each of his words. Her tears had stopped. Her mind was clear and her body glowed. Her heart swelled at hearing his words. Suddenly he hugged her, and then kissed her tenderly. She felt herself respond in full, and when he gently ended the kiss she blinked away the tears several times, trying to focus on his face, and then she did and she smiled, as he was smiling.

He rose from the bed. She did as well, and dressed quickly.

He walked her to the door, holding her hand in his, no more words needed. She understood. She smiled goodbye, contented, her precious Greek virginity gone for all time, and with no regrets, but definitely not forgotten. She felt strangely wonderful inside; tired and tender, but wonderful. Perhaps being a natural female was working already.

After Appolonia left I closed the front door and smiled. Maybe they would be in my life today, or tomorrow, or next week. But eventually they'd come. It was only the dance of time, but they would accept me, one and all, unconditionally, as their first male, as their first mate... and as their first master.

Now all I had to do was sit down and conclude matters with their mother's friend.

More exciting titles available from Chimera

***

Sales and Distribution in the USA and Canada

Client Distribution Services, Inc
193 Edwards Drive
Jackson
TN 38301
USA
(800) 343 4499

Sales and Distribution in Australia

Dennis Jones & Associates Pty Ltd
19a Michellan Ct
Bayswater
Victoria
Australia 3153